I0647263

Lalita's Power

Book One – The Mystical Healing Trilogy

By RP Mickelson

Filidh Publishing

Lalita's Power
Book One – The Mystical Healing Trilogy
By RP Mickelson
Copyright © 2023 by RP Mickelson.

ISBN: 978-1-927848-91-3

Published by Filidh Publishing Corp,
Victoria, British Columbia, Canada   filidhbooks.com

Cover Design: Danny Weeds
Cover Art by Zoe Duff and DALL-E software.

All rights reserved. This book cannot be copied, printed or reproduced in any form without the author's written consent via email (rick.mickelson@telus.net)

Other Books by RP Mickelson:

Stone House (2021)

Inspirational Short Stories (2023)

Preface

This novel involves the power of mystical healing and reveals a new way to understand the universe. Despite the veil of suffering covering all aspects of modern civilization, there's a perfect harmony of peace, happiness and bliss lying at the core of Life. The existence and personal development of Lalita Fitzgerald exposes the key insights to spiritual living:

- Every aspect of life in the present moment is absolutely   sacred.
- The transformation from suffering to ecstasy occurs when all the barriers to bliss are consciously removed.
- To abide knowingly in one's soul is where permanent happiness can be found.

Mystical Healing is unsuitable for anyone younger than eighteen because it has mature themes and involves complex situations that only adults can fully understand. All of the characters in the book are imaginary and bear no witness to anyone living or dead. Any likenesses to real people are purely coincidental.

RP Mickelson Victoria, BC
(email) rick.mickelson@telus.net
October 1st, 2023

'Follow knowledge like a sinking star, beyond the utmost bound of human thought.'

---Alfred Lord Tennyson

PART 1

Jack Turner

Chapter 1   <u>The Twins</u>

Jack Turner had a tough life growing up in North Surrey, British Columbia. His father, Rory, was an itinerant construction worker who drank heavily and beat his wife and children regularly. Jack's saving grace was the love he received from Jimmy—his twin brother--and Sylvia, his mother.

Rory was often out of work, and when that happened, he sold heroin and cocaine to pay the bills, which brought his family into contact with some very unsavory characters. Usually, these druggies slinked in and out of the back door, but sometimes they just lingered in the front yard sitting on two benches beside the overgrown blackberry bushes, smoking, swearing, or spitting while waiting for Rory. But often, there wasn't enough money to pay the bills, so the Turners had to go on welfare, sometimes forcing them to the brink of homelessness. They moved often and usually stayed in cramped, slummy apartments or trailers— dwellings way too small for a family of four. So, the twins grew up feeling insecure, vulnerable and generally on the defensive. People who looked like pimps or mafia men were too often seen hanging around the Turner abodes, like bats nesting in a dark barn. But that meant the twins grew up tough and developed thick skins very early on.

Sylvia Turner was an attractive woman with a striking head of red hair, a sleek figure and a face with classic features. She played delightfully harmonious folk songs on her guitar. She tried to sell the exquisite paintings she created to keep her family's head above water when times were challenging. Her favorite medium was watercolor, and she'd developed a distinct flair for capturing the essential beauty of objects that captured her interest. She bought her paints from the *Salvation Army*, using old bed sheets for canvas and wood scraps for frames. She sometimes even framed the paintings of her artistic friends, which periodically brought in a little extra cash. To her, beauty was an expression of love, and creative endeavors made her feel alive and helped her cope. Any money she could make from the pure creativity flowing out of her consciousness was perceived as a bonus. On a physical level, she was a beautiful woman—tall, blonde, curvaceous, slim, athletic and vibrant.

Her parents were working-class people who'd emigrated from England in the '50s. John Simpson, her father, was a welder from Bristol who worked hard, voted conservatively and was very set in his ways—a stubborn man, chauvinistic, but honest. His favorite pastime was stopping for a couple of bitters after church on Sunday, even though Julie, his wife, never joined him there. She worked as a midwife and also cooked all the family meals, did all the laundry, housework and patio gardening. She loved to sing and had hoped to make records when she was young, but that never materialized. Both John and Julie were devout Anglicans. Sylvia had rejected traditional Christianity at an early age. However, her love of spiritual books and sacred places had never disappeared. She was raised in an environment of love and acceptance because both parents adored her. So much so that she didn't receive much discipline from them or many restrictions--even as a child.

Rory grew up in a trailer park with three brothers and a single alcoholic mother. All the boys in his family adapted quickly to living in a slum and learned to fight, steal and do drugs at a very early age. What brought a touch of sanity to his life was learning how to play the drums at sixteen. After high school, he joined a band and supported himself by playing music, hustling at pool and selling marijuana. That's how he met Sylvia, a singer in another band. She was attracted by his masculinity, virility and toughness. Still, when those qualities got twisted by alcohol later on, her marriage to him became an unmitigated disaster.

Rory and Sylvia formed their own band with two friends-- *The Crashers*--a hippy folk group that toured western Canada. Rory could bang noisily away on the drums while his wife saved the day with her lilting, harmonious voice and talented guitar strumming. Sam Stanley played the bass guitar, often going off-key, and George Diamond tapped out tunes on a fiddle he bought for five dollars at a garage sale. They got together out of a genuine love for music and a dream to make enough dough to supplement what was often their sporadic and meager wages. It was a group that made music and partied hard but actually never made much money. Once Jack and Jimmy arrived, the music scene ended for Rory and Sylvia, and the band fell apart, like wounded soldiers deserting their posts and disappearing from a bloodied battlefield after the war.

Despite the chaos of growing up poor in a violent setting-- without discipline, order or predictability, Sylvia inculcated in her boys the idea that a good education was critical. No matter how bad things got, she always read to them, taught them how to write, made sure they did their homework and insisted they graduate from high school—which they both did. She was the glue that held her family together. The boys were fed their favorite foods at mealtimes, and Sylvia was an excellent cook. They both loved fried chicken, toasted tomato sandwiches and exotic salads and their mother only ever prepared foods they loved.

Jimmy was the only true friend Jack ever had. From the beginning, the twins were inseparable. They defended themselves from bullies, played and studied together and never abandoned each other during innumerable predicaments. Until they were fifteen, they slept in the same bed. Even though Jim was morose and pessimistic, Jack never did anything without consulting him. He, on the other hand, had a happy nature-- always trying to see the positive side of things—including the many disasters he experienced in his youth. His relationship with Jimmy kept him focused and helped him survive psychologically. They had a language of their own which nobody else understood. At times, they could even read each other's thoughts. In the end, they grew up as real partners, both tough as nails.

Jack was six foot one after high school graduation--thin, athletic and extremely handsome. He was well coordinated, could dance with uncanny rhythm, run as fast as an antelope and climb trees effortlessly. By the time he was fourteen, his body was chock-full of testosterone, so from then on, he was fixated on women.

Jim, on the other hand, was clumsy and had a drooping left eye, which made him look sleepy. He loved junk food and developed a slight pot belly before his fifteenth birthday, which never left him. He was not nearly as successful as Jack at attracting women.

Both boys did well at school and helped each other study to stay on the honor roll. They loved their mother and wanted to please her by achieving academic excellence, the most important thing to her. She constantly boasted to her friends about how smart her boys were.

In June 1973, Rory got busted for trafficking drugs and was sentenced to four years in <u>Matsqui Prison</u>. He never lived with Sylvia again and didn't see Jack for three years. By that time, both he and Jimmy had completed undergraduate degrees at UBC. During their teenage years, both boys worked at various lousy, minimum-wage jobs to help support themselves and their mother. Any kind of work was acceptable as long as they could help her. The only way the boys could afford to go to college was through massive student loans. Jack worked as a line cook at *Subway* throughout his post-secondary school years, and Jimmy served as a waiter at *Surrey's Colony Inn* when he wasn't in classes. They both graduated with over $25,000 in student loan debt.

The fundamental problem with their parent's marriage was Rory's mental disorder. He had a split personality—the Dr. Jekyll, Mr. Hyde syndrome. She could forget about things like his lack of interest in spiritual things and his love of junk food and beer. But his psychosis was a much deeper problem.

In good times, he could be loving and generous—a kind and skilful husband and parent. But when he was upset, uncomfortable or depressed, a devilish character emerged. That's when he began to drink. Once alcohol was in his system, he'd demand obedience from his wife and kids. When that obedience wasn't forthcoming, he'd swear at them loudly and lash out impulsively—often beating them cruelly. Sylvia tried her best to cope but could never change the marital dynamic. When her husband was sent away to jail, she was upset at first but later realized how much better life was in a peaceful home. She willingly filed for divorce when her parents pressed her on it.

Jack and his brother worshipped Sylvia and fiercely supported her in every way. She, in her turn, was devoted to them and resolved never to date another man until her sons were wholly independent and living away from her. That resolution was never broken.

Despite the fact they were heading in different directions after college, the twins remained extremely close, like a double-headed clover leaf. Jim thought the only way to escape the generational welfare cycle was through some kind of high-powered career, so he enrolled in law school after college graduation and specialized in corporate studies. He was on his way to becoming a partner at Laxton—Fields, the largest corporate law firm in Toronto. Jack, on the other hand, became a hippie.

While studying philosophy, he was attracted by the teachings of Baba Ram Dass—a former Harvard psychology professor who'd become a spiritual guru in the West after spending time in an Indian ashram and embracing esoteric Hinduism. Jack lived in a community of seekers in his early twenties—a group of vegetarians who meditated daily, practiced free love and shared all their possessions. They tried to live as a collective, like ants toiling in their pulsating hills. Jack worked part-time at a *green cuisine* restaurant on Cambie St. in downtown Vancouver and shared his earnings and most personal feelings with his friends in the collective.

In the summer of 1976, he was passed the community phone one hot August evening.

"Jack, it's your Dad—can we meet soon? I'm staying at the YMCA on Burrard St."

"Dad, are you out of the slammer *already*?"

"Yeah, only did three years--got out early for good behavior."

"Sure, when do you want to meet?"

"How about tomorrow morning for breakfast at the Denny's on Burrard--across the street from the YMCA?

"Okay, I'll be there at 7 am."

Rory had aged a great deal in just two years. All his hair was now white; his face was full of wrinkles and red pock marks. At first glance, Jack thought he had German measles. The red-blue snake tattoo on his forearm was scratched and faded, like a moldy water color with frayed corners--hung too long in the same damp place. He smelled like stale beer.

"You never visited me, kid, or sent me even *one* letter."

"Dad, I've been incredibly busy these last few years, but it's good to see you again. How'd you track me down?"

"Jimmy told me where you were staying. How's your mother?"

"Not very well—her body's riddled with arthritis, and she's going downhill fast. She shakes a lot these days and limps when she tries to walk—but her mind is still sharp. When I see her, she looks senile and wizened, and her physical beauty has evaporated completely. It's pretty depressing. It was her parents that made her divorce you officially, and she eventually ended up marrying a retired Anglican priest. But he left her six months ago, so now she's all alone."

And you were mainly responsible for her demise, he thought.

"I'm sorry to hear that, son, but I'm sure you'll be able to help her as she ages. What about you—what are your plans for the future?"

"I want to open my own vegetarian restaurant with Cathy, my girlfriend."

"Now, that sounds like a great plan, and I think I can help you with it."

"How would you do that?"

"Two of my buddies, Jake Symons and Butch Billy have a line on a bank job. It's a *sure* score because Jake's sister works at the bank and has given us inside information."

"I'm not interested, Dad."

"Just a minute—this is a 1.2 million dollar gig, and all I want you to do is drive the getaway car. Two Loomis drivers are delivering a load of cash next Wednesday to the CIBC on Hornby at exactly 10:05 am. We'll be waiting for them. Our rendezvous is in the town of Aldergrove, so you'll only have to drive 42 km. The job will put $200, 000 in your pocket, which is enough to get that diner started. I'm sure Cathy would love that."

"Dad, I'm not a criminal; the risks are too great anyway. The answer is **no**."

"You've never done anything for me, and now I'm desperate. If you can't help me with this little caper, my relationship with you is over forever."

"Give me a bit of time to think about it. I'll let you know in three days."

"Thank you, son--I knew you'd come through for me."

That night, Jack went to bed early and lay motionless on his mattress, staring at the ceiling.

"What's the matter, Jack?" asked Cathy.

"Nothing—I'm just in a bad mood."

"Come on, guy, you've been lying here for three hours. I know something big is bothering you. Let's make love. That'll take your mind off any problems you've got," she stated enthusiastically.

"I'm not in the mood right now."

"But you're always in the mood for sex. Now I *do* know your head's screwed up."

At 3 am, Jack woke up with a start and sat bolt upright. He poked a naked Cathy, who was by then sound asleep.

"What's up?" she moaned groggily.

"My Dad wants me to drive a getaway car for him and two of his buddies. They're planning a robbery and have inside help. The payout is 200k—enough to get us started in our restaurant."

"You can't do it, Jack. If something goes wrong, you're screwed for life."

"It's not the money, Cathy. My Dad needs help, and I'm racked with guilt."

"Why?"

"He *is* my father, and he did try his best to raise us. It's just that his childhood was horrible, in fact, extremely traumatic. He says I owe him because I've never done anything to help him in my whole life.

"Jack, you owe him nothing. If you do this, our relationship is over. I don't need you for sex because there are two other dudes in this commune who can provide me with that, and quite nicely. I don't want to live with a criminal, and I won't."

For the rest of his life, Jack remembered what happened next as the biggest mistake he'd ever made. Maybe the money tempted him; perhaps he felt guilty about ignoring his father for so long and just wanted to help him—but on that fateful day, he was pushed into a plan that was dead wrong—and he knew it. Years of profound regret were about to unfold.

Following a tip-off, the RCMP shot both Butch and Jake in the legs. Once down, they shot at two cops hiding behind a huge oak tree, but their bullets kept missing their targets by a mile. Rory lay motionless under a nearby hedge after getting hit in his right arm, just above the elbow. After a two-hour shoot-out, a huge sergeant pulled out his megaphone and yelled,

"Drop your guns now, or we'll shoot to kill."

At that point, all three of the robbers rolled over, lay still and sobbed loudly. They were quickly taken to the *Vancouver General Hospital* covered in blood. Jack drove a measly fifty feet before nine cops in two road-blocks stopped him and threw him in the back of a paddy wagon, fully handcuffed.

Rory was sentenced to seven years in <u>Kent</u> for armed robbery, and Jack got a four-year sentence at <u>Matsqui</u> for being an accessory to the crime. It was his first criminal offence, but Judge Harriet Reynolds wanted to make an example out of him. The real tragedy for Jack was that all his friends deserted him, including Cathy.

"You're dead to us now," they told him after the trial.

That left him with only one person in the whole world who cared whether he lived or died--his faithful twin brother. What follows are some of the most important letters Jimmy and Jack Turner sent each other from September 12th to March 15th, 1977.

Chapter 2   The Letters: September, 1976 to March, 1977

September 12th, 1976

Jimmy—

Today, I went through a two-hour admissions process at the jail. After putting my clothes in a creaky metallic locker, two guards searched my naked crevices, issued me a wrinkled orange jump-suit and demanded that I put it on. The on-duty officer made me feel like an object, not a person, and maybe to him, I am. My prison number is 90142.

I'm staying in a living unit with five other guys on the third floor of the central control tower. Security is tight. Food will probably be adequate but plain—for supper tonight, we got salt-less white sole, cold, limp carrots and artificial scalloped potatoes that tasted like the newspaper. There were no condiments---just stale, warm water in used plastic cups, and the salt was lumpy in a dirty glass shaker. The utensils were plastic, too.

My bed's a cot with two frayed, gray wool blankets on it and sits on a concrete deck in a small cell adjacent to five others. There's a seat-less toilet in the corner with rust in the bowl and a stainless steel sink right beside it, with a flimsy cold water tap—pretty simple and not much space. I'm all alone here, except for one other creature—a skinny rat with a very long, black tail, protruding yellow teeth and a spot of dried blood on its fur. He comes in and out of my cell through an exposed drain pipe. My goal is not to be bitten by him—he's one ugly sob. He likes to sit on his hind legs, stick his big belly out, wiggle his whiskers and nibble on kernels of rice in the corner of my cell. His eyes are like brown glass marbles stuck in a pile of Philadelphia cream cheese.

Jack

October 2nd, 1976

Jack—

Looks like you're settling in okay. Don't get too stressed; time will fly.

Working for Laxton is like being your rat but on a spinning wheel. You just keep going round and round in circles, and the harder you work, the faster it whirls. My boss is an asshole who keeps loading me up with more case-work every time I win a court case.

Jill's pregnant again and acts like a bitch most of the time. She constantly complains that I work too much and won't do anything with Jeff. The kid wants to sign up for hockey, but I'm just too busy to get involved. I haven't had sex for six weeks now because she's always tired, sick, or angry. I can't win with her, Jack. Sometimes, I even feel jealous of you, sitting in a cell all alone--in peace.

Are you staying in touch with Mom?

Jim

October 25th, 1976

Jimmy—

I phone Mom every Sunday. She says she's doing well, but I know that's not true. If she was, she'd come to visit me. Even her voice is shaky now, and she's got some memory loss.

Your job sounds awful, but I bet the money's great. Sorry to hear Jill's not happy these days, but be patient; she'll come round. Don't forget she's pregnant and likely nauseous, tired and depressed most of the time. It's a physical thing, nothing more. Relax and smell the coffee.

My counselor got me a laptop because I agreed to teach a beginner's guitar class to some of the inmates. That means I can now do research and watch YouTube videos if I get bored. Last night, I watched an interesting documentary on Ram Dass. He's an inspirational guy. Fully enlightened.

I've decided to get fit, so I do sixty push-ups every day in my cell—thirty before breakfast and thirty after dinner. I can already feel the difference—sleeping better and looking younger. I'll increase the number by five each month. It feels good to sweat again.

Jack

November 17th, 1976

Jack—

*Glad to hear you're staying in touch with Mom. Getting fit? You **do** make me jealous—just wish I had the time, something you've got lots of right now! So appreciate it!*

*The money **is** pretty good at Laxton. I make 165k annually, plus quarterly profit sharing and stock options. But who cares—the work's terrible, even vicious. I hate it. You've been in criminal court, so you know how intense it is—there's always heavy antagonism and conflict in the air. And it's a high-pressure job—lots of money's at stake if you make even a small mistake.*

Last night, Jill told me there'll be no sex until the baby's born. That's seven months from now! So, I'm sleeping with one of the paralegals at least twice a week. Her name's Suzie and we go to her apartment at lunch time. She's a twenty-two-year-old bombshell and very passionate in bed. Like me, she's a sex addict. She looks exactly like Marilyn Munroe and has Marilyn's sex drive. Maybe they're sisters.

Jill doesn't know about Suzie, but she's still unbearable to live with. Her latest kick is telling me I'm an alcoholic. Two nights ago, she slapped me across the mouth when I told her she was a bitch.

Good to hear you're online-- maybe a good creative writing course will become available. I've gained twenty pounds but plan to start a non-carbohydrate diet next week.

Ciao, Jim

December 10th, 1976

Jim—

I can't believe you make over a hundred and sixty grand a year--in fact, it boggles my mind. I can't even imagine making that kind of money. Sorry to hear about your marital challenges, but no doubt you'll solve them over time. If you're imbibing more than two drinks a day, it's time to cut back. Don't forget what alcohol did to Dad.

I've started an online <u>Creative Writing Course</u> through the Continuing Education Department at the <u>University of Victoria,</u> and it's going well. Maybe I'll never be the next Stephen King, but my instructor says I've got some talent. My aim is to write a novel about a tortured character falling into a life of depravity but somehow surviving and redeeming his soul.

*Carl Tara Sandheim is a senior Zen monk who offers a meditation class every Wednesday morning at 5 am, and I've joined his group. The monk demands perfect posture in the full lotus position, which is unbelievably painful. Still, if you persist, it **does** make you calmer and more aware of what's happening around you. This guy's very wise and gives great advice on the art of living. He's charismatic, for sure. Write soon.*

Jack

January 3rd, 1977

Jack,

Jill found out about my affair and is demanding a divorce. Her temper tantrums ruined any kind of harmonious family Christmas, that's for sure. I moved into Suzie's place last week only to learn she's pregnant too! I don't know why that condition renders women angry and depressed, but at least my new woman still loves sex—so that part of my life hasn't disappeared yet. We make love at least once a day, and if I want it more than that, I get it.

*Jeff won't talk to me, and I haven't seen him in three weeks. I **did** sign up for <u>Alcoholics Anonymous</u> and must admit it **is** helping. However, Suzie's a heavy drinker, too and likes to binge-drink every Saturday night. However, she won't come with me to the AA meetings. Says she doesn't have a problem and can quit anytime she wants. I don't believe that.*

The sex is definitely great, especially when I'm drunk—but I don't love Suzie and can't stand living in her dingy, under-furnished little bachelor suite. She uses old wooden liquor boxes for chairs. Right now, I have to pay Jill $1500 a month for alimony and child support. That hurts.

The diet backfired, and I put on seven extra pounds. I know I'm depressed because suicidal thoughts are starting to look attractive, and Suzie tells me I'm always in a bad mood. Gawd, I wish you were here.

Jim

February 2nd, 1977

Jim—

One of my short stories got published in the <u>Malahat Review</u> out of Victoria, and it's getting excellent reviews. It's about a criminal who's transformed by life in prison. When he gets out, he becomes involved in a church specializing in inner contemplation and outer rehabilitation work. I think my meditation practice is helping the creative process and revealing to me just how much suffering there is out there in the world.

All the fat on my body is gone due to my consistent push-up program, and I'm now up to eighty a day. Blood pressure and heart rate are low. I feel great!

My guitar class plays weekly concerts for the whole prison population, and we plan to produce a CD before Christmas. Creative acts make a person feel more alive, like an injection of energy into your life. Jimmy—take up a hobby! Why not go back to golf?

*Life in prison is good. I've had tons of time to reflect on my existence on earth and what's really important. Significant changes **will** be made on the other side. I live a disciplined life, and it's paying off.*

I just finished reading a book by Victor Frankl, <u>Man's Search for Meaning</u>. He survived four Nazi concentration camps using his philosophy which he later developed into what he called 'logotherapy.' He believed that human beings are motivated by a 'will to meaning,' which is nothing more than a desire to find meaning in life. He argues that life can have meaning **even in the most miserable circumstances,** *and the motivation for living comes from finding that meaning. He said, "Everything can be taken from a man but one thing: the last of the human freedoms—to choose one's attitude in any given set of circumstances, to choose one's own way (in life)."*

That's why I think I can't only survive prison life but use it to improve everything about myself. I urge you to read this book.

Hope things are changing for the better, and I wish I was there, too!

Jack

March 15th, 1977

George Laxton
Laxton—Fields
Toronto

To: Mr. Jack Turner
<u>*Matsqui Prison*</u>
British Columbia

Dear Sir:

Please find enclosed a Xeroxed copy of a cheque for $250,000, which is the amount James Turner's Will allocates to you, effective March 3rd, 1977. A copy of the section in his Will that specifically pertains to you is attached to this document. These funds have been forwarded to administrative officials *at your prison. They will become available to you upon the completion of your full sentence.*

We trust these details are acceptable. If you have any questions regarding this matter, please address them to MS Thompson, our Director of Human Resources.

Sincerely,

George R. Laxton
Office of Legal Management
Laxton—Fields

Chapter 3   On The Road To Recovery: July 1980

Jack Turner was released from <u>Matsqui Prison</u> into a work program on July 8th, 1980—one year earlier than his original sentencing date. He was thirty years old and had no family or friends.

"If you want to work outside the prison for the final year of your sentence, you have two choices," his sweating and obese parole officer told him. "One is living at the <u>Salvation Army</u> in downtown Vancouver--and working there full time as a janitor for minimum wage. The other is staying at the <u>Zen Buddhist Monastery</u> in Richmond. The pay there is fifty bucks a month plus room and board. But you'll have to do hard labor for twelve hours a day. Your meditation instructor, Carl Tara Sandheim, has personally recommended you for that one."

"I'll take the Zen Monastery," replied Jack tersely and without hesitation. "What better way to be completely rehabilitated?"

"That makes sense, Jack—you seemed to really enjoy Sandheim's meditation class," spluttered the official.

"Will I be able to access the money from my brother's will after one year in the monastery?"

"Yes," answered his officer. "If you successfully complete your program and are officially released, you'll get the inheritance."

Two uniformed sheriffs drove Jack to the monastery for his first tour and introductions. They escorted him to the entrance, where he was met by Nishida Kitaro, the guest master, who was standing like a serene statue, waiting patiently for him to arrive. Jack handed him the letter of introduction given to him by Sandheim.

"You're Jack, then," Nishida stated after reading the letter carefully, slowly—pausing after every sentence, moving like a honey bee flying in slow motion.

"Yes," responded Jack.

"Follow me through the main temple doors, and I'll show you the guest quarters."

As soon as they passed through the thick, steel-hinged swinging doors, which were by this time open, Jack noticed how different the setting was from anything existing in the outside world. Everything was immaculately clean and ordered. Smooth cobblestone pathways weaved through stately pine trees, beds of fresh green bamboo plants and grass boulevards that looked like putting greens. Several monks performed maintenance tasks such as clipping bushes, raking leaves or mowing lawns with manual machines. They all had their heads shaved bare and wore long black robes with stiff, bright red collars. Strangely, the environment was enveloped in silence as no one was speaking. The residents moved slowly, methodically, like quiet caterpillars slithering over dry leaves in a dream. There was a faint smell of orange incense in the gentle breeze, which made the air feel clean, sweet and fresh.

Eventually, after walking around several well-maintained, newly varnished wooden buildings, they came to a long wooden enclosure with a peaked roof and spotlessly clean sliding glass windows. On it hung a sign that read: **Guest**

House. Inside, there were neat rows of cubicles—each containing a simple futon about six feet square on top of which lay a quilt wadded with cotton-wool and two small black cushions.

"As soon as you wake up, put the bedding on the common shelf overhead and then go out that rear door to the general wash-stand. That area holds one big basin filled with fresh water that can be accessed by using a number of small bamboo dippers. They're small to emphasize we don't use the gifts of nature lavishly. Water *is never* to be wasted. Bed time is 9 pm, and a gong will ring at 3:45 am, signaling the start of *zazen* at 4 am," said Nishida.

"Do I have to get up *so early*?" inquired Jack.

"Yes."

"Can you show me how *zazen* is practiced here?"

At that point, the guest master took Jack to an open area, placing a small blue mat and a black, round cushion on the floor.

"*Zazen* at the monastery is very similar to the basic meditation methods you've been learning at the class in prison, just slightly more difficult, so I'll quickly go over it carefully," he said, pointing to the mat. "Put your butt on the cushion and your knees forward together. Keep your back rigidly straight at all times—as though a steel rod was penetrating it and then riveted to the floor. When ready, put your hands together like this," said the monk as he showed Jack a basic meditation *mudra*. Breathe normally, but *watch* your breaths and remember--a meditation session starts with the chanting of applicable sections of the <u>Heart Sutra</u>—one of our most important sacred books.

"He has no emotion in his voice," thought Jack, *"He's completely detached from his speaking and my reaction."*

"Breakfast will be served at 6 am. You'll receive two local fresh fruits and one piece of dry whole wheat toast," said the coordinator. "Please clean your plate after the meal and prepare for work in the vegetable gardens."

At that point, the monk bowed gracefully and said,

"I hope you enjoy your stay. Before you settle in, Mr. Sandheim would like to speak with you."

"Where can I find him?"

"In office number 12 inside the <u>Karuma Building</u>. Just walk toward the giant granite *Buddha Statue* beside the kitchen and turn left at the flowering bodhi tree.

When Jack reached Sandheim's office, he knocked on the door and heard a rich, deep voice,

"Come in, I've been expecting you. Jack, it's highly unusual for a prisoner on work release to be accepted into this institution. But I highly recommended you because you made so much progress in the meditation class. I know you've dabbled in spiritual practices before and are interested in finding life's higher truths. So this is an ideal place for you. Everything that happens in a Zen monastery is designed to train you in *reality*, not worldly illusions. And the way that's done is through discipline, labor, gratitude, service, prayer and meditation. We shun luxury, comfort and *any kind of commercialism.* Now, am I right that your goal in life is to achieve spiritual enlightenment?"

"Yes, sir, *it is.*"

"Do you have any questions?"

"Will I have to shave my head and wear a robe?"

"Yes—but the only mandatory meditation I've scheduled you for is the morning one. After that, you'll be doing hard labor all day. Don't' forget—the purpose of that labor is to free you from selfishness. Make sure you work in silence and put all your energy and attention into the tasks at hand."

"Will I have any free time?"

"Yes—I've allowed for you to have weekends off. But you must *not* leave the city limits of Richmond, and you must be back for the evening meals."

"Yes, sir, and thank you--I'm definitely on a spiritual path, and this will reinforce my search. Your explanations are very clear."

"Jack, is there anything in particular you'd like to accomplish while you're here?"

"Yes, Mr. Sandheim, there is. I suffer from two addictions and would like to get rid of them so I can live a healthier life. These are self-destructive blocks that cause me a great deal of suffering."

"What are your addictions, Jack?"

"I'm addicted to sex and alcohol."

"Can you be more specific?"

"If I feel uncomfortable, upset, angry, or frustrated, I crave alcoholic beverages. When I come across a beautiful woman, I see her body as an object and experience lust-filled desires. When I'm in that mode, a woman is no longer a person; rather, just a means to satisfy me and give me momentary pleasure."

"Those addictions can be healed, and I will teach you how. But let's start with a basic program of meditation and work. That's the foundation for any kind of personal growth."

Initially, it was difficult for Jack to adapt to Zen living, but, in some ways, it was like prison life--which he was used to. After about a month, he was fully integrated into the Zen way of life. He'd learned to resist the pain in his legs during meditation and quiet his mind for long periods of time. Unending work in the fields where onions, squash, lettuce, radishes, and cucumbers flourished enabled him to tap into powers of concentration he didn't know he had. Fresh organic vegetables exude a healing energy once you learn how to absorb it. Working in total silence helped him focus totally on the tasks before him—usually watering, digging, weeding, picking vegetables, carrying boxes, or stacking empty barrels in the storage sheds. No labor-saving devices were allowed. Jack could continue a physical regimen that kept him lean and fit.

"I'm going to give you a koan to work on, Jack," said Sandheim at one of their weekly meetings.

"What's a koan?"

"It's a question that can't be resolved by the thinking mind. You have to live in the puzzle it poses and place it at the core of your being until answers arise from deep within. If you solve the koan, it'll lead to mini-satoris—a space of timelessness and spacelessness where a blissful and direct realization of truth explodes into your consciousness. It's like a peak experience in sports--what professional athletes call *being in the zone*."

"When will you give it to me?"

"Now—***What is the sound of one hand clapping?***"

Jack immediately internalized the question and repeated it under his breath. He had no idea how this koan was going to affect him or if he could successfully complete his final year of training. But he *did* know that he was definitely now on the *road to recovery.*

It felt to him that everything in monastic living was designed to counter the effects of chaos, carelessness and crudeness. Everything that happened was intentional-- nothing was left to chance. From the very beginning, Jack was being taught how to take control of his own consciousness and generate life from within himself, just the way spiders generate webs from within their own bodies. Those webs are their own, individually designed as a space for the insect to interact with life *on his own terms.* No matter what happens, the spider is at home on his web.

Jack moved into the monastery on July 15th, 1980.

Chapter 4   Junko: August, 1980

On weekends, Jack invariably spent his time in Steveston. This was formerly a quaint fishing village on the Fraser River that had become a suburb of Richmond. He loved walking along the river's edge, wading into the cool, fresh water and talking to fishermen as they repaired their twine nets like owls fixing their nests. His favorite coffee house was Anita's. It sat just off the river, beside a sandy boulevard, and served expensive trail boss coffee and snacks like caramel popcorn and moist fruit cake. Anita herself and a young assistant served their customers with enthusiasm, friendliness and dedication. Both wore immaculately clean white aprons and had their hair done up in a bun. Each table had turquoise-tinted salt and pepper shakers with stainless steel tops, a sugar jar with little black swans on it and a spotlessly clean orange napkin at every place setting.

"Why did you shave your head?" was a question that floated with the breeze into Jack's right ear as he sat at a granite patio table by an outside iron railing overlooking the flowing water, while sipping his hot, black coffee. Turning to his right, he saw a tall, slim Japanese woman smiling at him.

"Because I'm staying at the *Zen Monastery* in Richmond and studying meditation," he replied.

"That's cool," she answered, "I spent time in a Zen dojo in Kyoto."

"You did?"

"Yes—why don't you join me so we can discuss it?" she replied, smiling mischievously.

Jack may have wanted to find out about this woman's Japanese Zen experience, but in the moment, he was overcome by her beauty. She had shiny jet-black hair curled into a page boy down to her neck. Her eye lashes were long, sitting over black pupils on pure white retinas and highlighting thin lips touched by a tinge of crimson. She was slender but had exquisite curves. Her low-cut, long-sleeved *Gore Tex* top revealed cleavage that demanded his attention, and her skin was flawless and as white as a newly starched Zen priest's collar.

"Okay, I will," Jack stuttered, as he stumbled over to her table, almost knocking over an unoccupied chair on the way.

Her scent was subtle, delightful and powerful. Jack knew immediately it was expensive *Tamarind* perfume made in Cairo, one of his favorites. She smelt like a fresh Egyptian rose.

"What's your name?" He asked her.

"Junko Yamamoto—what's yours?"

"Jack Turner and I **am** interested in finding out about your Zen pursuits."

"Why are you shaking and blushing?" she asked

"I'm just nervous, I guess."

"You can relax now--I never really *pursued* Zen but used to visit my uncle who lived in a <u>Rinzai</u> <u>Priory</u>. He taught me how to meditate."

"How did he do that?"

"He showed me the full lotus position, explained all the *mudras* and then emphasized the importance of watching my breath."

"Do you still meditate?"

"Only if I'm stressed out, depressed or overwhelmed by life. It always calms me down and relaxes me. Do you come here often?"

"Yes," answered Jack, "I visit this waterfront every weekend. There's something about the flow of the river that attracts me. I can watch the current for hours and never get bored. The water's teeming with life. If you look closely enough, you'll notice jumping fish, dragonflies landing on floating chips of wood and frogs hiding beside patches of lotus leaves like children playing hide and seek: that kind of thing.

"I spend a lot of time around here, too. Perhaps we'll run into each other again?"

Jack and Junko then talked non-stop until a waitress interrupted them to say the restaurant was closing. Their conversation was animated and featured lots of direct eye contact, laughter and animated hand gestures. Jack found her energy contagious, seductive, even and magical. But when the subject of family came up, he became sad and morose.

"Jim was the best friend any one could ever have," sighed Jack. "But he couldn't conquer his demons, and eventually, it got so bad that he killed himself by overdosing on sleeping pills. I just can't let it go, can't forget about him. He was my best supporter—always there when I needed him."

"I can really feel your pain, Jack. This is such a sad story. But I can't take any more of it right now—sorry."

Jack then glanced at his watch and yelled,

"I completely lost track of time!" We've been sitting here for almost five hours! But, I'd like to continue this conversation sometime."

"Oh my God—it seems like we've been here for just a few minutes," she responded. "Would you like to meet again next weekend?"

"Yes! Yes! Why don't we have breakfast here next Saturday, say about 9 am?"

"Sounds great," she whispered, getting up and gently touching his bare left forearm, sending shivers up to his head and putting goose bumps all the way down his arm. He felt like he'd been penetrated by a minor electric shock. "I'll be here."

Jack was clearly shaken. He didn't have much experience with Asian women and hadn't had a girlfriend for years. But he was extremely attracted to Junko and couldn't wait to see her again.

As a matter of fact—he couldn't stop thinking about her all week. Mental images of a stunningly beautiful Japanese woman disturbed his morning meditations, and he lay awake for hours, dreaming about kissing and caressing her. She was incredibly seductive, *even in his dreams*. Only when he delved deep into his koan he got any psychic peace.

"I must find out if we have anything in common," he kept thinking. *"I hope there's more to this attraction than pure physicality and lust."*

When he arrived at <u>Anita's</u> the next weekend, she was waiting for him, smiling and drinking a steaming hot cup of clear, green herbal tea.

"You showed up on time, Jack, and that's good. Thank you."

"Of course," he replied, smiling back at her.

She wore a thin, red, short-sleeved cotton T-shirt and tight black Nike track pants. There was a foot of bare skin showing between the top and her slacks, and Jack couldn't help quickly glancing at her belly button, which had a tiny red stone implanted in it.

"Do you find my apparel offensive? You seem to be staring?" She asked.

"No, quite the contrary—it's sexy and attractive. What kind of gem is that embedded in your stomach?"

"I'm glad you asked. It's a present from a former boyfriend who was extremely wealthy. He knew I loved South African rubies, so he bought me one, and I glued it into my belly button. It was my favorite birthday present four years ago."

They then began other intense conversations, but this time, Jack was asking most of the questions. Over the course of two hours, he found out she was fluent in French, English *and* Japanese and worked as a translator for the federal government. She was a vegetarian, an accomplished tennis player and an avid reader of erotic novels.

After a light breakfast of fruit, toast with honey and black coffee, Jack asked her,

"Where do you live?"

"I'm staying in an A-frame bungalow at the river's edge-about a kilometer from here. My Dad owns it, but he lives in Tokyo and rarely comes to Canada. Do you want to have a look inside? I've got some powerful homemade Saki we could sample."

"Yes, I'd very much like that," he added with a gleam in his eyes.

As the sun reached its nadir, it became very hot and sticky at the river's edge. The slight wind that was blowing stopped, leaving nothing to cool the air. Perspiration and flecks of sand stuck to Jack's forehead like grains of pepper on spaghetti. He was nervous and didn't know why.

Junko's abode was full of light as it had nothing but windows on the south wall. Three futons lay in symmetrical patterns adjacent to the living room, surrounded by tall bamboo plants, various species of cacti and a climbing leafy-green rhododendron. At the top of a twenty-foot vaulted ceiling hung a whirring fan, which was at least moving the hot air around.

Junko and Jack talked on and on, sipping warm Saki and nibbling on fresh shrimp sushi and crispy seaweed chips. Presently, she moved close to him and whispered seductively,

"Will you kiss me now?"

Jack hesitated but then slowly bent forward and pressed his lips lightly into her right cheek.

"You can do better than that," she said with a mischievous smile.

When he put his mouth on hers, she immediately pushed her tongue through his lips and teeth. He then opened his jaw wide and welcomed her passion. As he necked with this beautiful woman, his state of being became ecstatic, his body burning with red-hot desire.

"I want you to make love to me," she moaned, throwing her bra-less T-shirt onto the floor, revealing the beauty of her tanned bare skin and perfectly symmetrical breasts with taught nipples, each over one inch long. When her panties came off, Jack was mesmerized by her overly hairy pubic area—a black triangle that was soaking wet.

"Let's stop for a moment, Junko. There's something I need to tell you,"

"What could that possibly be *at this moment?*" She moaned.

"I made a terrible mistake a few years ago and, influenced by my father, got involved in a bank robbery for which I was sentenced to four years in jail. I'm now serving the final year of that sentence in a work release program at the Zen

Monastery. Trust me--I'm no criminal—this was the first and only illegal act I've ever committed—and it'll be the last. Nothing like that will ever happen again. I can promise you that."

"Thanks for sharing that with me, Jack, but I still want you to make love to me **now**. Do I have to beg you to?

"Junko, I'd love to do it, but I must be back at the <u>Monastery</u> for the evening meal. Can I see you again tomorrow?"

"Yes, of course. Come back in the early afternoon. I'll be *completely* naked, waiting for you in my bed."

Chapter 5   A Buddhist Wedding: December 1980 to
August 1981

By Christmas, Jack had fallen madly in love with Junko, and she was by then his official girlfriend. They were now spending every weekend together.

"When will you be able to leave the *Monastery*, Jack?" she asked him.

"In the summer—just six months from now," was his reply.

"Would you like to move into my place once you're free?"

"Is that what you really want?"

"Absolutely--because I'm smitten with you, and I love the idea of seeing you every day."

"My dear, I'd be honored to live with you."

At Easter time, Jack's mentor and sponsor, Carl Tara Sandheim, requested a meeting with him in his office.

"I've got some very good news for you, Jack," he began, "Your progress here has been going so well that I've secured an early release. You'll be able to leave on April 1st. Do you have a place to stay?"

"As it turns out, yes, sir, I do. My girl friend has invited me to move into her place on the Fraser River in Steveston. I'm very happy about the early release you've secured *and* about *all* the support and encouragement you've given me. I thank you from the bottom of my heart. I feel that you're a dear friend as well as my revered teacher."

"I've scheduled a farewell interview with you at 11 am on April 1. After that, you'll be a free man."

"I'll be like a honey bee in summer," thought Jack.

When that day came, he approached Sandheim's office with a spring in his step. The monk had set up an informal tea ceremony for them, which was part of the Zen lifestyle. A large tea pot, inscribed with a flaming red dragon breathing fire, was brewing chamomile tea. Two small, round, handle-less cups—also with fire-spewing dragons painted on them—were lying ready. Steam rose up as the tea was poured to meet a rotating ceiling fan. In the Zen tradition, the room set-up and preliminary discussion were as important as the conversation. Every act was performed *meticulously* in that culture, like the inner workings of an intricate Swiss watch.

"Have a seat and enjoy your tea, my friend," said the master mindfully. "How are you doing with your koan?"

"Not so well, teacher--focusing on it is the only thing that calms me down in chaotic situations. But I'm stuck with the actual koan."

"Let me give you *one* small clue. What is the *source* of sound? If you dive deep into yourself with that question, solutions will come. The only other clue is to continue meditating *every day*--no matter what happens in your personal life—and that's not easy to do. Sooner or later, you *will* have breakthroughs. Then you'll feel like a chick breaking out of its egg shell, entering a fresh new world for the first time. I've enjoyed working with you. Don't forget that you're always welcome back for a retreat, a meditation or a counseling session."

At that point, Sandheim bowed deeply, with great humility, before handing Jack a money order for $250,000. It was the money from his brother's estate.

"If I were you, the first place I'd go would be a bank."

"You're right, of course," returned his pupil, his face all lit up. "And when that's done, I'll be making a donation to the *Monastery.*"

"That's most generous of you, Jack, and it'll be greatly appreciated."

As he left the institution, Jack had nothing but fond memories of his stay. He also had a strange feeling that someday he'd be coming back.

Junko was waiting for him beside her flashy, white, brand-new SUV as he passed through the main swinging steel gate.

"Hello darling," she said, running into his arms, clutching him tightly, "Are these the only worldly possessions you have now?" she asked, looking with curiosity at his small backpack and the Steinway guitar hanging from his shoulder.

"Yes, I'm afraid to say *they are.* Now, can you drive me to the nearest CIBC?"

"Sure, but why do you need to go to a bank?"

"As soon as we get home, I'll tell you."

After a light lunch of miso soup, vegetable tempura and brown, whole-grain rice cooked in Junko's steam cooker, Jack started to explain.

"I've told you how much my twin brother Jim loved me, and I loved him. He was really my only true friend growing up. We lived like Siamese twins. Well, he became a very successful, wealthy lawyer and decided to leave me a quarter of a million dollars in his will. I went to the bank this morning to deposit that money."

"Oh, my God—what are you going to do with all that dough?"

"I want to open a vegetarian restaurant specializing in Japanese food. Would you be interested in helping me with that?"

"Absolutely—I only work four days a week now and get off every day at 4 pm. I'm also free on weekends. And I've achieved mastery of authentic Japanese cooking."

"You're hired!" said Jack, laughing.

He'd spent a great deal of time meditating about his future and was certain about Junko's role in it. He loved being in her presence. She was charismatic, beautiful, practical and extremely feminine. To top it off, she was a passionate, creative lover and wanted sex on a daily basis and sometimes twice a day—which suited Jack perfectly.

"Before I start my café, I'd like to ask you a very personal question, Junko."

"Yes, what is it?"

"Will you marry me?"

"Of course, I will, my dear," she replied, jumping into his arms. "I was praying that you'd ask."

At the time, Jack was delighted by her response but later often thought her lack of hesitancy was suspicious. It was almost as if she was in a hurry to tie the knot.

Their wedding, a sacred yet simple affair, was held at the *Monastery* on August 21, 1981. Carl Tara Sandheim served as both the master of ceremonies and the priest conducting the service. The ceremonial party consisted of only five people. They were Junko's bridesmaid, Rebekah Leslie, her boss at work; Jack's best man, the Monastery's cook, Haru Kazan; and a fifth member of that small group--Fuji Yamamoto, Junko's father—a man Jack disliked from the start. He was short and fat with beady eyes inserted into a sweaty, swollen face, and he kept asking his daughter to harass her fiancé with stupid questions about his financial future.

"Why does he want to know how much money I'm going to make in my life, Junko," he asked her.

"Think nothing of it, my dear; he's just making conversation."

Silence permeated the ceremony as the bride and groom followed Sandheim while he led their small procession through the temple's lush, green gardens, ending up in a white-shingled gazebo on the south lawn. Green ivy leaves were interwoven with the pillars holding the structure up, and planters full of marigolds hung all around the frame.

Jack felt like he was in a movie that had been muted and slowed to a snail's pace. But the scene was beautiful and became etched into his mind forever as he glanced at his gorgeous bride standing tall beside him--a bride who was replete in a short, pure-white dress, red headband and crimson leather sandals that matched her lipstick. A gong broke the silence, which had the effect of snapping everyone to attention like a parade of soldiers following the orders of their dominating commander. Sandheim then read three verses from the Heart Sutra, using the Japanese language. Before the exchanging of rings, he intoned,

"We are gathered together today to join two people in marriage. May their lives together be filled with love, peace and compassion. May their hearts be joined together as they move forward in life with one purpose, one plan and one intention. Let us now observe two minutes of silence."

After what seemed like an eternity of quietness, during which a pin drop could be heard, four monks standing beside the gazebo gave a short chant, and then the bride and groom were pronounced *man and wife*. As he kissed his bride, Jack felt like he was an eagle flying high above the earth.

This was the start of an intense relationship between a man and a woman that would produce great heights of bliss mixed with unexpected and surprising challenges, along with a good measure of suffering.

Junko was stunningly beautiful and, without a doubt, a very brilliant woman. She was multi-lingual, well-read in all the current trendy books and well-versed in the arts of cooking, tennis and communication. Unfortunately, she had a character trait that tended to create problems in her relationships with men—a quality that Jack was unaware existed on his wedding day. This was her habit of sinking into narcissism or self-absorption around the areas of sex and money. She frequently flirted with other men and did not share Jack's innate financial generosity.

She expected to receive multiple orgasms every day and was critical of Jack when he didn't produce them for her on a consistent basis. He was an excellent lover and held back nothing when Junko made her demands, but he was also human. Sometimes, he got tired or felt ill and fell asleep when his wife was anxiously waiting for him to perform.

"I know you can do better if you try." She'd say the next morning when the nights did not meet her expectations.

And where money was concerned, she was obsessive.

"I'll go to make the deposits today," she told Jack at the end of business each day. Nothing pleased her more than going to the bank to deposit money into their accounts. She liked to hold the cash and count it several times before actually arriving at the teller's wicket.

"Why do you spend so much time studying our online accounts, dear?" Jack would ask her.

"Well, someone has to keep track," she'd invariably respond, with a distinct edge to her voice.

Chapter 6 The Zen Café

Jack had a clear idea of how he wanted his restaurant to operate. It would have a massive salad bar and offer delicious vegetarian foods like exotic rice dishes with spicy golden curry and many varieties of vegetable tempura and Japanese sushi. There'd be many brightly covered tables and servers who were friendly, polite and attentive. Lastly, there'd be melodic, relaxing background music played by live musicians. He wanted all his future customers to feel inspired and uplifted while they ate.

By mid-September 1981, he'd found a deserted fish and chip shop with twelve tables that was renting for only $1400 a month. It was located in a quaint strip mall in Steveston overlooking the river near a wharf for fishing vessels and recreational boats. This place was like a derelict shop in a ghost town, but Jack saw potential in it because it was on the waterfront.

"This is it!" He told his wife the minute he stepped inside the old eatery and glanced around. All the tables were damaged, and there were cobwebs everywhere—but the full-length grill and stainless steel stove were in working order—even though covered in layers of dust, rat droppings and intricately hanging spider webs, like booby traps in a haunted house.

Junko agreed with him, as expected. She was quick to support her husband in many ways. As it turned out, her father knew an elderly Japanese lawyer-accountant doing business out of a small office near the waterfront in the basement of an old, run-down character home. His name was Basu Mishikori. Unfortunately, he spoke very little English but *was* willing to set up the books for Jack's business for fees significantly below market rates.

"Mr. Mishikori says we should put the eatery in my name, darling," said Junko after a private meeting with him.

"Why's that?" asked Jack.

"Your prison record could create problems if we ever have to travel outside Canada. Also, people who have criminal records must abide by several restrictive conditions which could hamper us as we expand."

"I wish you hadn't visited him without me, but I don't mind if we put the restaurant in your name. Everything that's mine is yours, too. Tell him to go ahead and draw up the documents."

"Why are you frowning, dear?"

"It's nothing, just a bit of a headache," replied Jack.

It *was* a headache, and it was caused by small elements of tension that were seeping into their marriage. Junko's obsession with money and financial success was getting on Jack's nerves a bit. For him, accumulating money was a very low priority in life. He wanted his work, writings and business to make a difference in people—to inspire others and lift them up.

The Zen Café opened for business on November 15, 1981. Jack and Junko had renovated and painted it and had all the cooking equipment cleaned--rendered spotless so it could work as if brand new. They'd purchased a salad bar counter from a derelict *Subway shop* in Steveston, along with a coffee machine, soup maker and fridge for drinks.

Jack hired one person—Sarah Graham—an attractive forty-eight-year-old former cook and waitress who looked ten years younger than her real age. Her job was to keep the café clean, prepare all the salad bar vegetables and wait on tables. He cooked the food until his wife showed up after work. Junko also prepared all the sushi at home in the evenings so Jack could take it in fresh first thing every morning.

From the very beginning, Jack's restaurant was a smashing success. He was charging $10 for unlimited access to the expansive salad bar and $5 extra for salads with *any* regular meal.

Sarah was adept at keeping the over fifteen varieties of vegetables at the salad bar fresh and delicious, and, as well, she created seven original dressings. That vegetable bar became a hot attraction. Jack played folk songs and sacred meditation music on his guitar for four hours a day, and customers loved the calming effect this had on them. He also hired talented buskers to play either the flute or a second-hand Stein piano he bought for a song at a *Kelly Brother's* auction. It turned out Junko was a master chef, and her squash tempura and avocado sushi dishes became best sellers. The eatery had a six-foot-tall wooden Buddha statue that stood beside a tall palm tree near the front door to welcome all visitors. The placemats were illustrated by Buddhist art and contained sayings from the *Heart Sutra,* along with all the menu choices, printed in a bolded calligraphy font. By Christmas, Jack had obtained a liquor license for beer and wine. White Saki, in attractive but small handle-less cups, became an item in constant demand.

As time went on, Jack became very close to Sarah—so much so that his wife complained about his attachment to her. She worked incredibly hard in the coffee shop, did whatever her boss told her and made it obvious that she adored him. She was a tall, blonde, buxom woman with powerful maternal instincts. She also shared a deep interest in spirituality with Jack, *something his wife did not.* Sarah was a devout Roman Catholic but was willing to hear about other faiths and try to understand them. She was in the progressive movements in Catholicism and supported women priests, birth control, gay rights and liberal sexual practices. Her favorite religious authors were Richard Rohr and Thomas Merton.

Jack could talk to her about Zen, and she listened intently, asking questions and explaining how her religion differed on key points. He even told her about his koan and how he struggled with it. She wanted to hear all about it. Jack meditated every day, and she prayed ceaselessly, which put them on the same wavelength in some magical way. When Jack went to the *Monastery,* she went to *St. Michaels' Sacred Heart Church.*

"You know that Sarah's in love with you, don't you, Jack?" Junko commented sarcastically one evening as they sat on a futon watching the movie *Titanic*, starring Kate Winslet and Leo DiCaprio.

"No—she just loves the business, that's all," he replied sharply, maintaining a serious look.

"Do you still love *me*?" she asked with a quizzical frown.

"Why do you ask?"

"Because you seem to be irritated at me quite a bit lately."

"It's because of the stresses of running a business and has nothing to do with you," replied Jack unconvincingly. "Let me prove how much I love you," he countered, moving close to her, running his hands through her jet-black hair and kissing her crimson, welcoming lips.

After they made passionate love for two hours on a thick Persian rug in front of burning cedar logs in the fireplace and experienced many exotic activities that thoroughly satisfied Junko on a physical level, he said,

"There's no woman in my life but you, darling. Can't you see and feel that?"

"If you say so," she muttered under her breath.

But it was true. Jack adored his wife most of the time. She worked tirelessly for their restaurant, complimented him constantly and performed vigorously in bed whenever he requested it—always until he was completely spent physically. In his mind, her only flaws included greed for money and the way she allowed men to come on to her— never discouraging the frequent advances made upon her by the opposite sex. However, he was so in love with Junko that he was willing to overlook her minor transgressions.

The *Zen Café* made an operating profit of $107, 642 in its first eight months in business.

"Have you ever thought of expanding to other locations, dear?" asked Junko in mid-July 1982.

"No, I haven't, but that's not a bad idea. We could certainly consider it someday," he answered.

"I think we should expand immediately, Jack, and I've got a great guy we can hire to be a manager of the second store. He could start training here before we put him in charge of our next restaurant."

"Who is he?" asked Jack.

"Butch Cassidy—a person who owned his own successful *Harley Davidson* business for ten years."

"Is that the bulky, bearded biker who comes here every morning for coffee and flirts with you?"

"He doesn't *flirt* with me--he just likes to talk about business and economics—subjects I'm *very* interested in."

"I don't like the idea, but let me think about it for awhile."

"Alright, honey, you don't have to decide on this right away. Take your time," she said with a sarcastic smirk on her red lips.

She looks like a Cheshire cat that swallowed the goldfish right now, he thought.

There were a few details about Butch that Junko neglected to tell her husband. She forgot to mention that he'd spent ten years in *Kent* for armed robbery and running a heroin operation out of his motorcycle dealership. Jack was also unaware that he'd been married six times and had been sued for sexual harassment twice by ex-wives.

From the first day he hired Butch, Jack felt uneasy about him. He was loud, crude and insensitive to the people around him. He swore constantly and was a chain smoker. Jack could not understand what his wife saw in him, and it made him very uneasy. For the first time, he began to doubt Junko's judgment and they started to argue on a regular basis. He didn't think this man was a fit for his business but was hesitant to disappoint Junko. He knew that forbidding him to become an employee would send her into hysterics. It was only recently that he discovered that his wife had a temper. On certain occasions, she could become very volatile and violent. Jack preferred to avoid heavy confrontations if he possibly could. He was always attracted to peaceful, compassionate resolutions.

Chapter 7   A Mini Awakening

It was definitely against his better judgment that Jack gave in to his wife and allowed her to bring Butch Cassidy in as a trainee. It didn't take long for him to realize his intuitions were correct. The biker was an unsavory character, like one decaying potato in a sack, starting to stink. And one rotten potato soon begins to affect the others around it. He was six feet tall, wore a torn, black leather jacket at all times and had a bushy brown beard with a dirty black mustache. He was rude to customers and smelled like stale whiskey.

"It's not going to work out with Cassidy," Jack told Junko after his first two weeks.

"You promised to give him a month, Jack and he's improving and learning more *every* day. **Please keep your word**."

"Please don't scream at me, Junko. Customers and staff are complaining about this guy."

"I'm sorry, *asshole,* but I thought your word was your bond," Junko answered, scowling and gritting her teeth.

One week later, Jack left his business to buy avocados at *The Organic Place*. When he got back, Sarah whispered to him,

"Can I talk to you outside?"

"Of course," Jack replied, walking gingerly into the street after her.

"When you were out of the restaurant, I had to go into the pantry closet to get a towel. Junko was in there passionately kissing Butch, and she had no clothes on below the waist."

Jack's face turned bright red as he ran past Sarah, barging through the café's front door and banging his way into the kitchen. He found Butch there cutting up an orange Hubbard squash with a long, extra-sharp and serrated butcher's knife.

"You son of a bitch—you're having an affair with my wife. Leave the premises immediately—YOU'RE FIRED."

Butch quickly stuck the knife into Jack's left side, just below the ribs, then banged him hard over the head with a rubber hammer that was sitting on the counter. Hot red blood spurted out all over Butch's dirty white apron and ragged jeans. On his way to the floor, Jack hit his head on the corner of a cutting table and lapsed into unconsciousness. This occurrence put him into a coma that was to last for over six weeks.

During his convalescence in the *Richmond General Hospital*, Sarah visited him constantly. She stayed with him for at least eight hours *every day*. Sarah mopped his head with cool antiseptic cloths, gave him Reiki treatments until his heartbeat slowed down and read him spiritual books for hours and hours on end. She had plenty of time to nurse him back to health because Junko had fired her the very same day her boss had been injured and knocked out.

Jack would later discover that Butch Cassidy and Junko closed the Zen Café, drained all his bank accounts and flew directly to Tokyo, Japan. He'd been left penniless and near death. Luckily, his BC Healthcare plan was in full effect, so all his medical bills were fully covered.

While he lay in his private hospital bed, Jack's body was sound asleep, and his eyes were tightly shut. But his soul was wide awake, and he was *very much alive*. All his physical senses had been suspended, but he could still think and understand the precariousness of his situation. He could not hear Sarah's voice as she read to him or see any human form, but her loving presence was deeply felt.

"Nurse, Jack's skin goes slightly red, and his throat quivers when I come into the room and start reading to him," she said to Ms. Rachit.

"He must like your books then," she replied sarcastically.

"Please don't mock me, nurse--he knows I'm here; *I can feel it.*"

Jack dived deep into his being and noticed that he could hear a flute playing delightful meditation music.

"The sound of this exquisite music is arising from within," he realized. "It's not coming from outside of me."

Then something snapped in him, and he got it—"*the source of sound does not come from an outside world. There are no sounds in the outside world! Sounds are integral to my sense of knowing—and all there is to sounds is my knowing of them.*"

"Maybe I'm starting to crack the mystery of my koan," he thought.

Two weeks later, as Sarah sat reading to Jack, listening to the steady bleeping of his heart monitor, his left eyelash flickered and moved.

"Oh my God, he is waking up!" whispered Sarah to herself, noticing the change immediately.

And it was true. After six weeks, two days and sixteen hours, Jack was coming out of his coma. Sarah placed her hands on his chest, closed her eyes and began pouring her love into Jack's being as she chanted a Christian prayer to herself--over and over again,

"Dear Lord, your grace is my sufficiency in all things. Thank you for bringing this beautiful man back to life."

Three hours later, Jack's eyes were wide open, and he smiled at Sarah. His usual speedy thoughts had slowed right down, and, in his new world, everything moved as if in slow motion--like a video clip shot at half speed. He felt totally present in the moment and understood the *power of now* at a deep level. His appreciation for all of life had definitely intensified.

It would later become clear to Jack, after speaking at length to his mentor--the monk Carl Tara Sandheim--that he'd had a mini spiritual awakening in that hospital bed. His life would never be the same again.

"Sarah, everything looks more colorful than it used to," he whispered. "Where am I?"

"You're in a hospital recovering from the wound in your ribs and a massive bump on your head."

"How long have I been here?"

"Over six weeks."

"Oh my God, I don't remember anything since we last talked outside the café."

"Don't worry, Jack, I'll tell you all about it when you're feeling better. Right now, you've got to rest and heal."

"Have you been taking care of me, Sarah?"

"Yes, I have, and it's been my pleasure."

Sarah's loving energy had helped knit his bones together and heal his wounds. That love was so intense Jack could feel it surrounding his whole being.

"You're lucky to have such a dedicated friend, Mr. Turner," said Jack's surgeon, Dr. Ken Paltrow, after he entered the room. "You were in pretty bad shape when you arrived here."

"How do you mean doc?" replied Jack.

"The knife wound missed your liver by half a centimeter. Had it entered your body a bit to the right, you wouldn't have made it. And we had to cut your scalp open to relieve the pressure on your brain. I consider your recovery in such a short time nothing short of a miracle. We're going to discharge you tomorrow. Do you have someone to look after you?"

"Yes, he does," intervened Sarah. "I'll be his primary care giver until he's completely healed."

"Again, Mr. Turner, I say you're a lucky man. Count your blessings," stated the doctor as he exited the room.

"Sarah, I can't impose on you like this. You owe me nothing."

As she clasped his right hand, Sarah smiled down at Jack and remained silent as she stroked his bare arm. To him, she looked like an angel. He could smell her exotic perfume, newly starched white tunic, and the honey shampoo in her hair. Sarah's hair was blonde, wavy, clean, thick and shiny, and the skin on her face was flawless, white and soft. As she touched him, an electric current ran through his entire body, making the blood in his veins flow faster, and the warmth in his heart expand. He felt completely alive and aware. There was no need to talk. A silent bond was forming between them—a bond that ran deep.

"Why are you taking such good care of me, Sarah," he asked.

"Because I love you, Jack," she replied.

Then she sat down and began reading to him from the <u>Holy Bible</u> in a calm, loving, sweet voice.

The Lord is my shepherd;
I shall not want.
He makes me lie down in green pastures;
He leads me beside the still waters.

He restores my soul;
He leads me on the path of righteousness
For his name's sake.

Yea, though I walk through the valley of the shadow of death
I will fear no evil;
For You are with me;
Your rod and Your staff,
They comfort me.

You prepare a table before me in the presence of my enemies;
You anoint my head with oil;
My cup runs over.

Surely goodness and mercy shall follow me
All the days of my life;
And I will dwell in the house of the Lord forever.

"Is that Psalm 23, Sarah?"

"Yes, it is, Jack."

"Those are the most beautiful words I've ever heard in my whole life."

"I'm glad you liked them."

"I truly did, and there's something remarkable happening right now. I feel a contentedness that nothing could take away. And I can't help feeling that I can call on that happiness anytime, anywhere, to visit me again. Sarah, you're the agent that's facilitating that feeling."

"That feeling exists inside you, Jack. I'm only triggering it."

"Well, I sure hope you can continue triggering it."

"Jack, I'd like you to move into my apartment until you're better. That way, I can take proper care of you."

"But Sarah, I have no money."

"That's fine—you don't have to pay me *anything*. This is what friends do for each other."

"How can I ever repay you?"

"You don't have to repay me at all. This is something I really want to do."

Chapter 8   Sarah's Place: Fall 1982 to September 1984

Jack moved into Sarah Robinson's one-bedroom apartment in the fall of 1982. Her suite was on the edge of *Fairview Park*, overlooking a grove of stately pine trees, a quaint pond full of white swans and a family of Mallard ducks. It had a small balcony, and Jack often sat there in a curved beach chair beside two lavender plants with his eyes closed in contemplation, feeling the subtle, calming energy of the lush green trees washing over him and the pungent scent of pine needles and exotic herbs penetrating his nose. Those were some of the times he slipped into a state of contemplation centering on his koan, trying to penetrate the mysteries of sound, like a meandering river trying to find its source. But even in this setting, he was often besieged by sadness over his broken relationship with Junko. That relationship started with so much hope, promise, beauty and fanfare but ended disastrously.

"I'm going to sleep on the sofa, Jack," said Sarah one day, "Until you've recovered. Right now, you need a proper bed to sleep in--so you can use mine," she stated with definite authority.

"Thank you, Sarah; from the bottom of my heart, I'll never be able to repay you for all you're doing for me," he replied, feeling overwhelmed with gratitude.

Despite the fact that Sarah was an attractive middle-aged woman who worshipped him, Jack Turner had no romantic feelings for her. But, as time passed, he grew very fond of this motherly woman. She was an amazing cook, had healing hands and could engage him in a multitude of conversations because they had so much in common. Like Jack, she was not a conventional person, did not buy into materialistic middle-class values, did not hold conservative economic views and considered herself very progressive in political and spiritual matters. She was pro-choice, non-racist and deeply pious.

Her place was a compact living space, slightly crowded with two people living in it—but all the essentials *for a* high-quality existence were present--and that was what she strived for--high-quality living based on loving relationships, simplicity and living in the present.

She found another job as a waitress at *Quon's Sushi House* on 43rd Street. Also, she made extra income doing healing Reiki treatments on the weekends. Jack was not yet ready to venture into the world, but did start to write short stories and even sold a few. He even went back to writing his novel. There was no doubt about it-- creative inspirations were coming back.

By the summer of 1983, they'd settled into a set of routines that helped Jack move beyond his tragic experiences with his ex-wife, even though he still sometimes sipped whiskey to dull the psychological pain. They rose at 7 am, breakfast with coffee was over by 8:30, supper happened at exactly 6 pm, followed by a long, meditative walk through a nearby forest. Bedtime was 10 pm.

Jack was ready to look for employment at last. Sarah regularly administered healing physical treatments to him, including massages, Reiki treatments and the kneading of his feet, using well-known acupressure techniques. By the end of July, she decided to increase the intensity of their relationship.

"I'd like to start sleeping in my own bed again," she said late one evening after slowly polishing off two glasses of Pinot Red on the rocks.

"Of course," responded Jack. "I'll be happy to move back onto the couch and start looking for my own apartment."

"No," she said sharply without the slightest degree of hesitation, "I want you to stay in my bed with me. You need someone to keep you warm at night." His blushing, quivering, goose bumps, and shaking knees did not go unnoticed.

From that day forward, they lived as man and wife, and Jack began to find himself falling in love with this woman. She was so devoted to him, so sensitive and so physically sensual that he could no longer resist her. At the heart of their relationship was a mutual commitment to spiritual goals. While Sarah prayed and worked hard to become closer to the Christian God, Jack meditated, sought to expand his enlightenment experiences and worked endlessly on solving his koan. He went to the Monastery every Sunday morning to meditate with Carl Tara Sandheim's Group. At the same time, Sarah attended mass at St. Michael's Sacred Heart Church. She was a lay reader there and spent many hours in their soup kitchen helping homeless parishioners and destitute women.

"How are you coming along with your koan, Jack?" asked Sandheim early one Sunday afternoon in August.

"I've had a breakthrough, sir," he answered respectfully.

"Tell me about it."

"When I was in my coma, I noticed that sounds were present, yet my ears weren't working. That observation led to the realization that the source of sound doesn't exist in an outside world, but rather *within me*. That's to say, sounds don't come to me from outside of myself. The sound of one hand clapping can't come from an external world. Maybe an external world doesn't actually exist, which would make reality *totally subjective*."

"You *are* making progress, Jack. Keep working on it, and many more insights will come--just be patient."

Jack eventually found work as a part-time journalist for the *Richmond Times*. This included researching and writing scholarly articles and penning a daily column he titled, *Insights*. At that point, his life had settled down nicely, and his physical healing was almost complete.

He also started adding erotic sections to his novel based on his experiences with Sarah. When they had sex, it was full of love, caring and sensitivity. She taught him how to access pure love during even the most passionate physical acts. In fact, no act was forbidden with her as long as it was soaked with love, like a sponge full of fresh water. For the first time in his life, Jack learned to put love before lust and move sexually with exquisite intention and joy. Sometimes, a blue ring of light would encircle them as they united as one. Intercourse could then last up to three hours because they used it as a meditation: a device to achieve the state of flow. Sarah's hands would massage every part of Jack's body until his very cells were expanded, alive and awake. Their bed became a sacred space, almost like a medieval monastic church, when the nuns sang mystical hymns. Their actions there were definitely consecrated.

The only area of tension between Jack and Sarah involved Jennifer Black, Sarah's only daughter. She was a stunningly beautiful model married to jet-setting real estate developer Bernard Black. The couple lived in a luxurious penthouse west of Vancouver's Stanley Park. Jennifer was adamant that Jack was far too young to be his mother's partner.

"He's younger than me, mother, and that's completely unacceptable. You *must* kick him out immediately," she screamed at her in a tense, private telephone conversation.

"Jen', Jack's the love of my life. I've never been happier with any man, *including your father.*"

"That's disgusting," Jennifer spewed--then abruptly ended the call, slamming the receiver down so hard it cracked the plastic receiver.

"I don't think my daughter will be talking to me for quite some time, Jack," said Sarah.

"Why do you say that?"

"Because she's very judgmental, and, in her eyes, it's sinful that you and I are living together."

"Is that simply because I'm eighteen years younger than you?"

"That's part of it, but I think she's jealous of us."

"Jealous—I thought you said she was married to a very wealthy, charismatic man."

"Let's just say I don't think she loves him. I'll bet they hardly ever have sex, and Jennifer is a very passionate woman. When she looks at me, she knows I'm very much in love with a man who satisfies me totally in every possible way."

"Thank you, darling—does she know I'm in love with a woman who satisfies me in every possible way?"

"I don't think so. But Jack, haven't you noticed that she's very attracted to you herself?"

"No, I have not."

"Jack, trust me—I'm a woman—she'd like to be in a relationship with you. Don't take it personally--this has nothing to do with your character. She doesn't even know what your values are. No—it's purely physical with her. She wants to make love to you; I know it."

"Well, it's never going to happen, I can tell you that," laughed Jack.

Over a year went by before Sarah heard from Jennifer again, and during that time, her life was not going well. What her mother had said was true: she did **not** love Bernard Black in the first place and only married him for his money and status. As it turned out, he didn't have nearly as much money and status as she thought, and his many affairs added fuel to the fire of a miserable marriage. They argued constantly and had separate bedrooms in the down-sized apartment that had become their home. He was emotionally abusive, often cruel and insensitive. He gave Jen an allowance that was just barely enough to keep her alive. Bernard demanded that she cook all his meals, clean their apartment and run constant errands for him. Sometimes, he slapped her across the face when his wishes weren't obeyed. She was desperately looking for a way to escape the suffering her life had begun to include.

The beginning of the end happened when Bernie started to drink. As his business began to flounder, he found solace in beer, wine and whiskey. When Jen's husband was drunk, he became physically violent with his wife. On one occasion, he kicked her in the stomach when she denied having an affair with his brother. On another, he tripped her when she walked by him in disgust as he watched a pornographic movie on their TV.

"My knee's bleeding, you jerk," she yelled. "Get me some band aides, or I'm going to bleed to death."

Bernard Black then just looked down at her and laughed.

"You're a whore and a bitch, Jenny and I can't stand you. Get your own bandages."

After that, Jennifer stayed in bed and cried for two days.

"This is never going to work," she thought.

Chapter 9   <u>Infinite Healing: January to April 1985</u>

As time passed, Jack became very clear about one specific aspect of Sarah's character. She was a natural-born healer. Her voice was as soft and full of compassion as an angel's. She knew how to listen intently to anyone conversing with her, just like a musician listening for the song of a nightingale in the evening breeze. She was an expert at reading the maladies of her clients and could see directly into the karmic source of their suffering. Her hands were supple, soft and expressive, and when she touched you, a healing energy was released. After she gave someone's wound a <u>Reiki Treatment</u>, the cut healed very quickly—far faster than would normally be expected.

"I think you should start a healing center," he said to her as they lay in their king-sized water bed one Saturday morning after making love slowly, tenderly and mindfully for over two hours.

"How do you mean, Jack," she replied, gently rubbing the silk sheet underneath her with the smooth skin of her right hand. She watched the water ripple to the end of the plastic mattress like the waves of a pond after a pebble plops into the still waters.

"You love healing people and have magic in your body. Wouldn't it be wonderful if you could help *more* injured, broken or sore clients and actually make a living doing it?"

"What kind of center?" She asked.

"One with a studio and a couple of breakout rooms for <u>Reiki Sessions</u>, relaxation massages, meditation workshops and classes in the healing arts."

"Do you really think I could make such a business *profitable?*"

"I *know* you could, and I'd be willing to support you fully and help you get started."

"Thank you for saying that, my dear," she responded. "I love you."

"Sarah, do you have any capital?"

"Yes, as a matter of fact, I do. After my second marriage ended, we sold our three-level townhome in Burnaby. That left me with a nest egg of sixty-five thousand dollars, and I still have forty-eight thousand left."

"Would you be willing to put some of it into your healing center?"

"I probably would," was her hesitant reply.

Jack then began searching for the right property to get his partner set up in business. After some frustrating internet searches, fruitless telephone inquiries and long viewing appointments, he stumbled upon a massage clinic for sale. The owner was pregnant and *had* to leave her practice to start a family--so negotiating with her was easy.

"I'd like to show you a great site for your center, Sarah. It's just past the Highstream Mall on the harbor in downtown Richmond. If you're willing to take over the lease, you can get it for ten thousand five hundred, and that includes a large foyer, three massage rooms, a small kitchen and all of the owner's furniture and massage tables."

"How much would the lease payments be?" Sarah asked.

"Fifteen hundred and fifty dollars per month, but don't worry--you'll make that in one week of operations."

"It sounds fabulous, Jack—when can I see it?"

"How about right now? I've got the master key."

"Yes, let's go look at it *now*," she answered without hesitation.

"By the way, have you thought of a name for your center?"

"Yes—I'll call it *Infinite Healing*," she blurted out quickly in an excited voice.

On January 6th, 1985, Sarah opened <u>Infinite Healing</u>. She held an Open House the following weekend attended by all her current clients, the Richmond City Clerk, Father Jerome Santoro of <u>St. Matthew's Anglican Church,</u> twenty-two friends, fifteen members of the general public and the Buddhist monk Carl Tara Sandheim. Jack introduced them, after which Sarah made one long cut into a large, two-layered, strawberry-covered angel food cake and then sidled up to the microphone and gave a short but heartfelt speech. She said,

"Friends, I can't express my gratitude to all of you for attending this event and supporting me in making this Center happen. From here on, my life will be about helping people and serving them by healing any brokenness in their lives, including all of you. Please circulate now and enjoy all the delicacies and liquid concoctions Jack has prepared for you."

Infinite Healing became a highly successful Center of Wellness from its first day. Sarah did no advertising or marketing, yet she was as busy a practitioner as any in the *Lower Mainland*. It was all about word of mouth. Her patients were amazed at how thoroughly her treatments made them better in short periods of time.

Jack started giving *Zen Meditation* classes every Wednesday evening at the Center. Once a month, Carl Tara Sandheim attended the class and spoke for an hour on a topic related to some aspect of transformation through Buddhism, which was definitely his area of expertise.

Father Santoro offered a Centering Prayer Workshop, held every Saturday from 9 am to noon. This Workshop was based on the work of Richard Rohr's non-dual approach to Christianity. Father Santoro taught his students to repeat the chant, "*Lord Jesus Christ, Son of God, have mercy on my soul*," until they reached the profound silence lying at the core of their Being--a silence the Bible claimed was beyond human understanding.

"Centering prayer is very much like zazen," Jack told Sarah.

"Yes, it is. Both practices are based on *experiencing* the soul, not talking about it," responded Sarah. "Experiencing reality is far more powerful than believing something about it."

"You could say it that way, and I'd understand," replied her partner.

The survey questionnaire guests completed after visiting Infinite Healing revealed the key elements of the Center's success:

- Exquisite background meditation music.
- Powerful physical, emotional and spiritual healing sessions.
- Spaces of silence: creating a calming, peaceful environment and
- Caring, empathetic and professional healing practitioners.

"Aren't you happy you took the plunge?" asked Jack after one of Father Santoro's Sessions.

"I certainly am, darling, and you deserve most of the credit for the Center's success," she replied.

"We certainly have some wonderful programs, Sarah, but the heart of the Center's power lies in your healing massage sessions. How do you affect such profound changes in your clients?"

"There's no secret to it really, Jack. First, I have to get centered and become fully present. That's why I always do a short meditation before I touch anyone. Then, I have to completely disappear as a person, so I visualize all my boundaries evaporating until I become nothing but a golden pool of light. Then I guide my hands onto a person's body, and they move by themselves without any direction from me. My hands can feel lumps of suffering, pain, tension and resistance, so they knead those spots until the blockages disappear. I can then actually feel the blood flowing freely. Once that happens, physic energy arises and buzzes throughout all the patient's chakras. Once the chakra centers are flowing, the disease usually evaporates."

"That's amazing, my dear. It's totally miraculous. Will you give me a treatment now?"

"Of course I will. Where are you feeling uncomfortable?"

"My right hip and upper thigh are very sore and throbbing with pain."

"Then lie down on this massage table, and I'll see what I can find," Sarah whispered.

After sitting in a chair for five minutes with her eyes tightly shut, Sarah began to work on Jack's right leg. She moved her hands gently, slowly across the high part of his right leg, pouring feelings of love into him.

"You've got a lump the size of an orange next to your thigh bone, Jack. Can you feel me massaging it?"

"Yes, you've got the exact spot that hurts."

At that point, Sarah rubbed one specific spot on his leg. Once in a while, she'd stop and hold both of her hands on the hurting place, closing her eyes, humming, and pouring herself into his lower body.

"Your fingers feel so strong and powerful, Sarah. The pain is starting to subside."

"This is a particularly difficult pain body, Jack. It may take a few hours to clean up. Did you injure yourself there at any time?"

"Yes—when I was five years old, my father whipped my leg with the buckle on his cowboy belt, and it was swollen for over a year. Actually, it's been sore ever since."

"The pain there is more than physical, Jack. Your father violated you in a way that hurt your psyche, too. I want you to close your eyes and think about your father now. Think of him when he was good to you, when you felt love for him."

Jack saw his dad in the fast-flowing Sooke River, teaching him how to fish. He was complimenting him and showing him how to tie a fly. The water was cool on his legs, and he could smell the fresh forest and the bright green pine needles on the shore.

"Now feel love for the man. Yes, love him—forgive him, Jack—for what he did to your leg. Let it go."

Jack fell into a deep sleep and had a vivid dream. His father was playing the role of Santa at Christmas, handing out gifts to his two five-year-old sons. He was strong, generous and full of fun in the dream.

"I love you, Dad."

When he woke up, he saw Sarah sitting on a bamboo chair in the corner of the room with a beautiful smile on her face.

"How does your leg feel?"

"Sarah, it's a miracle—all the pain has vanished, and the lump's completely gone. I can't believe what you've just done."

From that day forward, Jack never felt pain in his right leg again.

"You're a saint, Sarah, no two ways about it," he said, tears slowly trickling down his face.

Chapter 10   Cara: April to September, 1985

Just after the Easter holidays, Sarah's website received an unsolicited email with an attached resume from Cara Shrum.

I'm looking for permanent work as a professional massage therapist. Having just graduated from <u>Richmond Community College's</u> Registered Massage Therapy Program puts me in an excellent position to deliver quality massages to the clients of <u>Infinite Healing</u>. I'm also an acupuncture and Reiki practitioner. Please find my resume enclosed.

Most sincerely,

Cara Shrum
RMT

"Jack, look at this resume—it's awesome!" Sarah said to him as he sat drinking from a cup of steaming, green herbal tea at their kitchen table.

"Is someone looking to work at your <u>Center</u>?" he countered.

"Yes—and she's a registered massage therapist, an acupuncturist with <u>Reiki</u> experience, and she also holds a degree in philosophy from the <u>University of Victoria.</u>"

"Wow—sounds perfect. You could hire her and let her work for you from the spare room or just rent her the space on a monthly basis."

"I'd prefer to hire her directly if she's a fit."

In her email reply, Sarah wrote,

Dear Cara,

We'd like to schedule an interview with you next Saturday afternoon at 2 pm to discuss working at Infinite Healing as a massage therapist. Please meet my partner and me at the Center then.

Sincerely,

Sarah Robinson,
Owner--Infinite Healing
16—2708 Harbor Road,
Richmond, BC.

Cara arrived at precisely 1 pm and bounced into the Center with confidence and high spirits. She was over six feet tall, slim, straight back, and perfect posture. Her hair was brown, held together at the back in a floppy pony tail and her eyes were large, clear, bright and sparkling with anticipation. It was obvious that her hands were powerful because she had long, slender fingers with beautiful, unpainted nails. She wore no make-up but didn't look unfinished. She was attractive but wholesome, clean and vibrant.

"You must be Cara," stated Sarah with authority.

"Yes," she replied, with a broad smile that could melt ice, revealing white, perfectly formed teeth against a background of slightly tanned skin—the same color as Roger's Golden Brown sugar. She was full of a wonderful kind of positive energy.

"Please come into my office. We'd like to ask you a few questions."

After some brief introductions, and once Cara was comfortably seated, Sarah paused, looked directly into her eyes and asked her,

"Do you see yourself as a healer?"

"Yes, I most definitely do. I've undergone many intense training sessions to be able to break down people's inner blocks, which would subsequently allow them to experience peaceful, integrated spaces within their own being."

"What were your favorite courses at Uvic?" interjected Jack.

"I specialized in Eastern philosophical studies and particularly enjoyed studying Tantric Buddhism and Sufi Mysticism," she responded, to her questioner's delight.

"Are you a meditator then?"

"I don't do formal meditations, but I'm constantly looking to experience the flow state through athletics and my massage practice. I'm addicted to peak experiences and try to turn all my physical activities into sacred dances."

"Would you be willing to participate in Jack's Meditation Classes on Wednesday evenings and a Centering Prayer Workshop run by an Anglican priest every Saturday morning?"

"Why yes, *of course*," she replied effortlessly.

"And are you willing to work for 65% of your customer's fees, providing we supply your table and all the necessary accessories?" asked Sarah.

"Yes, that sounds *more than fair.*"

The interview dragged on for another fifty-five minutes, but as soon as Cara agreed to the financial terms of her employment, Sarah made the decision to hire her immediately. Jack concurred.

Cara's work at Infinite Healing unfolded seamlessly. She took on some of Sarah's clients and soon began building her own loyal customers. She actively participated in the existing Center Programs and frequently noticed ways to improve the business. Before too long, she was contributing in a significant way to the bottom line.

In the summer of 1985, Sarah called a staff meeting to discuss leasing the vacant Starbucks Coffee Shop next door.

"It's a tiny operation," she said, "But Starbucks has moved across the harbor into the Surfside Mall. There are only four tables because the whole shop is only six hundred square feet. But all their equipment for hot beverages is available, and the rent is only $800 a month. This feels like a great opportunity to me, but I want to know what you all think. Should we take on the lease?"

"We could also serve herbal tea, energy drinks and coffee with our own brand of muffins, croissants and fruit squares," added Jack.

"Can we have a look inside?" asked Cara.

Once inside, they were surprised at how dark and cold the place was. The walls were all finished in teak mahogany but stained with a deep brown varnish, and the tables were painted jet black. However, all the equipment was spotlessly clean stainless steel—ready to go--and as good as new.

"We'd have to brighten it up, don't you think?" questioned Cara.

"Absolutely," added Jack.

"Yes, I'd paint the whole operation white--with a red trim and crimson tables," said Sarah.

"But who'd you get to run it?" asked Cara.

"I think I can find someone to do that," responded Sarah, "Let's do this--I intuitively know it's a great idea," she said, dancing out of the store.

As of May 1st, Infinite Healing included an empty snack and juice bar named Healing Foods & Drink.

The next day, an advertisement appeared in the Richmond Times under the Service Staff Wanted Column. It read:

Coffee Bar Attendant Wanted

High Integrity Company needs a juice bar attendant with the following qualities:

- **Honest.**
- **Hard-working.**
- **Team player.**

- **Coffee lover.**
- **Good customer service skills.**
- **Meditation practice is preferred.**

The successful candidate will receive good wages and tips, a profit-sharing plan, two uniforms and free coffee while at work.

Sarah was surprised to receive thirty-eight resumes over the next two weeks.

"Can you review all these applications for me and give me the five best, Jack?"

"Of course, I can," he replied.

He enjoyed this task despite most of the applicants being underqualified, overqualified or poor writers.

The first one he gave Sarah was from a young male university student who wanted part-time work. But during the interview, he swore twice, criticized the décor of the Juice Bar and asked if he could smoke.

The second interviewee was a more mature, friendly, polite, and experienced woman. But she was morbidly obese, had greasy hair and didn't know why she wanted the job. A discussion with her lasted only twelve minutes.

The following person Sarah talked to came close. She was an attractive, articulate young woman who was very qualified for the job but wore a low-cut dress to the interview, which exposed over half of her huge breasts.

"She'd definitely distract our male customers," Jack noted with a gulp that Sarah overlooked when they discussed the applicants later that night.

"I think she'd do more than just distract them, added Sarah. "I didn't know it'd be hard to get the right person for this job, Jack."

"Well, let's just keep on looking. The right person will turn up; I just know it," he responded. "Besides, you've still got two more interviews to conduct.

The fourth applicant aced the interview. He had lots of experience and was very enthusiastic, even aggressively interested in the job. He was young, handsome and full of energy. However, when Jack checked two of his references, he was shocked to find out that number four had a criminal record and had been fired from his last job for assaulting a customer.

The final interview happened in the evening due to scheduling conflicts. The potential employee was experienced, calm, professional and articulate. Her resume was immaculately put together and stressed all her good points in an orderly fashion. She answered the question about how much money she wanted by saying emphatically,

"I won't work for under $21 per hour."

"But that's six dollars more than we're paying," replied Sarah. "However, you'll make good money with us because we'll give you 50% of the collected tips and 5% of the monthly profits."

"That won't do," replied the interviewee. "Twenty-one per hour is my bottom line."

"I'd never hire someone so interested in money," Sarah told Jack at the end of the day.

Over the next month, Jack did most of the renovating and cleaning of the Juice Bar. He painted the whole space with pure white latex, and all the tables were tinted red with white trim. He scrubbed the place until it was sterile and got all the equipment working and ready for service. Then he bought a large fridge to store items that needed to be kept cold, as well as a glass buffet to show off their muffins, cookies, cakes and sugary squares. He also had to install and learn how to use a cash register. By Labor Day, the Bar was finished and ready to open. It looked even more trendy than the Starbucks it replaced.

During the month of September, Sarah received many more resumes. Still, she was generally too busy to read them or too uninspired to keep looking for the right server. Jack read every application, but not one that came in over the summer was appropriate.

"Are we being too fussy, Jack?"

"Not at all," he replied. "Trust me, getting the right employee is 75% of the secret of a successful business, and sometimes you just have to be patient and wait until someone who's a perfect fit comes along."

"It's frustrating having everything ready to go but not being able to start this part of our operation."

"I know, but be patient. The right person will come along when we least expect it."

And, as it turned out, Jack was right about that.

Chapter 11   A Surprise Guest: September, 1985 to January, 1986

Three days before the end of September that year, a traumatic event occurred in Sarah's life. At 2 am on Monday the 27th, she was awakened by three loud knocks on her front door.

"Mama, I need help," spluttered Jennifer through the small crack between the door and its frame once Sarah opened it slightly.

"Jen, what are you doing here at this time?" moaned Sarah, trying to see her daughter through closed eyes glued together by sleep, like two pieces of cardboard stuck together with contact cement.

"I'm in trouble. Can I come in--**please**?"

As Sarah opened the door, she was shocked by Jennifer's condition. She was soaking wet, and her dress was torn badly, exposing a dirty brassiere. Her bare left foot was bleeding profusely into an old worn-down thong, like ketchup running out of a hot plastic bottle.

"I haven't seen or heard from you in eight months, Jen. Where have you been?"

"I've been living at the *Salvation Army* downtown in the Woman's Quarters. Tonight, I got accosted by a drunken homeless guy who was wandering through our residence, so I can't stay there any longer. He actually nicked my leg with a Swiss Army Knife—luckily, I jumped away just in time and ran away. It's like being in prison down there."

"Does that backpack contain all your worldly possessions now?"

"Yes," bawled Jennifer.

"Do you have any money?"

"No—I have **no** money."

"Where's Bernie?"

"He's in jail awaiting trial for bilking seven of the investors in his *Silver City Project*," she replied before bursting into tears again.

"Here, drink this," whispered Jack as he stepped out of the background and handed her a cup of steaming hot decaffeinated chamomile tea.

"Mom, I can explain everything later, but please let me stay here tonight," she pleaded.

"Sure, Jen, that's fine, but you'll have to sleep on the couch. Jack sleeps in my bed now. But I'm going to have to dress your wound."

"Thank you *so much*, mother. Can we talk more about this in the morning?"

"Yes—have a bath, dry off so I can put a band-aid and some antiseptic on your leg--and then *go to sleep*. I'll get you some clean pajamas while you're in the bathroom.

Jennifer's face lit up as tears streamed down her nose into an open, blubbering mouth. She looked like a stranded sea otter just reunited with her mother. She'd mistreated Sarah over the past year, and yet, here she was, forgiving her daughter without any questions *or conditions*. After she cleaned herself up, put on fresh bed clothes and let her mom fix her cut, Jen went directly to bed and fell into a deep, dreamless sleep.

When she woke up, Jack and her mother were eating breakfast and chatting at a small vinyl kitchen table as the sun streamed through open Venetian blinds, smattering bright light throughout the apartment, shining directly on plates of hot scrambled free-run chicken eggs, freshly buttered olive-bread cheese toast and steaming hot black coffee.

"Come and have some eggs and toast with us, Jen. You must be starved," murmured Sarah.

"Yes, I am," she winced.

As they ate together, Sarah began to seek some answers.

"I thought you had a great marriage—at least, that's the impression you always gave me."

"Mom, Bernard started abusing me over a year ago. When his business began to flounder, he drank like a fish—as much as two bottles of Crown Royal whiskey a day. If I questioned him on *anything*, he beat the shit out of me. He turned violent and kept accusing me of having affairs. One night, I swore at him, and he punched me as hard as he could in the stomach; then, he threw me against a wall until I collapsed onto the floor. I was unconscious for over an hour. He left me there and went to a neighborhood pub to drink and play darts. Just after Christmas, I left him and ran away to a <u>Women's Shelter.</u> They eventually found me semi-permanent housing at the *Sally Ann*."

"Why didn't you contact me then?"

"I still thought it was wrong that you were shacked up with someone half your age. I'm *so* sorry," she moaned, glancing sheepishly at Jack.

"You can stay here temporarily until you get back on your feet. But if you do so, you'll have to completely accept my relationship with Jack. Can you do that?"

"Yes, I can."

"Are you interested in getting a job?" Sarah blurted out.

"Yes, absolutely and *as soon as possible*. But what can I do in this condition, and who'd hire me?"

"Would you be willing to run our new <u>Juice & CoffeeBar</u> at <u>Infinite Healing</u>?

"What would that entail?"

"Serving our clients hot and cold drinks and healing snacks, doing some marketing and getting involved in the Center's Classes and Workshops."

"What would the pay be?" Jen asked.

"You'll receive minimum wage plus 40% of the profits from all food and drink sales."

"Yes, I'll do it," she responded eagerly and without hesitation, jumping up and down and breaking into a huge smile before hugging her mother tightly.

"I'll give you a chance, but you must take this assignment seriously. All of us at Infinite Healing are committed to succeeding in business, healing and personal service.

"You can count on me to make the Juice Bar a smash hit. I promise you I'll be great for this position."

As time passed, Jack noticed that his stepdaughter's attitude toward him began to change radically once she moved into her mother's place. He was surprised at how quickly she became integrated into the overall work of the Healing Center. She actually began to treat him very well and attended his Meditation Class regularly, even showing an interest in contemplative practices. He also noticed that she was extremely attractive and sexually provocative. But by January 1986, Jen had become a respected and valuable member of the Center's team.

"You have a magnificent body, Jen," Jack said to her one morning when Sarah wasn't around, "But when you walk around with just your underpants on, it throws me off."

"What are you saying *exactly*?"

"I get sexually aroused looking at your naked body, and that's *not* appropriate."

"Okay, Jack—good to know. I'll try to correct that in the future," she responded, winking at him quickly with her right eye.

In actual fact, Sarah's apartment was too small for three people, and that reality began to splay Jack's nerves. He knew that any intimate noises made in bed with his partner were clearly audible to Jennifer. When Jen brought a friend over, male or female, it was inevitably going to be awkward when both Jack and Sarah were present. Jennifer was a very fussy eater and craved junk food, so she rarely ate the nutritious delicacies her mother prepared. Perhaps that's why she was so skinny. Most of all, she was extremely messy and never cleaned up after herself, which added to the tension beginning to accumulate in Sarah and Jack's world.

Jennifer was five feet ten inches tall and had large breasts and a very thin waist. There wasn't an ounce of fat anywhere on her body other than at her bust line. She had two large tattoos—one on each arm. On the right was a blue dragon breathing red fire, and on the left was a demon in a blue dress with two red horns sticking out of his head.

"I'm trying to be discreet now, Jack," she said when they were eating alone for lunch one day. "But you still keep staring at me."

"I'm just studying your tattoos—they seem so unusual. Why did you get them done?"

"A friend of my ex owned a tattoo parlor and got me drunk on two occasions. Both times, he talked me into having the tattoos done—at no charge. Do you like them?"

"No, I don't, Jen. They look crass and crude. And what if you decide you want to get rid of them someday?

"I love them, so I won't ever want them gone. They're symbolic. The dragon stands for my sexual passion and the devil for my addictions."

"What do you mean sexual passion?"

"Jack, this is personal. Please don't ever tell anyone. I'm a nymphomaniac."

"How do you know?"

"I crave sex every day."

"And what are your addictions?"

"Swearing, tobacco, grass and whiskey."

"Jen, if you want to get clean, we can help you at <u>Infinite Healing</u>. That's what the <u>Center </u>does. Your problems are curable if you want them gone. Do you want me to talk to your mother about putting you into a program?"

"I'm not ready for that now, Jack. But I must say, I *am* enjoying your <u>Meditation Class</u>."

"That's good to hear. Now, will you let me just talk to your mother about your sexuality and your addictions?"

"Sure, go ahead."

Two days later, Jack started a conversation with Sarah about her daughter.

"Did you know Jen's addicted to sex, drugs and booze?"

"I know about the drugs and alcohol, but not the sex. How do you know all this?"

"She told me the other day and then gave me permission to mention this to you. Personally, I think putting her into one of your programs at <u>Infinite Healing</u> could really help her get through all this. Unfortunately, she says she's not quite ready for that yet."

"Jack, I've never told you this before, but I think you need to know. The reason I left my first husband is he was sexually abusing Jen. He was having full-on intercourse with her regularly when I caught him. I filed for divorce the next day. But Jennifer has never been the same since. Before that happened, she was an innocent, precocious twelve-year-old doing well in school. After I left Frank, her grades plummeted, and she started biting her nails, smoking and hanging around with the wrong crowd. By the time Jen was fourteen, she was drinking hard liquor daily. She got expelled from high school in the middle of Grade 10 and never went back."

"That's horrific, Sarah, I didn't know. Now I think I understand your daughter a little better. But I still think she'd benefit from one of your intensive programs."

"Time will tell, Jack. I appreciate your concern."

Chapter 12   Flashbacks: January to March, 1986

Three weeks after Jen started working at the Juice Bar, Jack got a phone call from the Richmond police.

"Is this Jack Turner?" asked a woman on the other end of the phone, with an authoritarian voice, like that of a Nazi prison guard.

"Yes, it is—who am I speaking to?"

"It's Staff Sergeant Jean Mattis of the RCMP. Are you the same Jack Turner who spent time in Matsqui and whose father is Rory Turner?"

"Yes, officer, that's me. How can I help you?"

"Mr. Turner, we've been trying to track you down for two weeks. It's important that you call the Kent Institute right away regarding your father."

"Is there a problem with my father?"

"Sir," replied the sergeant hesitantly, "He passed away suddenly three weeks ago. I'm sorry for your loss. Please call the warden at Kent as soon as you possibly can. He's desperately trying to get a hold of you."

Two hours later, Jack was on his way to Agassiz, BC, his head throbbing and his heart aching, like an antelope's pulsating brain being eaten alive by turkey buzzards. When he arrived at the maximum security prison in question, he went straight to the main entrance, handkerchief to his face, and spoke directly to a security guard posted at the large oak desk just inside the front door.

"I'm here to speak with Warden Simpson about my father, Rory Turner. Apparently, he died inside this prison almost a month ago," he spluttered.

The guard quickly called on his cell phone, asked Jack to sign the <u>Registry,</u> and then buzzed the inside door open. Another uniformed prison official was standing on the other side, waiting to escort him to the warden's office. They walked down a long, sterile, marble-floored corridor that was as smooth as glass and shone with freshly polished wax and up two flights of shiny stairs before arriving at a large door with the boss's name on it. The guard opened it, and Jack immediately saw the warden.

"Come in, Jack. I've been waiting a long time to meet you. I can see you're upset, but we must talk," said Simpson.

He was a very portly man, over 300 pounds, with a baby face, double chin and handlebar mustache. As he waddled toward his desk, sweating profusely, Jack glanced at the bookshelves lining the walls and saw they were full of legal reference texts and law journals. Once the warden was sitting behind his desk in an extra-large, reinforced and cushioned swivel chair, he began to speak.

"Jack, I'm very sorry you've lost your father. He was a violent man, frequently punished for his outbreaks, but he *did* have some strengths. He couldn't tolerate anyone being bullied, he was loyal to his friends, and he worked hard to learn the welding trade."

"My dad had a serious drinking problem, and when he drank, he beat me and my brother when we were growing up. But we also had some great times with him. He taught me many important things. How did he die, Mr. Simpson?"

"Unfortunately, he got into an altercation with another inmate who stabbed him three times in the chest with an ice pick before any of our staff could intervene. One of the jabs penetrated the center of his heart, and he transpired immediately. Again, I'm terribly sorry. But now I'd like to take you down to the morgue so we can positively identify him."

When Jack saw his father's head, he gasped and recoiled in shock. His face and chest were scared with cuts, and all his hair was gone. He lay there with glassy eyes, looking straight up at the concrete ceiling, stiff as a board, like a frozen mummy. All of a sudden, Jack's consciousness was overwhelmed by flashbacks.

He remembered times when his father was sober and working. He loved to go fishing in those days and taught his sons how to cast and catch rainbow trout. On one fishing expedition, Jack fell into the <u>Fraser River</u> and was being swept downstream by a powerful current. Rory plunged into the icy water, swam hard to retrieve him and pulled his son to safety, catching him just before he went over a waterfall.

"He saved my life," thought Jack.

Then he remembered how his father would give Sylvia flowers on her birthday and make her breakfast, bringing her a tray of her favorite foods with hot herbal tea while she lay in bed.

What about the times he played music with Mom," he pondered. *She loved the way he played the drums.*

"This *is* your father, then, Jack?" interrupted the warden.

"Yes, it's him, no doubt about it," he answered tearfully.

"Do you want me to arrange to have him cremated at the *Fraser View Sanctuary?* I can do that for $400."

After a long pause, Jack replied hesitatingly,

"Yes, sir, that would be acceptable."

"Fine, just sign these papers, and you can pick him up in a metal box in two weeks."

For three days, Sarah noticed that her partner was drinking whiskey again. She tried hard to cheer him up because he was very depressed.

"Let's get you out of the doldrums, Jack. Why don't we have a Celebration of Life for your Dad?" I could ask Father Santoro to officiate so his soul gets a proper sendoff."

"I think that might help the grieving process for me. Let's do it," responded Jack, a faint smile on his lips.

The funeral was held on March 7th, 1986, at St. Matthew's Church on Sandringham Drive in Richmond, with Father Santoro officiating. In attendance were Jack, Sarah, Jennifer Black, Cara, Warden Simpson and Carl Tara Sandheim. Everyone was dressed in black except Jennifer and the priest. Jen wore inappropriate clothes: blue jeans and a white T-shirt covered by a cream overcoat. The priest wore a green robe tied at the middle by a black rope frayed at the ends. It was a short ceremony with several periods of silence. In conclusion, the padre prayed that Rory be forgiven all his sins and that his soul progress *straight into heaven.*

"May the Lord be praised, may the Lord be praised, may the Lord be praised," chanted Santoro to end the rite and, after three minutes of silence, said,

"Thank you all for coming today. Let us now reconvene in the *Church Hall* for refreshments and a social time."

No one but Sarah noticed the tears staining Jack's face at the luncheon. Everyone but Sarah's daughter tried to console Jack. She, on the other hand, stood back away from the crowd against a hardwood wall, smoking Du Maurier cigarettes and staring at some strings of colored lights hanging from the ceiling. Her eyes darted furtively around the room—a sign that she was distracted and not present to the solemn event happening around her.

Father Santoro went right over and stood beside her.

"You seem to be deep in thought, Jennifer. Can I help you with anything?"

"No, I was just thinking about the hopelessness of life."

"How do you mean?"

"There's a criminal lying down over there who had lots of problems in his life. But what does it matter—he's gone now. Soon, no one will know what he did and why. What's worse, nobody will care. What was the point of his life anyway—or anyone's life?"

"Jen, the Lord has a purpose for each and every one of us. Our job is to find that purpose and live it with passion, honoring Him in everything we do."

"What if we can't find a purpose?"

"Then, my dear, we'd have to pray for one. God reveals his secrets to every faithful heart."

"Thank you for your kind words, sir," said Jen wistfully as she left his side and went to sit down at an empty bench outside the church hall.

I don't have the nerve to tell him I don't believe in his God, she thought. *Where was his God when that Roman Catholic priest at summer camp made me give him fellatio every day for two weeks?*

There were many memories that invaded her mind on the tail of that one. Her father had been a very devout, strict Catholic who went to Mass three times a week and followed the dictums of the church to a letter. When she was twelve, he put her in the church choir and sent her to a Catholic school for two years.

She was innocent then and devoutly believed in the Catholic God. But it was around that time her Dad started abusing Jen sexually when Sarah wasn't around. He was rough with her, fondled her and made her satisfy him in adult ways.

She concluded that no God would allow His people to do these things to her. Soon afterwards, she dropped out of the choir, went to public school and stopped believing in Catholic theology. Something deep inside her had been wounded, and the wound wasn't healing. As soon as she broke down and finally confided in Sarah, her parent's marriage was over.

Jen found herself attracted to sex in dark ways after that. Once she started dating, rough treatment was desired and requested. She wanted to be slapped, spit on and ravaged. She craved physical contact but hated foreplay or any kind of emotional bonding with boys. Her distance gave her some form of control.

In those days, Jack was emotionally detached from Jen and made it obvious he wasn't interested in her—emotionally or physically. This fact aggravated her and made her try hard to get under his skin, to make him vulnerable. But he was, even then, trying hard to move in another direction.

After his father's passing, he redoubled his efforts to solve the 'one-hand-clapping-koan.'

If sounds don't come to me from an outside material world, and all we really are is pure knowing, how can death end everything? He thought. *Perhaps living in this question will create new openings,* he mused to himself.

Chapter 13   Confronting Death: March, 1986 to July, 1990

As time passed, it became clear that Cara was also a natural healer. She worked with Sarah to develop more effective *Reiki* treatments. She collaborated closely with Father Santoro as he set up the healing Order of St. Luke. This was a Christian movement that used *prayer* and the *laying on of hands* to heal people who were sick or suffering. Every Wednesday evening, he held a meeting of this group at Infinite Healing, with Cara assisting. After playing hymns on his guitar for about twenty minutes, the minister had everyone in the group form a circle and hold hands. The person desiring healing would enter that circle and sit in the middle of it on a chair. All the other participants would close their eyes, lay their hands on the sick and pray out loud for recovery. It was like a small revival meeting where everyone talked in *tongues*—but it created a healing space that worked!

She and Sarah had become kindred spirits and began to have positive results curing diseases such as early-stage cancer, gout and asthma. Infinite Healing was gaining a reputation as an effective, perhaps even *miraculous,* healing Center. The only missing piece was Jennifer's attitude and behavior. She attended the Workshops only sporadically, often arrived late to work, flirted openly with some of the male clients and constantly took smoke breaks.

However, she did become part of the working family at Infinite Healing, and for four years, the Center prospered and gained a reputation as the best alternative wellness operation in the Lower Mainland. During those years, Jack and Sarah became a loving couple living and maintaining an idyllic lifestyle. They never argued or became bored with each other and continued to have a robust sex life. In lovemaking, the mutual goal was to satisfy the other person. It was always a selfless act for both of them, which manifested profound loving and caring actions.

But in early July 1990, Sarah woke up complaining of a stomach ache.

"All of a sudden, my stomach's on fire, and I've got heartburn, Jack."

"That's strange—you never get sick, and you're a mystical healer," he responded.

These symptoms persisted and got worse over the next ten days until finally, Jack insisted that she make an appointment to see Dr. Keith Chen, her GP.

"I don't think you're seriously ill, Sarah," said the doctor after examining her thoroughly. "But let's do a few tests to be absolutely sure. I'll call you if anything develops."

Over the next week, Sarah went for extensive blood work at Life Labs and chest X-rays at West Coast Testing. When the doctor finally called, she was exhausted.

"Sarah, I need you to come back to my office first thing tomorrow morning," said Dr. Chen over the phone.

"What time, sir?"

"Please be here by 7 am."

An appointment that early made Sarah extremely anxious. When she arrived at his practice with Jack, she was ushered directly into the main examination room, feeling heavy and stressed out. Her stomach was aching.

"Sarah, I hate to be the one to tell you this," Dr. Chen whispered, "but you've got *Stage Four* pancreatic cancer, and there's no cure for it at this point."

Sarah turned bright red and covered her face with her hands, gasping for air but not actually speaking for several minutes. After a long, heavy pause, she asked,

"How long do I have to live, doctor?" Her voice was quizzical and shaky.

"No longer than a month. I'd like you to move into the Richmond Hospice tomorrow morning. A bed has already been reserved for you. Now it's time to get all your affairs in order."

Jack then slumped over and knelt on the floor, sobbing unreservedly and beating his chest with clenched fists.

"This can't be," he kept repeating. "It just can't be. You haven't had any symptoms up until now."

Unbeknownst to Jack, his common-law wife had only one week left to live. During that week, he visited her every day, often staying for eight-hour stretches or more. He usually sat beside her bed, holding Sarah's left hand, watching her shrivel and grow wizened before his very eyes.

"I've never loved anyone as intensely as I've loved you, Jack."

"I love you too, Sarah," he replied, staring directly into her adoring eyes.

"I wish you'd spent time healing yourself before it all came to this. Perhaps you absorbed some of the illnesses you spent so much time curing," muttered Jack.

"My illness was just too far along in the end, and if I picked it up from others, I can live with that. Healing was my destiny no matter what that involved," stated Sarah.

"I can understand that, my dear."

"Now--will you make sure Infinite Healing survives and keeps doing healing work?"

"Yes, I'll certainly try, darling."

"Will you keep an eye on Jen and make sure she stays alive and well?"

"Of course I will; you don't have anything to worry about in that regard," said Jack, not realizing at the time how difficult that was going to be.

Sarah's funeral was held at St. Matthew's and was directed by Reverend Santoro. Over one hundred and fifty people attended the two-hour service, including most of the church's congregants, virtually all the past and present clients of Infinite Healing, every one of Sarah's close relatives and friends, as well as the Buddhist monks, Carl Tara Sandheim and Haru Kazan.

Jack's eulogy lasted for fifteen minutes and left everyone crying profusely. Cara's final words were equally as powerful. She shared how closely she and Sarah had become as they worked as a team to heal others. When she finished, Jack hugged her, compassionately holding her shaking body tightly.

After the ceremony, Sarah was lowered into the ground in a stainless steel casket covered with crimson roses, as all her friends and relatives lined the grave, weeping and gnashing their teeth.

At the solemn wake, held in the cavernous Church Hall, Jack had set up an open microphone, and twenty-three people attended to it—all speaking in glowing terms about Sarah Robinson. She didn't have an enemy in the world and was loved by everyone who ever knew her. Light refreshments were served and a live folk quartet played Sarah's favorite songs quietly in the background. Jack was racked by grief but somehow managed to effectively organize all the *end-of-life* arrangements and events.

Conrad Steinbeck was the lawyer who called Jack and Jennifer to his office three weeks after the funeral so he could instruct them on all the matters pertaining to Sarah's will.

"Jennifer, your mother has left you the sum of $50,000 in a savings account. I'll have a certified cheque drawn up for you that'll be ready for pick-up in two weeks. Jack receives the rest of Sarah's estate, which includes all her possessions, her art work and Infinite Healing-- plus a cash amount in the sum of $15,000."

"I'll be giving the business, <u>Infinite Healing,</u> and all Sarah's art work to Cara Shrum, sir, so could you draw up all the requisite ownership transfers?"

"Yes, as per your wishes, then."

"But Jack, won't you have anything to do with the <u>Center</u> anymore?" asked Jennifer.

"Yes, I'll still be involved in some ways, and I'll do everything I can to help Cara continue to succeed."

After signing all the necessary documents, Jack and Jen left the lawyer's office and stopped at the Starbucks on 53rd Street for coffee on the way home.

"It's best if you find another place to live now, Jennifer," said Jack.

"Yes, I think you're right on that score. But I can't get out until I find the right apartment."

"Well, you can certainly afford a nice place now," Jack answered back.

During the last two weeks of that month, Jack struggled. It seemed like Jen had no intention of moving out. He stopped doing his daily push-ups and ceased working on his novel. On two occasions, he drank from Jen's hidden bottle of Crown Royal when she wasn't around. After he did that, he'd stare at his father's ashes in the metal box that was sitting on the mahogany mantelpiece above their fireplace.

The depths of depression were reached a few weeks later when he received notice of his mother's death from advanced dementia.

She was the glue that held our family together, he thought as tears poured down his puffy red face. After lying in bed alone for two weeks, he knew he had to get some support.

I've got to see Sandheim soon, he thought, *I'm not dealing well with death. It's difficult to find any meaning in life when everyone knows it's going to end sooner or later.*

At that point he sat down and composed a note to his mentor. It read:

Dear Master—

My life partner has now passed away from pancreatic cancer, and I'm struggling with her death. It all seems so final. Can I meet with you next week to discuss my profound grief regarding this matter?

Jack

As it turned out Sandheim was delighted to meet with his pupil and had much to say on the subject of death.

"Consider human life to be like a river that runs deep and wide. Occasionally, the water comes together in a whirlpool. Imagine that whirlpool is a person. One day, the whirlpool will unwind and cease to exist as a phenomenon—it'll become just part of the river again. That's what happens to human beings. They unravel just like the whirlpool. But they were never separated from the river in the first place. In other words, they were always just water in the river. Once back in the current, all traces of their former existence are gone. They're again just water in the flowing river of life. So while it looks like people die and evaporate, really they just transform into something that's different but paradoxically exactly the same."

"Does that mean all memories of the whirlpool are gone, too," asked Jack.

"It's quite possible that people maintain memories of themselves in the whirlpool state, even once they're back in the flow. That would help to explain why some people remember their past lives."

"Master—it sounds like you're saying that death doesn't actually exist because all the essential elements of a whirlpool remain intact even after it's disintegrated."

"You're absolutely correct. Death, as believed by most of the people on Earth, is fictional. The reality is based on experience and is simple. Consider that the water in the river is pure awareness. When the whirlpool disappears and flows with the river, it's gone. But infinite awareness, which is the river's deepest reality, remains intact.

"It sounds like you're saying death is like deep sleep. Awareness is present, but no person is there—it's just pure awareness."

"Yes, Jack, you've got it. You practice 'dying' every night when you fall into deep sleep. In that state, you're fully aware, but there is no *you* present."

"How do you know awareness is present?"

"Let me ask you a question: What happens when you're in deep sleep and your alarm goes off?"

"I wake up."

"Exactly-you wake up because you're aware and have been so all along. Your petty sense of self disappears, but awareness doesn't go anywhere--it just keeps flowing like the river."

"That means I can now relax when the stress of death arises within me," added Jack.

"Yes," replied the master.

Somehow, all that the Master said was logical, but even his wisdom couldn't help Jack from feeling depressed and demoralized.

Chapter 14   Monastery Life Revisited: Summer 1990 to September 1990

Jack thought it was strange living with Jennifer Black after Sarah died. It didn't feel right to him, and her strange, self-centered behaviors made him tense and irritable. One night, approximately three weeks after the funeral, he was very tired and decided to retire early.

"I'm going to bed now, Jen—do you mind putting the dishes away for me?"

"Not at all, Jack."

Just before he entered the sleep state, Jennifer slipped under the covers of his bed, completely naked. Jack lay frozen, breathing heavily and pretending to be asleep. Soon, her soft, large, bare breasts pushed up against his rigid back while her right hand began to slowly and erotically massage his right thigh.

"I'm in the mood for love, Jack. Can you help me out?"

What she started was later to haunt him--but in *that* moment, Jack was unable to resist Jen's exquisite sexuality. She was a beautiful woman in her prime who was extremely skilled in the art of love-making. Every night for the next month, Jack was taken to the heights of ultimate sexual pleasure--allowing his new lover to push him into long, intimate encounters—making him feel like three geisha girls were working on him all at once.

Despite being racked with guilt about what was happening, he couldn't help but continually think, *I've never had sex this great before.*

However, everything else about this relationship was wrong. He had nothing in common with Jen, finding her crass, materialistic and superficial, and he *did not love her*. They rarely spoke during the day, and Jack began drinking rum and beer on a daily basis. He stopped meditating, writing, playing music and exercising. That old, repressed family addiction to alcohol was seeping into his life again, starting to take hold like the tentacles of an octopus squeezing an otter. He was powerless against it.

In early August, he made an appointment to see his old mentor, Carl Tara Sandheim. Walking into the monastery brought back pleasant memories and immediately calmed him down.

"I need to change my life, master," he said, even before sitting down and sipping his steaming hot cinnamon tea.

"What's the problem?" asked the monk in a slow, tranquil voice.

"I'm in a dysfunctional relationship with Sarah's daughter, and it has to stop. She's driving me crazy and killing my spiritual life."

"Why don't you ask her to leave the apartment?"

"Because I'm afraid she'll end up in the wrong crowd."

"May I suggest you let her stay at her mother's place permanently while you move back into the monastery?"

"Would the administration let me back?"

"Yes, but only if you officially registered for *Phase One* of the <u>Zen Priest's Introductory Training Program</u> and agree to do all the work required. This is a three-month initiation into monastic living and is the first stage everyone has to pass through before moving on to become a Zen priest."

"What kind of work are you referring to?"

"It's the same life you led before, only there'd be more meditation requirements and less physical labor in the vegetable gardens."

"I'll do it," replied Jack with virtually no hesitation.

That night at supper, Jack decided to inform Jennifer of his decision.

"I'll be moving out on Saturday, Jen', so you can call this place your own now. I've spoken to Cara, and she's going to watch out for you. Please contact her at the <u>Healing Center</u> if you have any problems."

"You're leaving me? That's crazy--don't you enjoy our life together?" she muttered with a crooked smirk on her face.

"In some respects, I do--but I've decided to become a Zen monk, and this lifestyle just isn't compatible with spiritual living."

"What about your job at the <u>Richmond Times</u>?"

"I'm taking a three-month leave of absence, which they approved as long as I can finish and submit a twelve-part series on monastic living by Christmas."

"It doesn't matter to me because I've got another boyfriend. Just make sure you leave everything that was my mother's behind when you go."

That his connection to Jennifer ended quickly and acrimoniously bothered him, but the complications involved were soon forgotten as soon as he re-entered the monastery.

I told Sarah I'd watch out for her, and someday I will, he promised himself, *but right now, I need a break from her craziness."*

He wanted to live a life of meditation and service, a life that would *never* include toxic sexual relationships. He was searching for transformation like a prospector mines for gold.

The disciplines, rules and orderly living of the Zen way of life were a difficult adjustment at first, but Jack gradually began to adapt. For weeks on end, life progressed in a boring, repetitive and unbending cycle. But the more tedious it became for life in the world, the richer it became for his soul. He was up every day at 3:45 am to meditate for an hour, then worked in the kitchen helping prepare breakfast for the community, meditated some more, did hard physical labor in the gardens, ate his meals in silence, chanted for hours on end and then meditated again before falling asleep every night on a hard bamboo mat.

As his life in the external receded, real openings began to occur in his inner life. Time slowed down to a standstill, and ordinary things took on a deeper meaning. He noticed things like the exquisiteness of an opening sunflower, the symmetrical breathing of a Siamese cat or the rhythm of a mosquito's buzz. The marigolds outside <u>Buddha Hall</u> came alive—their deep golden colors were now striking to Jack, and he could feel each flower breathing, their buds rising and falling in a pattern synchronized with the sun. Everyone seemed to be moving in slow motion, and Jack began to see right into the heart of anyone who spoke to him. All the struggles and addictions of daily living evaporated—he was living in the *flow of life* itself.

These esoteric shifts in consciousness lasted right up until the end of this particular training period. When it was over, Carl Tara Sandheim called him back into his office.

"Have you made any progress with your koan, Jack?" asked the master.

"Yes—I now see that in deep sleep, there *is no sound,* and my personality and character have disappeared. But I'm not dead—I'm still alive and aware. As you said before, it's like practicing for death."

"How do you know for sure, Jack?"

"Because, just as you told me, when my alarm goes off, I jump up—awake in the world and ready for action. Yet while in the state of deep sleep, my personal sense of self is completely gone."

"Yes, you *have* made progress because you're now experiencing what I told you intellectually—but don't stop working on the secrets of the koan."

"Do you want to enter <u>Stage Three</u> of your training now?"

"Perhaps, sir—but first, I need to take a break to see if I can maintain my inner strength, calm and awareness while living back in the world. When that happens, I'll request further training."

"That makes sense, Jack. We'll be waiting for you to come back. In the meantime, don't forget to meditate every day and keep working on your koan."

Sandheim then shook Jack's hand and passed him a letter.

"Here, this came for you yesterday," he said, as Jack got up, took the envelope and mindfully walked out of the monastery again—a happy man.

The first thing he did after leaving the monastery was call Jennifer Black. He'd promised Sarah to keep an eye out for her, and yet, when he left her, there was definitely a bad taste in his mouth, like rancid cream.

"Jen, how are you?" he called into his cell phone.

"I thought you'd be a priest by now."

"No, I was just in an introductory program for the ministry. Can we get together for coffee?"

"If you insist, but there's not much to talk about, is there?"

On Labor Day that year, Jack met her at Anita's, outside on the promenade so they could watch the river flow by as they talked.

"This is where I first met Junko," he said.

"Who was she?"

"My first wife—we had a great time here, but the marriage didn't go so well."

"What did you want to talk about, Jack?"

"Have you been participating in any of the programs at Infinite Healing?"

"No, and I'm not even working there anymore. My last boyfriend told me to quit. He said I didn't need to work because he had lots of money."

"How is that relationship working out?" Jack asked her.

"It's over now, Jack. He *did* have lots of money, but it was all obtained from the sale of illicit drugs. He's now in jail."

"Are you single again?"

"Yes, very much so," she responded. "Why don't we get together again? You're welcome to move back into my place."

What Jack said next was difficult for him. Jennifer was wearing a tight sweater with no bra underneath it. She was taunting him with her body, and despite the fact that he'd had many spiritual breakthroughs over the last few months, he was mesmerized by Jen's figure and the memory of all those delightful nights of passion he'd spent with her.

"I'd love to, my dear, but I'm on a different path now. I called you because I wanted to know if I could help you in any way."

"No, you can't. I'm fine, Jack."

"Well, let's stay in touch then. I'd like to be a part of your life now."

"Sure, that'll be fine. But if you ever get horny again, come to see me. Right now, I'm lonely and available."

"I'll keep that in mind, Jen. Take care of yourself, and I'll be in touch."

"Good-bye Jack," she winced, getting up and walking briskly out of the café.

Chapter 15   Jack's Nephew: September to October 2nd, 1990

After meeting with Jennifer, Jack booked himself into the Savory Hotel on a monthly basis. It was a modest establishment on the east side of Richmond, not far from Infinite Healing, and it offered shelter to low-income pensioners, former homeless people on welfare and groups of students attending Kwantlen Community College. The letter Sandheim had given him was one that shocked Jack. It was from his brother's former secretary and temporary common-law wife, Susan Fitzgerald, and read,

Dear Jack,

I've sent this letter to the Zen Monastery in Richmond because your brother, Jim Turner, told me you used to take classes with one of the monks there. I hope it somehow finds its way into your hands.

My name is Susan Fitzgerald, and I'm the mother of your nephew, Rodney Jack. He's thirteen years old now and looks exactly like Jim. I left the madness and chaos of Toronto some years ago and now work as a paralegal for my father at his law practice in Stewart, BC.

My hope is that you'll someday visit us and get to know Rodney better. He doesn't have a father figure in his life right now. If you do come, you can stay in my Dad's home--free of charge. There are three spare bedrooms on the top floor, and I live downstairs in a self-contained basement suite. My father is single and only lives in his Stewart house every other week because he also has a law office in Terrace.

Sincerely,

Susan F.
(email)suzfstew@shaw.ca
(phone) 250-782-3500

Jack started shaking after reading the letter and had to sit down to stay calm.

"Oh my God," he thought, "Rodney's my only living relative. *I have to meet him.*"

After further contemplation, and a night of fitful sleep, he replied to Susan's email saying,

Dear Susan—

Jim told me all about you but I never dreamt I'd ever get to see you—but thanks so much for reaching out.

I'd love to visit you and Rodney but can't get away for a month as I have to give notice at my hotel. How do I get to Stewart?"

Jack
(email) jacer@telus.net
(phone) 250-479-1800

Two hours later, Susan answered.

Jack—

Just take a regular flight on an <u>Air Canada</u> 727 to <u>Terrace</u>, then book yourself onto the <u>Goose</u> to <u>Stewart</u>. It flies back and forth into this town every Friday afternoon. Just let me know when you'll be arriving, and I'll pick you up at the <u>Goose's</u> dock.

Sue.

Over the next month, Jack readied himself to travel again and met twice with his boss at the *Richmond Times*. The upshot of those meetings was that he could keep his job writing *Insights* from any distance away via his laptop—for the princely sum of $950 per month.

"We value your work, Jack, and we hope to put all your columns into a book one day," said George Copeland, Editor of the *Richmond Times*. "Your insights into the human condition, spiritual living and ideas for rehabilitation after prison are intriguing to many of our readers, and there's no reason why you have to work out of our bricks-and-mortar office."

"I'm not sure I'd have this gig if George wasn't a Buddhist and a good friend," thought Jack.

He then informed the hotel staff that he'd be leaving in early October, giving them a month's notice. He booked his return for November 1st.

Two days after reading Sue's last email, he wrote back, saying,

Susan—

I'll be arriving in Stewart on Friday, October 2nd at 3:42 pm-- can't wait to meet you and your son. I'll be staying for four weeks which will give me lots of time to get to know my nephew.

Jack

Flying down the <u>Portland Canal</u> into <u>Stewart</u> aboard the <u>Goose</u> was a frightening experience for Jack. The pilot was Bill Tracy, a disheveled ex-gold miner who chewed tobacco, mumbled to himself under his breath and limped onto the plane; a retired WW2 vintage yellow seaplane. Its fuselage was chipped badly, revealing rusty iron underneath and one of its windows was badly scratched. This plane was like an injured eagle with bleeding feathers and several claws torn off in the wind.

"Are you Jack Turner?" stuttered Bill, spitting out a lump of dark black, gooey tobacco.

"Yes, sir, I am," replied Jack, noticing the smell of beer on the pilot's breath.

"Well, hop aboard and let's get going—you're my only passenger today."

Inside the cramped vehicle, Jack strapped himself in and shut his eyes tightly while Bill fired up the propellers and lurched down the harbor waterway, bumping over the waves. The noise was so loud he wasn't able to talk as they jerked into the air. The extra-long wings shook violently and appeared to be detaching themselves from the body of the plane, which was by this time rattling noisily and shaking all over. Jack squeezed the arm rest until his knuckles were bloodless and as white as a delicate pianist's hand caught in a closing vice.

Gradually, however, the noise stabilized slightly, and Jack was able to open his eyes wide enough to see endless groves of stately evergreen trees below, dusted with pure white, fresh snow. Majestic mountain ranges stood on both sides of the channel as Bill navigated his wobbly craft dead center down the valley, but very low to the ground— sometimes barely missing the tops of tall trees. The beauty around Jack was breathtaking. Finally, after what seemed like hours, a long wharf appeared. The plane's floats hit the water with a loud splash, and the Goose slowly puttered up to the dock.

As soon as the rickety, rusted door opened, Jack glanced beyond it to see a stunningly beautiful woman standing by the <u>Goose Administration Office</u>. She wore a long brown furry parka with a thick red scarf tied around her neck and held the hand of a freckle-faced boy. She was forty years old but didn't look at day over twenty-one. By this time, Jack was thirty-four years old.

"Oh my God," muttered Jack under his breath, "*He does* look *just like* Jimmy!"

A toque covered the top of Suzie's head, but couldn't hide long waves of bouncy, well-shampooed blonde hair stretching down past her shoulders and fluttering in the icy cold breeze. Her face had classic features—an aquiline nose, large penetrating blue eyes and perfectly shaped lips touched with slight traces of pink lipstick. Smiling widely, she called out,

"Welcome to Stewart, Jack—it's great to see you."

As soon as he stepped onto the wharf, he extended his bare hand to Suzie and shook her hand firmly. A shot of warm, welcoming energy shot up his arm as her long, slender fingers wrapped around Jack's palm.

"I'd like you to meet your nephew, Rodney—he's been so looking forward to seeing you."

"Hi, Rodney," blurted out Jack with enthusiasm.

"Hello, Mr. Jack," responded the boy.

"How old are you, Rod?"

"I'm thirteen," he answered.

"C'mon, let's hop in my Land Rover and head home," chirped Suzie.

Darwin Fitzgerald's home was a large rancher on a quiet cul-de-sac just outside town. As Jack walked up the concrete front steps, he could see that what used to be a carport had been converted into a basement suite for Suzie.

Inside the main house, many of the walls were lined with dusty legal books from the floor to the ceiling while others had rare art hanging on them—works like Tony Onlee's <u>Sunset</u>, Emily Carr's <u>Forest Line,</u> a white print on black done by Pat Martin Bates and Thunder Cloud's <u>Black and Red Crow</u>. Furniture throughout the home was sparse. There was a faint, musty smell in the air and a touch of mold in one of the corners of the ceiling, like the scent of a dank wine cellar.

"Let me take your coat, Jack," said Suzie as she then hung it up, along with her own. "You can stay in one of the back bedrooms on this floor, but for now, let's go down to my suite for refreshments," she said slowly while descending a flight of steep stairs. "Now, how'd you like a cup of tea?"

"That'd be perfect right now—I need to get warmed up. That fall weather outside is definitely on the cool side."

Once inside her digs, she asked,

"What would you like, cinnamon, chamomile or green tea?"

"I'll have cinnamon, please."

"Okay—come and join me in the kitchen."

Jack couldn't take his eyes off the woman who was now hosting him in her father's home. She had a figure demonstrating curves in perfect proportion. When she took her coat off, she was clad in a bright red tight sweater buttoned from the neck down to a pleated skirt that drifted down to her knees. Her waist was thin, and her bare shins were sleek and athletic.

She could be a professional model, thought Jack, and, at that point, he remembered his brother mentioning in his letters that this woman loved sex and alcohol.

The tea was served in a sterling set with cups that had elaborate handles on them like they'd come from a nineteenth-century museum display taken from an aristocratic Chinese household.

"Rodney's in need of a father figure right now, Jack."

"Why do you say that?"

"He has trouble concentrating for long periods of time and tends to hang out with the wrong kind of people. They smoke and hang around downtown—just loitering, spitting and jostling each other. He's much too young for this kind of thing."

"How's he doing in school?" asked Jack.

"Not well. He's smart as a whip and has tons of ability but is unmotivated, lazy and wayward. I'll be honest with you— he's a C student, and I find that frustrating, given his natural abilities. I need to tell you something personal that's affected Rod in a significant way. Some years ago, I lived with a man for about a year. That man bullied Rodney, called him stupid and criticized him constantly. That abuse started him down a very rocky path."

"Did he physically abuse Rod?"

"No, he never did that. But he thought my son was getting in the way of his exclusive right to my time and life. That's why our relationship only lasted a short time."

"Did this guy drink a lot?"

"Yes, he did, Jack."

"I think I can help Rod, Sue. He sounds a lot like me and Jimmy were when we were thirteen. My dad could be emotionally abusive, too--and he was definitely an alcoholic. Times were mostly tough."

"Anything you can do will be appreciated."

"Does he ever ask you about his Dad?" asked Jack.

"Yes, he does—all the time. He's very curious about him. And he asks me why most of the kids in his class have fathers, and he doesn't."

"What do you tell him?"

"That his Dad was brilliant and handsome and successful, which is all true."

"Sue, have you told him that Jim committed suicide?"

"No, Jack, I haven't. That's a stretch too far. Do you think I should have?"

"Not if you think it's inappropriate. What kinds of things do you think I could do with him that'd have an impact?"

"Fatherly things like teaching him how to fish, or play hockey or build kayaks. Helping him with his homework wouldn't hurt, either."

"I'll do my best, Sue. I'll do my very best in the short time I'm here."

Chapter 16   Stewart   October 2nd, to November 30th, 1990

The autumn of that year was particularly spectacular in Stewart, BC. All the deciduous trees in the region had turned blazing colors—red, yellow, orange and brown. The Snake River on the outskirts of town was full of fat, spawning salmon, and the night sky was loaded with bright, flashing stars, like fireflies in a pitch-black cave. Jack enjoyed the peace and quiet of country living, always right up close to the natural world. This village was actually a mining town full of homes mostly owned by either Quartz Gold, The Le Duc Gold Mine, Stewart Regional Health or the Terrace District School Board--and you couldn't walk two hundred feet in any direction without encountering alpine meadows, tall evergreen trees or the open sea. A road two miles north led to Hyder, a village that was actually in the United States. It had a population of only one hundred twenty-four American hippies and contained five old-fashioned saloons that opened twenty-three hours a day. Time had stood still in Hyder; it reminded Jack of towns he used to watch in old B-rated American westerns. It was cut off from the rest of Alaska, so it had to be policed from Ketchikan via helicopter—which effectively made it a lawless community of vagrants. Along the way to the empty Canadian Customs Office at the border were long ribbons of decaying docks revealing that, in 1910, twelve thousand people lived in this area. Today, there were only twenty-two hundred.

Jack was in his element in this land, but most of all, he loved being around Rodney because he reminded him of his brother. The boy was a precocious child, full of aggressive energy, curiosity and mischief. He'd experienced the kind of environment growing up that Jack could relate to.

"I really appreciate you telling Rodney all those stories---he loves your exciting narratives," said Suzie one day. "You've got a writer's imagination."

"He's such a smart kid and listens intently to everything I tell him. Jimmy would have adored this little guy."

"Yes, I think you're right," replied Rodney's mother.

"What was your relationship like with my brother anyway?"

"I adored him. For me, it was love at first sight. He was handsome, charismatic, virile, funny and smart. Everyone at Laxton knew he was our most successful lawyer. All the women on staff were in love with him."

"What went wrong with his life, then?" asked Jack.

"He had one major character flaw—an addiction to alcohol. Booze seeped into his soul and grew roots there, like aging potatoes in a guinea sack. It destroyed his marriage and eventually even caused problems with us. After he moved in with me, I started drinking, too, and we began to fight a lot. But I never stopped loving him and was devastated when he swallowed one hundred zopiclone pills, fell asleep and never woke up. I gave up drinking for over a year after that fateful day, but it took me a long time to get through the grieving process, that's for sure."

Jack was also enjoying Suzie's company: her stunning beauty and the way she treated him. Sidentifiehe constantly smiled at him, laughed at his jokes and complimented his actions. She also invited him down to her place every evening for supper and, as it turned out, was a superb cook. Soon his favorite meals were being produced--chicken cordon bleu with white rice and freshly baked Idaho potatoes smothered in butter or piping hot chicken Chow Mein covered with bright green, lightly steamed broccoli. Usually, when the meal was done, Jack would have a glass of home-made red wine and then play folk songs on his guitar while Suzie and Rodney sang along. Before he left her suite, he invariably tucked Rodney into bed and told him a long, magical story full of wizards and giants and goblins. He was a natural story teller. He even started writing some of his children's stories down so Rod would have a record of them. Rodney did the illustrations.

On the weekends, they went on several memorable adventures. On one occasion, the threesome borrowed an authentic, hand-crafted *Huron* canoe from Suzie's next-door neighbor and paddled over a mile down the <u>Portland Canal</u>. The sea was protected on all sides by high mountains, so the water was glassy calm, but it was glacial run-off; deep, dark and icy cold.

"Thanks for teaching Rod how to fish," said the boy's mother. "But that dogfish he just caught is full of prickles. His grandfather's a great fisherman too, but he's always too busy to take Rod out."

"Wow—that little shark sure put up a fight, Uncle Jack," yelped the kid.

"Don't touch him, my boy; there's poison in those prickly scales," answered his uncle, as the mini-shark jumped around wildly in the boat's bottom before Jack whacked him hard with the blunt end of a gaff, like a Roman gladiator finishing off his opponent.

Later, they hiked all the way up to <u>Premier,</u> which was an abandoned mining community way up in the mountains.

"These old shafts are spooky," said Suzie, "I can't imagine anyone descending into those pits for ten hours of back-breaking work every day in the pitch-black darkness."

"Yeah--and those broken down train carts are how they went into the depths and transported the tailings."

Sometimes, they just went to the <u>Town Camp Site</u> and roasted wieners on a roaring bonfire. As time went by, they became closer and closer.

"It's starting to feel like we're a small family," muttered Suzie. "Is there any way you can stay another month, Jack?"

Without too much thought, he quickly decided he was having way too much fun to go back south in November. "Sure, that sounds like a great idea," he exuded.

Jack discovered an active *Anglican Church* on the edge of town that held regular services every Sunday morning. The priest, Reverend Blaine Stephens, preached and gave communion to a congregation of twelve, most of whom were over seventy-five years old. But he was also an up-to-date member of the <u>Healing Order of St. Luke</u> and held "laying on of hands" sessions every Wednesday evening, which Jack attended. The Reverend's wife, June Eagle-

Feather, was a very charismatic woman, only forty-two years old, with a reputation as a powerful healer. She was a First Nations Shaman and Church Army Priest before marrying Blaine. Her specialty was running week-long sweat lodges for large numbers of Indigenous people. She'd take a group of twelve participants canoeing up the Nass River to Greenville, a native fishing village on the coast. It was in Greenville that she held her lodges. The Church Army was the First Nations version of Anglicanism, and almost every member of that group had been to at least one of her retreats. This guaranteed her a leadership role in that side of the church. On top of that, she had the reputation of being a mystical healer. For that reason, she had a following of people who came to all the sessions of the Healing Order. These meetings were much more dynamic and alive than the regular Sunday services, and many attendees reported significant healing effects from their participation in these specific gatherings.

"Do you want to come to church with me tomorrow, Suzie?" He asked her one Saturday night.

"No, I'm not the religious type, and I don't believe the Christian doctrine, do you?"

"No, I'm not a Christian either, but this church is a peaceful place to go for quiet reflection and contemplation. There's a healing energy there as well. The minister and his wife are very dynamic."

"I've got to stay here all day tomorrow anyway because my Dad's in town."

Darwin Fitzgerald had found a lady friend in Stewart and often invited her over to spend the night with him when he was home.

"Jack, do you mind staying somewhere else this weekend— Georgina and I would like some privacy," he proclaimed one Friday evening. "Sue told me you could stay down at her place until Sunday night."

Later that evening, after Rodney went to bed, Jack and Suzie watched the movie <u>Notting Hill</u> and ate three large stainless steel bowls of hot, salty, buttered popcorn.

"Do you want another glass of wine?" she asked him lovingly.

"Sure, why not."

"Those embers are so hot," sighed Suzie, staring at the fireplace and then taking off her kimono and wiping the sweat off her forehead.

Unfortunately, her pajamas were transparent, and Jack couldn't help but notice her upper body, fully revealed. He started to perspire profusely.

"I'm going to bed now. Why don't you join me?"

"I'd like that," he gulped.

"Why are your knees knocking together, Jack?" she asked him, smiling mischievously.

"They sometimes do that when it's very hot." His words came from a face that was crimson.

When he got under the thick, clean eider down, he could feel Suzie's sexual energy vibrating like a meat stew in a pressure cooker. She was lying on her back, naked, hot and aching for love from Jack. She put her right hand on his left thigh and started massaging it.

"How does that feel, Jack? Do you like it?"

"Yes, don't stop, darling—I really do like it."

"Can I kiss you now?" she asked.

"Yes, you can," he moaned.

Their passionate kissing started off a night of luxurious love-making that lasted for over four hours and brought both of them to heights of unending orgasmic bliss. Suzie was highly skilled in the art of love and was soft, sensitive and experimental.

"You can do whatever you want to me, Jack and I won't hold back. I'm here to satisfy you totally."

"Let's just keep going, my dear—I wouldn't change a thing. You're a perfect lover."

For his final two weeks in Stewart, he stayed with Suzie and Rodney. When he thought about it later, he realized that this person was the most desirable woman he'd ever met on an emotional and purely physical level. As his day of departure drew near, Jack revealed to her why he had to leave.

"I'm seriously considering becoming a Zen monk, Suzie and for the next two months, my full attention will be focused on completing my novel. Would you and Rodney consider visiting me in Richmond?"

"I hate to see you go right now, Jack. But I commit to bringing my son to the Lower Mainland for Christmas."

"That's wonderful, Sue. We'll get to spend more time together in just three weeks."

"I can hardly wait," added Suzie.

Chapter 17   <u>Christmas: December 22nd, 1990 to January 1st, 1991</u>

True to her word, Suzie brought Rodney with her to Richmond at Christmas. Jack met them at the <u>Vancouver International Airport</u> on December 22nd and enjoyed being kissed passionately when the visiting woman jumped right into his arms and hugged him tightly. After picking up the luggage, they decided to stop at <u>Starbucks</u> for coffee and muffins.

"It's so fabulous to see you," stated Sue emphatically, smiling from ear to ear. "I really missed you. Rod did, too!"

"Yes, it's good to be with you again! How was your flight?"

"A bit choppy, but luckily, we had a good pilot."

Rodney sat between Jack and Suzie on the taxi ride to Richmond and seemed very content to be reunited with his uncle.

"It's going to be a bit crowded in my hotel room, but we'll make do," said Jack. "I've purchased a foam rubber mattress we can put on the floor for Rod, but you'll have to sleep with me in a single bed, Suzie."

"That'll be just fine, my dear," she glowingly replied.

Over the holiday season, the threesome had a wonderful time. Jack bought a four-foot-tall artificial Christmas tree, and they filled it with boxes of new Canadian Tire decorations: tinsel, flashing lights and little cartoon figurines. In the end, even toy animals hung from the branches on circles of string. It was a loaded tree that created a very festive mood, like chocolate eggs at Easter.

They went caroling door to door for two nights before Christmas and stood for hours in a light snowfall waiting for *Santa's Parade,* which Rodney loved, especially the painted models of all the reindeer—Rudolf with his bright red nose leading the way.

Jack and his nephew made a giant snowman beside the hotel's front door and used two lumps of dirty black coal from the furnace room for eyes, a discarded carrot for the creature's nose and a fresh bright-yellow banana for its mouth.

"Wow, that's the biggest snowman I've ever seen," shouted Rod with glee.

"Me too," answered Jack.

On *Christmas Day,* they rose early and, after a breakfast of hot mince tarts, fresh mandarin oranges and black coffee, opened several presents each.

Rod loved his <u>Canadian Encyclopedia for Teens</u> set and the fishing rod with reel.

"Thanks, Uncle—I love these presents so much," blurted out Rodney with obvious joy. "Can I call you Dad from now on?"

"You can call me whatever you want, Rod."

His mother was delighted to receive two romantic novels and a sheer negligee.

"This album is beautiful! Thank you so much," sighed Jack as he leafed through page after page of exquisite photos taken during his time in Stewart. "I didn't know you were a *professional* photographer!"

"I'm not, but I *do* like to take the odd picture."

For lunch that day, Suzie cooked a twenty-pound turkey full of sage-tinged stuffing and served it with bright green Brussels' sprouts, buttered mashed potatoes and cranberry sauce loaded with real berries. The smells of crackling turkey skin, sweetly cooked celery and hot sage wafted throughout the room.

"This is the best meal I've ever had," groaned Jack after it was all over. "The turkey was *so* succulent! But now I'm going to have to loosen my belt and lie down for a while."

On *New Year's Eve*, Jack asked the hotel manager's daughter to keep an eye out for Rodney while he and Suzie went to a ball at the *Fisherman's Club*.

The music was outstanding. It was played by the Raveens, a group of four folk artists specializing in classical songs from the sixties: Bob Dylan, the Beach Boys, Pete Seeger, Peter, Paul and Mary and the Beatles. Suzie turned out to be a great dancer—graceful, fluid, full of zest—and during slow songs, she pulled herself in and up close to Jack, gripping his back and shoulders so tightly that they turned red. She continually led him toward the many bunches of mistletoe that were dangling from the ceiling and insisted she be kissed at length when they drew near any one of them.

Despite his best intentions, Jack drank way too much velvety Johnnie Walker while his date imbibed more than two bottles of full-bodied Merlot.

"Let's go home and make love, *now*," she muttered as the last dance came to an end. "Then we can go out and get married later in the week."

Both of them slept in on *New Year's Day* and woke up with throbbing heads. After slurping water, nibbling on fresh cantaloupe and over-dosing on red *Tylenol Extra Strength* tablets, Suzie said,

"We were too drunk to have sex last night, but I meant what I said about getting married. We make a beautiful little family, Jack."

"Suzie," he replied, "I love you more than I can express in words and want to stay connected to you and Rodney *forever*. But over the last two months, I've thought very hard about my future and have decided to become a Zen Buddhist monk. My training starts up again in early February."

"I'm madly in love with you and want to become your life partner, Jack," she responded, "I'm happy you've decided to lead a spiritual life, but we *must* stay in touch. I want you to stay close to your daughter as she grows up because she's going to need a father figure."

"My daughter?" Came Jack's shocked reply.

"Yes—I'm six weeks pregnant, and I have a strong feeling that the baby is a girl."

"Are you sure, Sue?"

"Yes, I failed two pregnancy tests last week—that's to say they were both positive. But I also feel new life inside of me. Jack, this is real."

At that point, Jack's face turned white as a ghost, and he slumped down onto the bed.

"Are you alright, Jack?"

"Darling, I feel a little anemic and very fatigued. Do you mind if I lie down for a minute and have a little nap?"

"No, not at all—go for it!"

Jack then fell back onto the bed and slipped into a deep sleep, during which he had a very powerful dream. He dreamt he was back in the days of Cowboys and Indians and was being chased by a band of painted Cree warriors on horseback. He was running as hard as he could, but his blood-thirsty pursuers were getting closer and closer. Finally, he ran right up to a cliff and peered over. It was a thousand feet down to acres of pointed rocks. He then knew he had to face his foes—so he turned around.

A huge fighter, who turned out to be Chief Deer-Hunter, slowly dismounted and walked towards Jack. He wore a headdress with two massive buffalo horns holding up strings of brown eagle feathers and white bear teeth. He was covered in red grease paint and was carrying a spear, looking like a vicious caveman. Looking directly at Jack, he screamed,

"You've impregnated my wife and now must pay the price. Before we hang you by your feet and burn you to a crisp, my woman must be avenged. You'll watch her give birth before we stab her to death. Then we'll fry your baby on a spit."

Jack then saw himself at the side of a beautiful native woman with long, jet-black hair and chocolate-brown skin. She was naked and sweating profusely as she watched a group of her own people chanting, drumming and screaming around a bonfire while she was in the middle of her birthing pangs.

"Death to you both," they shouted—louder and louder.

Just then, she whispered:

"I love you, Jack," as a large baby girl emerged from her. But it was a strange baby--half eagle and half human with big hands, a large beak and two powerful wings. The child hopped over to Jack and picked him up before flying away, clutching him with her claws and eventually perching on a branch of the massive oak tree that was sitting on a nearby cliff.

"My mother has died," she moaned, "But it's going to be fine. I'll always take care of you, Father."

The newly born creature had large, luminous human eyes and an exquisitely shaped girl's body, like characters from a Rowling novel. Jack could feel her heart beat, and the light shining out of her eyes took away all his pain and all his fear. He was amazed that someone just born could talk.

In the dream, each scene was clear to Jack. He realized that the newborn had magical powers because she made some snacks materialize so they could eat.

"Here--have some seedless, green grapes and a ripe banana, Father—you must be hungry," she said.

"How did you know that, and how did you make this food appear?"

"It appeared because I visualized it in my head."

"And how can you speak—you're not even a day old."

"I've been sent here to heal a broken world, and to do that, I have to be able to speak," she answered.

"And how are you going to heal a broken world?"

"One person at a time, Father—starting with you."

Jack stared at this dream creature with awe. Her feathers were brown, orange, white, red and black, and her eyes were lit up like Christmas tree lights. Her hands were long and smooth as she began to massage his shoulders and arms.

"You've got pain bodies all throughout your being," she proclaimed. "I'm now going to get rid of them."

With that, she closed her eagle eyes and squeezed his arms. A white current penetrated his entire body like thunderbolts in a storm, and he lit up like a giant fluorescent light bulb.

"I pronounce you clean, Father," she stated emphatically, "I pronounce you clean."

In the dream, Jack felt like he was on fire, burning up from the inside out. But soon, the electricity passing through him stopped, and he felt renewed, relaxed and re-energized.

"I feel alive again and whole. Thank you so much."

"You're free now to heal others, so go and do that," she added.

"And what shall I call you?"

"Lalita," said the creature before flying into the distant sky.

Chapter 18   Preparation for Fatherhood: January 1st to February 2nd, 1991

Jack suddenly woke up to see Suzie lovingly staring down at him.

"Are you alright, Jack? You've been wiggling about and rolling back and forth."

"I feel fantastic, my dear, totally alive, in fact. I'm sorry I had to lie down, but what you told me was a real shock. Before I say anything else, let me tell you how pleased I am. Congratulations on this news; I'm really very happy for you."

"I thought you'd be happy for *us*."

"Well, I am, of course--but this news was so unexpected. I'll need some time to process it."

As it turned out, Suzie had to fly back to Stewart two days later, so they agreed to email each other and make the key decisions over time. Jack spent the first week of January going on long walks, meditating daily and consulting with his mentor, Carl Tara Sandheim. On January 7th, he wrote Suzie the following note—

Dear Sue—

I apologize for not responding with immediate joy upon hearing about the birth of our daughter—but I was in a state of total shock when you told me about it. This new state of affairs changes everything, just the way any human birth does. I've decided to move forward with Phase Two of my Zen training, which will last for five months. I'll be able to write or call you at various times during that period so we can stay in close touch.

If everything's going well with your pregnancy, when this part of my training ends, I'll be moving to Stewart to be with you. After a great deal of thought and contemplation, I've realized that I must join you so that we can raise our daughter together. Please play lots of music near her body, especially violin or piano songs.

Much love,

Jack.

Her reply was immediate.

Dear Jack—

*It sounds like the only reason you'd move to Stewart is if the pregnancy goes well, which I find a bit insulting. Nevertheless, I **am** glad you've decided to join me in the difficult task of parenting, and hopefully for the long term. My father says he'll give us his house if we get married. (He's glad you're the father!)*

I'll keep you updated on the pregnancy.

Sue.
PS *I'll be happy to expose the baby to violin and piano music.

Two days later, Jack reported to the monastery for Phase Two, and his introductory interview was intense.

"Are you really certain you want to enter this phase, Jack because it'll be much more challenging than any work you've done before at the Monastery," said Sandheim. "We don't believe in labor-saving devices because, to us, hard labor is *sacred*. We don't encourage luxurious living or comforts of any kind and certainly no feminine kindnesses. Ours is a life of grim and earnest self-denial in the search for life's higher truths. Your only possessions from here on in will be a bamboo hat, an undershirt, some cotton leggings and a pair of straw sandals."

"Yes, sir, *I am certain*. The discipline will forge me into a sword of awareness that I'm hoping will last a lifetime. I'm going to need that to prepare for what's coming in my life."

"I accept that, Jack. Here's your Certificate of Novitiate from me, signifying that you're now *officially* my disciple. For the rest of this week, you'll be in the dojo doing a sesshin—ten hours a day of sitting alone, staring at a wall in deep meditation--with only one meal of rice gruel in the morning and six pieces of sushi in the evening to sustain you. This will make your awareness sharp, like Sir Lancelot's medieval sword. The Buddha stressed the importance of that kind of one-pointedness, advising his disciples to remain at least twenty-five percent hungry at all times."

"Shall I focus primarily on solving my koan?"

"Yes—but also spend time noticing your power of witnessing or observing," replied Sandheim. "Don't change anything about your breathing—but *notice your breaths*. Watch them coming in and going out. And experiment with resisting urges. If your foot itches, *try not scratching it*— notice what happens to the itch if you simply watch it."

"Will I be given periods of free time in this Phase?"

"Yes—every Sunday is a free day, and you'll be given access to the monastery's library and computer lab on that day."

"Thank you, Master," said Jack as he placed his hands in the prayer position and bowed low, very low--like an obedient black slave in the days when American tobacco plantations thrived in the southern states.

It was particularly difficult for Jack to adjust to life in <u>Phase Two</u> because he had to spend so many hours kneeling with his back as straight as a ramrod, staring directly into a concrete wall, with unfocused eyes—like a death row inmate in solitary confinement.

The first thing he did after a Sunday lunch of one small fresh-cut yellow mango, a piece of dry sourdough bread and two cups of hot cinnamon tea was head to the computer room to communicate with Susan. He wrote,

Dearest Sue—

*It's been so hard for me this week—meditating motionless for ten hours a day and then doing slave labor in the vegetable fields. It's encouraging that your Dad is willing to give us his house if we marry, and yes, I **do want to do that**. Please start planning the kind of ceremony you'd like. Whatever you choose to do is fine with me.*

Continued exposure to the violin will give our child a head start in the world of music.

Love,

Jack.

Suzie's reply came quickly.

Darling—

I can't understand why you're putting yourself through such torture at the Monastery, but someday, I'm sure you'll explain that to me.

Rodney's fine, but misses you, and my pregnancy's going well. I went to see Dr. Wright this week, and she said everything was normal and healthy.

I thought we could have a small ceremony with about ten friends and the minister of the Anglican Church presiding, along with two or three church officials, my father and some of his friends. Dad says we should get hitched as soon as possible.

I love you.

Sue.

Jack replied as follows:

Dear Suzie—

I like the idea of having Reverend Stephens officiate at our wedding. That'll add a touch of the sacred to our affair and make it seem very official; consecrated by God. But I'm surprised you suggested that, considering your lack of a Christian foundation. Given our current situation, it does make sense that we get married right away. I'm so glad your pregnancy is progressing well. Soon, we'll be able to hold each other and make love whenever we want. I can't wait.

Jack.

She replied quickly:

Dearest—

I think about giving my whole being to you daily and miss you terribly.

But I must tell you my feelings for Georgina. I don't trust her. She keeps asking my Dad for money and, two weeks ago, demanded that he buy her a pick-up truck. Father caved, and now she drives around with a brand new, eight-cylinder, bright red Ford crew cab.

My best friend, Karly Jones, saw her in that very truck parked at Glacier Lake last week on a Sunday afternoon, sitting with a man in the front seat. They were making out right in public! That man is Pedro Lopez, a Mexican biker who lives in Terrace and is best known as a regional cocaine dealer. Everyone in our town avoids him because he spent seventeen years in prison on a murder charge. He was convicted of killing a young elementary school teacher from Kitwanga whom he was dating back in the seventies.

Should I tell Dad about this?

Love,

Sue

A week later, she received Jack's response:

Sue—

I've been meditating on your words to me about Georgina. There's something about her that's very disturbing and dark.

I feel you must tell your father about her dalliance with that Mexican drug dealer. This is not something that should come out after their marriage. He'll be devastated but you really don't have a choice.

How's everything going with your health, and is Rodney doing any better these days?

Jack.

Later that day, she responded by writing:

Jack—

I went to George Bowler's Esso station for coffee this morning with my Dad and told him about his fiance's infidelity. Of course, he was enraged and swore he was going to break up with her. I was surprised at how decisive he seemed to be. Actually, I don't know what he sees in her other than good sex, but she does seem to be able to cast a spell, so to speak, over him.

Rodney continues to be a troublemaker at school and hangs around with too many dubious characters.

I saw Dr. Wright yesterday for my weekly check-up, and she gave me a clean bill of health. My blood work is excellent; blood pressure is normal, and the baby's heartbeat is strong, very strong. She must have your constitution! I play violin tapes for her every day, and she seems to breathe in sync with the music. She's going to be an amazing child, that's for sure.

My love, as always,

Suzie

His reply was as follows:

Suzie—

You did the right thing telling your Dad the truth about Georgina. I applaud your guts! There has to be more to a marriage than great sex. Your Dad is a highly successful lawyer, but I think he's very lonely in his personal life.

When I arrive in town, I'll do whatever I can to straighten out Rod.

Keep up the violin sessions.

My love,

Jack

Chapter 19   <u>Contrasting Societies: February to July, 1991</u>

The months passed slowly for Jack, like snails crawling home after a rainstorm. But gradually, he was making spiritual progress. By May, he was able to sit motionless for up to three hours at a stretch--not moving to relieve bodily irritations one inch. His powers of concentration were definitely growing. He often noticed that the distance between thoughts expanded as silence permeated his entire being. The sound of one hand clapping was, for him, a way to realize that the waking state was very much like dreaming.

"Real wakefulness occurs when there aren't any sounds at all, and I'm grounded in awareness itself," was his latest insight.

He continued to email Sue every Sunday. On May 15th, he received the following note from her—

Dearest Jack—

Our baby's moving now and kicking the inside of my stomach hard on a regular basis. I've gained thirty pounds, and my belly protrudes far into space. Moving upstairs into Dad's place happened last week because he's moved out. One of the small bedrooms has been turned into a pink nursery. Even the crib and mobile are now pink. You'd be impressed with the work I've done to get things ready.

Rodney got a great report card last week but is having behavioral problems. Some of his bad friends are still hanging around, and he keeps getting into nasty fights. He needs a father figure in the worst way, and you are that person. He's fourteen next week, so this is a critical time in his life.

I think about you constantly and can't wait to hold your body next to mine.

All my love,

Sue.

PS *Have you picked out a name yet?

His reply came quickly.

Sue—

I'm delighted all's going well with the pregnancy, but can't imagine an enormous stomach on you!

Sounds like everything's unfolding as it should for life in a big family home—just think I'll be there in seven short weeks!

I've grown accustomed to a disciplined way of living, which will help me cope with the many challenges of parenthood and family living.

*As for a name, I like **Lalita,** which in Sanskrit means "beautiful woman." Rodney's progress in school is encouraging, but I'm concerned about the friends he's keeping. We must do something about that.*

My love to you,

Jack.

One day, several weeks later, another email arrived from Sue.

Dear Jack—

My due date is only two months away, and I'm feeling depressed that you won't be with me during the delivery. However, we'll soon all be together.

My father came over for dinner last night with Georgina, which means his threat to break up with her was hollow. Did you know she's twenty-eight years younger than him and dresses like a French whore? The whole scene was neurotic, but how can I criticize him after all he's done for us?

Rodney was involved in a robbery at <u>Stenberg's Groceteria</u> last Monday with some of his friends. On Tuesday, he was called into the principal's office and expelled from school for the rest of the year. I'm hoping you can help him with his academics over the summer.

Our wedding day is set for September 21st. I can't wait.

Your loving partner,

Sue.

His reply followed quickly.

Dear Suzie—

Your Dad's having a mid-life crisis, but there's no way we can judge him. Let's try to stay focused on his generosity and support him as best we can.

I'm shocked to hear the news about Rod. One of my highest priorities for the summer will be to work on getting him back on track.

Soon we'll be married; living together as a happy, fully-functioning family.

Jack.

On August 31st, Suzie's most important email was waiting in Jack's inbox.

Jack—

*I'm recovering slowly, but I just **have** to connect with you today. Lalita was born on August 25th after fifteen hours of labor, a last-minute episiotomy and using the largest set of forceps imaginable, which scratched her head on the way out. The doctor did the best he could, but he's only a third-year resident. Thank God his nurse was very experienced. However, I'm past all that now because our baby's the most beautiful eight-pound two ounce infant in the entire universe. Please see the attached photo of her suckling on my left breast ten minutes after birth.*

All my love,

Susan.

When Jack clicked on the attachment, a photo of his daughter came up, and he stared at her for twenty minutes in shocked silence. She was gorgeous—blonde curls of silk hair on perfectly formed limbs and a relaxed, tranquil posture—like a meditating Buddhist nun.

This is my own flesh and blood, he thought. *I must get back to Stewart as soon as I possibly can—I already feel bonded to her.*

On the last day of his <u>Phase 2 Program</u>, a small ceremony was held in the monastery's courtyard. Carl Tara Sandheim was the priest selected to be the master of ceremonies for the seven graduating students.

"You've all worked incredibly hard to pass this part of your *Zen Training,* and for that, I acknowledge and congratulate you. In our culture, it's important for monks to go out into the world periodically to test their levels of mindfulness and to contribute to the lives of others. After all, ours is a *life of service.*"

After handing out their certificates, they were entertained by music delivered by a Buddhist monk who was a flute master. His music was quietly inspiring, even other-worldly in its beauty—like a chorus of angels playing heavenly harps in perfect harmony. Then came a tea ceremony and light refreshments. It was an ordered and sacred event, unfolding with impeccable grace.

"I look forward to our final interview tomorrow, Jack," said Sandheim.

At that interview, the teacher was direct.

"You're making wonderful progress, my friend. Take what you've learned and let it guide your lifestyle. Be mindful at all times, meditate every day and don't do anything looking for a reward. Your actions must always be pure and work on your koan as hard as you can. You're on a path to the priesthood, so stay in touch with us and work to complete your training as soon as you can."

"We have a special bond, sir, and I want to keep in close touch with you. Is that possible?"

"Yes, of course, Jack. I can be reached directly via email and will always respond to your questions and comments as soon as I can."

During the last three days of this stage of his training, Jack threw himself into his meditations with intense purpose. He knew how difficult family life in a small mining town was going to be, so he wanted to consolidate and complete his Zen apprenticeship in a powerful way. He also made sure to say goodbye to his fellow monks who'd become close to him during the training.

Daryl Brown was a young American novitiate from Chicago who'd dropped out of college and was in the process of reassessing his life's path.

"I've enjoyed our periodic conversations, Daryl, as well as working beside you in the gardens. Your discipline is admirable. I believe you'll one day become a seasoned monk and serve many people in that role."

"Thank you, Jack—I'll miss your passionate discussions and your inspirational talks. The Zen way of life is hard on the outside, but the inner peace it leads to is well worth all the challenges and struggles. I had many successes in worldly living, but there always seemed to be something missing. I had great jobs and relationships but was mostly unhappy in my heart. At the monastery, I feel much more fulfilled and content with what's happening around me."

JJ Suzuki was a newly initiated monk—someone by whom Jack had been amazed. He walked up to him as he worked on his hands and knees in the hot sun, pulling weeks and clipping tomato buds. This man worked relentlessly all day long, often without breaks. His skin was tanned, almost black. Looking down at him, he said,

"Thank you for all the times you encouraged me when I was down and distracted.Your steadfastness and powers of concentration inspired me."

"Jack, you've come a long way in just three months," said JJ, slowly getting up from his work, standing straight and looking directly into Jack's eyes. "I'll be thinking of you in Stewart, hoping you don't get pulled away and sucked into the morass of life in mainstream Canadian society. Someday, I hope you'll come back to complete your training here. Don't ever forget how peaceful the Zen way of life is. Do you notice how quiet it always is around here? You'll find life in a mining town very noisy and full of commotions and distractions that signify nothing."

"Yes, JJ, I appreciate how quiet and ordered life is here, and I won't forget it--Good-bye, my friend."

Akiro Manami was an old Japanese monk who'd been ordained for over thirty years. Despite his eighty years, he was wiry, thin, tough and articulate. It had taken Jack many weeks to be able to understand his heavily accented English. Akiro was in charge of many garden work parties that Jack had attended and could not only lead his charges but keep up with them no matter how hard the work was.

"I'm leaving the Monastery for a while, Akiro—thank you for teaching me how to grow tomatoes, peaches and broccoli—my three favorite foods in the world. I'm going to miss you."

"You meditate, boy—don't stop. You see truth soon," he replied with the flicker of a smile on his dry, weathered face.

As Jack walked through the Zen properties for the last time, he couldn't help but notice the disciplined nature of the community. On his way out, he stared at the waterwheels that turned effortlessly, the orange goldfish swimming in the ponds, the buds of April opening on the Japanese maples, the black-robed monks working ceaselessly in silence and the beautiful, well-cultivated, lush vegetable gardens. The Zen society couldn't be more opposite than the one he was heading to.

Once out of the Monastery and back at the hotel, his drive to get to Stewart was intense. He missed his woman and wanted to test out the strength of his spiritual accomplishments. Jack Turner intended to take his accumulated Buddhist wisdom *into the world*. He looked forward to living the family life. Above all, he wanted to make a difference in the lives of others.

PART 2

LALITA

Chapter 20   Lalita: September 2nd to 20th, 1991

On September 2nd, Jack boarded Air Canada flight 7109 to Terrace. After an uneventful three-hour flight, he landed at 2 pm and had to run quickly over to Hangar B17 as his flight on the <u>Goose</u> to Stewart was scheduled to depart at 2:17 pm. Bill Tracey was again the designated pilot--but on this day, he was well-dressed—attired in a pressed white shirt and clean blue jeans. He didn't look inebriated to Jack but was again chewing tobacco, as evidenced by the dry black saliva crusted into the corners of his wide mouth.

"You're Jack, right?" he said. "I remember you."

"Yes, I am, and you're the Bill Tracey who flew me on the <u>Goose</u> last time I travelled on it?"

"Yes—now come along and hop aboard—there's only one empty seat left today."

That meant there'd be twelve passengers flying to Stewart on this journey. Flying low again, Tracey flew his plane right down the middle of the <u>Portland Canal</u>, just above the evergreen trees. Fortunately, it was a beautiful day with clear, blue, cloudless skies and a bright, warm sun illuminating all the glories of Nature in northern BC.

Suzie waved to Jack with both her arms as he sat inside the aircraft, waiting to deplane. She was wearing a tight, short-sleeved black sweater with matching track pants. In her arms, Lalita was wrapped in a pink blanket, and Rodney stood beside them, anxiously squinting and peering ahead in his attempt to see his uncle. As soon as Jack hit the pavement, Suzie ran up to him, kissed him lovingly and carefully placed their daughter in his arms.

"Do you approve, darling?"

"She's the most beautiful being I've ever seen," replied Jack, tears streaming down his face. He was transfixed, staring into her large, unblinking bright blue eyes. Soon, they were heading home inside a brand-new Jeep Cherokee that smelled like fresh leather.

"You didn't tell me about buying an SUV, dear."

"It's my dad's Jack, but he said you could use it for the time being. He also has a Toyota Prius and Georgina's crew-cab truck.

As they sped along, Jack caressed his daughter's cheek and rocked her in his arms. He was whispering to her—telling a story about butterflies and bees and flowers. Once inside the Fitzgerald home, they headed to the nursery and put the baby into her crib so she could gaze at the multi-layered Disney mobile dangling above her head, like an angel watching stars cross the Milky Way.

"Go down to your room now, Rod and finish reading *The Adventures of Tom Sawyer.* Maybe your uncle will teach you all about Mark Twain's characters," echoed Suzie.

"Yes, I'll definitely do that," noted Jack.

Once his nephew was gone, Jack asked,

"Is he sleeping in the suite now?"

"Yes, and he makes his own breakfast down there, too, which means we'll have lots of privacy."

At that point, Suzie embraced her lover and started kissing him passionately on the mouth.

"I can't make love for five more weeks, darling, but don't worry—there's lots of other things I can do to satisfy you."

Jack would welcome love-making with his fiancé at any other time, but right then, his thoughts were fixated on Lalita. Something magical had happened the first time he held her. It was simple spiritual bonding. He fell in love with his daughter at that moment, and it was a love he'd only ever felt before with his brother Jim. He knew that bond would last a lifetime, and whatever happened in his life, he'd be a devoted father--until the day he died.

And there was definitely something different and special about Lalita. She slept soundly throughout the nights, never cried, never fussed and smiled constantly as if she somehow knew everything in her life was going to work out perfectly. From the very beginning, she was calm, poised and focused.

Jack formed a new habit of entering the nursery every day at 5 am, sitting on the thick beige carpet beside his daughter's crib and entering a state of deep meditation. He could hear her breathing and feel her tranquility. The moment she woke up, he stood beside her crib, looking directly into her eyes. Then he'd pick her up, feed her breast milk from the prepared bottle in their fridge and sing her songs. Sometimes, he'd bring his guitar into the room to play soft lullabies and watch her coo with pleasure.

"Wow—you've really bonded with her, Jack—you're now spending more time with Lalita than with me," muttered Sue distractedly.

"She's a very special child, don't you think," he responded.

"Of course, I'd expect nothing less than someone who's *your* daughter."

"Sue, I've been having very strange dreams about Lalita lately, and I had another one last night."

"Tell me about them, Jack."

"When you first told me you were pregnant, I dreamt the baby was born as a magnificent cross between a princess and an eagle. She had brilliantly colored, red feathered wings and beautiful arms with strong hands that had long, slender, artistic fingers. Since then, I've had many more dreams—always with the same theme. I'm inevitably in trouble, and she saves me because she can fly and has magical powers. One time, she picked me up and flew me to a majestic oak tree just before I was going to be massacred by a group of wild, angry Cree warriors. Another time, I was up to my neck in quicksand, sinking fast. She flew down and put her fingers under my armpits, pulled me out of the muck, then flew me away to a natural hot thermal pool so I could clean up and heal."

"Jack, are these dreams vivid?"

"Absolutely, in living color--and the amazing thing is I can remember them in great detail. I've never remembered any other dreams in my life but the ones about our baby."

"That is so strange."

"One night last week, I dreamt that you and I were locked in a dark dungeon at the bottom of a medieval castle. We were hungry and terrified of all the rats surrounding us because they were frothing at the mouth. Lalita flew into our space through the prison bars, made the rats magically disappear and gave us each a bucket of deep-fried Kentucky Chicken and a plastic pot of potato salad for us to share. It was delicious!"

"What happened next?"

"She picked me up and flew me out of there. We ended up in a Spanish apple orchard harvesting big, ripe Macintosh apples and eating them. It was a hot sunny day, so we just leaned up against one of the trees when we were full and rested."

"What happened to me?"

"I have no idea other than you got left behind."

"That's kind of scary, Jack."

"Yeah, but they're just dreams and don't mean anything."

"You're so lucky—I can never remember any of my dreams. Maybe I don't dream."

"Suzie--everybody dreams, it just that often they're hard to remember."

"Well, okay then. What was the best dream you've ever had that involved our baby?"

Without hesitation, Jack began telling his partner about the amazing dream he had just two nights before.

I was living in a Buddhist monastery, sitting in a large meditation hall. It was empty except for me and my teacher who was sitting in a swivel chair on a raised dais at the front. It was Lalita! As usual, she was both a majestic eagle and a beautiful princess.

"I can give you one wish, but only one," she said to me.

After some consideration, I answered,

"My wish is to become enlightened. Can you make that happen?"

"Why, of course, but it'll be painful before you reach that state. Are you sure you want to go through all that suffering?"

"Yes," was my instant reply.

All of a sudden, she picked me up and flew me out of there, over hills and mountains and oceans until we came to a forest. In the middle of a strand of thick Douglas Firs sat a grassy hut in the middle of a clearing. Beside it was a massive bonfire with flames reaching over twenty feet high."

"What's that?" I asked.

"A sweat lodge--but before you enter, you must fast for seven days."

"How do I do that?"

"Just sit in the full lotus position and don't move. I'll be back in a week."

"During that week, I had many visions and temptations. I wanted to feast like a glutton, have sex like a stud, get drunk like a wino and fall asleep like a sloth. But I stayed in meditation without moving, drinking, eating or sleeping for seven whole days, like a camel in the Sahara waiting for his master."

"Jack, are you making this up as you go along?"

"No, honestly, this was my dream, and I remember it vividly. When Lalita came back to the sweat lodge, she told me to carry seven hot rocks—that were sitting in the fire—into the lodge, which I did."

"Did your hands get burned in the dream?"

"No-- but it was unbelievably hot in that sweat lodge, and I was extremely tired and hungry. She then told me to lie down but stay awake."

"Did you fall asleep?"

"No, but my mind was confused, and I had many terrible thoughts, including some suggesting I commit suicide. Three days later, Lalita shrunk herself and entered the lodge."

"Lie still," she said, "I'm going to suck all the poisons out of your soul."

"She then put her mouth on mine and sucked all my breath out like a vacuum sucking dust out of a filthy rug. Suddenly, it felt like I was floating in an ocean of bliss. Everything went silent, and I felt an overwhelming peace and sense of well-being come over me. I was deliriously happy for the first time in my life."

"Then what happened?"

"I woke up and saw your gorgeously naked body lying beside me. At that moment, I was back in reality, but the joy inside has lingered on."

"That's an amazing dream, Jack. But why don't you think I was a major character in it?"

"I just don't know, darling, but don't worry about it."

By the end of the summer, Jack was well on the way to perfecting the art of fatherhood.

Chapter 21   Employment: September 21st to September 30th, 1991

For the next few weeks, Jack trained as a nanny, learning how to change diapers, dress his baby, walk all over the countryside with her in a blue jean backpack and sing lullabies every night until she fell asleep.

"I can't believe you're such a natural father, Jack," exclaimed Suzie one day—"So loving and patient."

"Thank you, my dear. It's strange, but I feel so connected to Lalita. Every time I'm with her, I feel happy and inspired."

During that period, he also set up a learning program for Rod. It focused on reading comprehension, writing coherence and the mastering of complex mathematical calculations. Jack also made sure Rodney was getting enough physical exercise. He bought him a twelve-speed bike and a pair of Nike marathon running shoes.

"It's important to work out every day in some way, Rod," Jack told him.

"Rodney listens to you and does whatever you say," echoed Suzie. How do you do that?"

"Don't forget he's got my blood running through his veins."

Over time, especially when it came to wedding plans, Jack questioned their financial viability.

"How do you pay the bills, Sue?" he asked.

"I'm on an unemployment insurance maternity leave claim right now, but my Dad is also paying me a monthly top-up stipend. It's not much, but we'll get by."

"I'm going to meditate for a while before we talk about this again, Sue."

By this time, Jack had established his own contemplation area in a small spare bedroom. It was replete with a meditation bench, an altar covered in a soft, red felt mat, twelve metal jars full of sand with orange incense sticks stuck throughout them, like the crosses on Flanders Field. Several tall, white candles provided the lighting. That space had an enchanting and pleasant scent, like fresh fruit trees bathing in the sun. It was there that he went to meditate, pray and seek answers to any difficult questions. One wall of his study was covered with shelves containing books on Buddhism, Christianity, Shamanic Healing and Sufism.

The very next day, Jack received a letter from Conrad Houlder at the Richmond Times. It read—

Conrad Houlder,
Managing Editor,
The Richmond Times.

Dear Jack—

I write to inform you that the <u>*Richmond Times*</u> *has recently been purchased by the* <u>*Netcom*</u> <u>*Media Group*</u> *of Seattle, Washington. As a result, many changes have taken place in our paper's management approach. Our focus will now move away from many of its former trends and bring a more American slant to reports and publications. Also, there have been several key staffing changes. For example, our former editor, George Copeland, is no longer employed by our company. He decided that he needed to spend much more time with his family.*

We value the work you've done for us in the past but regret to inform you that your services will no longer be required. The last article you submitted will be published, but it'll be the final one from you that we'll accept.

A full accounting report will be completed soon, and a check mailed to you when it is done. We wish you every success in your future writing career.

Sincerely,

Conrad Houlder.

"Now we're going to have to make some big changes, Sue," he said after reading the letter.

"You look shocked, Jack—what is it?"

"I just lost my gig at the <u>Richmond Times,</u> so now money's become a real concern."

"Don't worry about it, we'll be just fine. But in case you did ever want another job, my father said he could help you."

"How would he do that?"

"I remember him saying once that if you ever wanted employment, he could make it happen, but I've got no idea how."

"Suzie, why don't we have your father and his girlfriend over for dinner? After supper and a few glasses of wine, we could talk to him about our wedding plans and this potential job opportunity."

"That sounds like a great idea. I'll invite them over next Saturday evening. What should I cook?"

"How about double cheese and vegetarian pizzas with Greek salad and a nice French red wine?"

"Consider it done," she replied. "But did you know that Georgina likes pepperoni?"

"That may be so—but she's getting vegetarian next weekend," replied Jack.

The following Saturday night, Darwin and Georgina showed up at 7:15 pm for dinner, which was forty-five minutes late.

"So sorry for the delay, Sue, but it took my woman a long time to get ready," said her father as he entered the home's lobby. "It's the make-up application that takes so much time."

"Don't worry about it. Just means we can start eating right now."

My future father-in-law's date looks garish and cheap, thought Jack as he stared at her.

She was wearing a bright purple dress so low cut that both her enormous breasts were eighty percent exposed. Her hair was a sticky strawberry blonde color, beehive stacked, greasy, and a foot high off her protruded, powdered and pasty-white forehead. A youthful Darwin, on the other hand, was dressed like the corporate lawyer he was—a black pin-striped suit with a starched white shirt overshadowed by a navy blue tie that hung down to his trim, athletic-looking waist.

"How do you like the pizza, folks?" asked Suzie while they ate.

"It's alright, but you forgot the pepperoni," blurted out Georgina through a mouthful of food, some of which escaped her mouth and plopped onto the table.

"That actually happened on purpose because Jack's a vegetarian," added Sue.

"Oh, sorry—I didn't know that," blurted out Georgina.

"Dad, we'd like to hold our ceremony right here in your home. Remember, we're only having a few friends and the Anglican Church officials."

"That sounds great to me," answered Darwin. "But I want to pay for a large reception in the Church Army Hall after the main ceremony is over."

"We weren't going to have a reception father."

"I insist. I've got a lot of friends and relatives to invite. This is a big event for our family, and I want to have a free, open bar and a real feast."

"How can we say no to you under those conditions?" interjected Jack.

"You can't," he replied.

"By the way, Dad, did you once mention there might be an employment opportunity in town for Jack if he wanted one?"

"Absolutely—one of my best clients is the manager of Le Duc, and he owes me big time. I could get Jack a job at their gold mine in a heartbeat. Now, it'd be just a laboring gig, but the pay would be very good. What about it, Jack? Are you interested?"

"It sounds like a real possibility, Darwin, and I've done this kind of work before--but let me meditate on it first."

After spending two mornings contemplating his latest job prospect, Jack decided to write his mentor and get some advice.

Dear Teacher—

I arrived safely in Stewart and met my daughter soon after the Goose landed. She's absolutely adorable!"

Since then, I've come to realize that money's going to be tight because I lost my job writing for the Richmond Times. However, Susan's father can get me work at a local mine. Should I take it?

I miss monastic living and all the peace, discipline and awareness it engenders. But most of all, I miss you.

Jack

His mentor responded two days later.

Jack—

I'm happy to hear you arrived safely in Stewart and met the newest member of your family. The job prospect sounds like a challenging but perhaps wonderful opportunity.

You'll have to be very vigilant with your awareness because there'll be many distractions and temptations associated with the mining lifestyle. Many years ago, I worked in a gold mine in Kalgoorlie, Australia, so my words of caution carry the weight of personal experience. Be especially careful to avoid noisy pubs, excessive alcohol consumption and loose women. Beer, wine and loveless sex will punch a massive hole in your psychic energy, and that may lead to bad decisions.

But, at the same time, if you can stay alert, there'll be many chances to build and enhance your personal power and inner freedom. That means remembering to meditate every single day and watching for any demons inside you that might get activated. Just remember that those demons are manifestations of your own past traumatic experiences. They can be nullified by meditation.

I can understand why you miss life in the monastery. We cultivate a life of peace through meditation and value an environment that maximizes the beauty of nature. One way we do that is through gardening. Since you left, we've begun to build a series of greenhouses to grow tomatoes, zucchinis and cucumbers year-round. We've also created thirty hanging baskets full of marigolds, nasturtiums and pansies, as well as rows of lavender plants along the sides of the Guest House.

I encourage you to grow vegetables and flowers anywhere you can in Stewart, Jack. Doing so will raise your awareness of life's authentic rhythms, give you the satisfaction of caring for other living beings and serve as an antidote to the darker kinds of human activities you're going to be exposed to.

In peace,

Sandheim

The next morning at breakfast, Jack told his fiancé he was going to take the mining job.

"Are you sure you really want to do this, Jack? Because we'll be fine without you working."

"Yes, I'm certain about it. There'll be aspects of the work I won't like, but the job will challenge me in many ways. Besides, laboring work is a great way to stay in shape, which I know will make you happy."

"When will you want to start then?"

"At the end of the month--but before that, I'd like to plant some lavender in the backyard and make up a few hanging flower baskets with plants that can survive the winter. Would your Dad be okay with me doing that?"

"It doesn't matter what he thinks. This property's going to be ours very soon."

Chapter 22   <u>Mining: September 30th to November 25^{th,} 1991</u>

The wedding ceremony, held on September 21st, was as informal as Suzie could make it under the circumstances. Reverend Blaine Stevens officiated, supported by his wife, June and his favorite lay reader, Jill Symons. Seven of Sue's friends were in attendance, along with her father, Georgina and Rodney. Lalita sat in her stroller, watching the proceedings with wide open and curious eyes. After the bride and groom exchanged cheap rings, were pronounced man and wife and signed the Registry, light refreshments were served. The happy newlyweds circulated and socialized dutifully. Suzie was wearing a green velvet dress with a mink fur collar adorned with two white orchids. Jack wore a white T-shirt, sparklingly clean blue jeans, a brand-new black sports jacket and sandals with genuine leather straps.

"My father has an announcement to make now," shouted out the bride above the general din of the event. At that point, Darwin stood up on a foot stool and made a brief announcement:

"I'm overjoyed that my daughter has finally married a fine young man this afternoon. Together, they'll make a wonderful family, continuing to live in this home indefinitely. Please join me in toasting this happy couple and wishing them a life of joy, happiness and unbounded prosperity."

After everyone had clinked their glasses and drank deeply, he continued.

"The reception will be held at the *Church Army Hall* on Third Street. There'll be lots of great music, delicious foods, exotic treats, sweet desserts and as much free alcohol as you can imbibe. Please join me there at 4 pm today and expect to have a long, glorious night of celebrating. We all love you, Jack and Sue."

By the time the newlyweds arrived at the Reception, all hell had broken loose. Music from a five-piece rock band—The Miners—blared so loudly it could be clearly heard in Hyder, Alaska, three miles away.

A fully grown pig was roasting outside the Hall, turning slowly on spittle in the middle of a roaring fire, like a wiener burning on a stick in a campfire. Inside, six folding tables were laden with salads, hot and cold vegetables, Idaho baked potatoes and a sizzling ninety-pound roast of beef. Beside the stage stood the drink counter serviced by two qualified bartenders dressed in tuxedos. Some of the guests were patiently lining up along the buffet while others danced wildly on an opening in the floor space. There was a long single file of people waiting to order drinks.

Darwin had invited thirty-two guests and many friends, clients and relatives. All of Suzie's local acquaintances were there, along with her children and the church officials. Jack was so stressed out he started drinking tall Bacardis, which went straight to his head because he'd forgotten to eat. He then started to dance with anyone available, hopping up and down as he whooped it up. His father-in-law slapped him on the back and yelled,

"You and I are going to do great things in this town, my boy—welcome to the family!"

And the party continued like that well into the early hours of the morning.

"You went crazy last night, darling," muttered Suzie in bed the next morning.

"I didn't do anything *really* stupid, did I?"

"Nothing other than stripping down to your underwear and jumping into a barrel of run-off water outside the hall."

"Oh no, can you forgive me for doing that?"

"Of course, I thought it was funny. The water was full of mosquito eggs," she laughed.

After swallowing two Tylenol Extra Strength red tablets and a full glass of ice-cold water, he sat on the bed and asked his wife an important question.

"Do you think I should go to work in the gold mine?"

"Yes--but only if you *really* want to."

"I've been meditating on it and have received advice from my Zen master.

"What did he say?"

"That it'd be a great way to test my spiritual progress. But, he warned me to be vigilant in my practice, saying there'd be lots of temptations coming my way in the mining lifestyle."

"There might be temptations for you, Jack, but nothing you won't be able to resist. I'm happy that you've made this decision but remember—it was *your* decision. Whatever you choose to do is fine with me," replied his new wife.

On September 30th, Jack started working at the Le Duc Gold Mine in Stewart, BC. He had to arrive at Jim Bowler's Chevron Station at 7 am to pick up the caboose that would take him all the way up <u>Premier Mountain</u> to the site.

On a plateau, halfway up, stood a large warehouse-like structure full of sixteen twenty-eight-ton diesel engines that drove power underground into the mine.

Jack's main job entailed cleaning out sixteen oil filters, helping the fitters lift heavy parts into the engines when necessary and steam cleaning all the outside driveways. To clean the filters, he had to unclip the heavy, round metallic capsules encasing them, open each hinged lid and remove all the coagulated oil sediments. Once the inside of each filter was clean, he had to shut the tops and polish their round domes. It was very dirty work. After cleaning each filter, his coveralls were soaked in oil, which crept into the pores of his skin—particularly along his thighs.

He was also responsible for keeping the entire building spotless, which meant sweeping all the floors, cleaning the staff lunchroom and bathrooms and wiping down all the diesel engines.

"You're getting the idea of how to do this job, but you're going to have to work faster, boy," shouted his boss, Bill Dougherty, on Day 1.

This guy turned out to be a ruthless man known for harassing any employee he didn't take a liking to. The working conditions were far from ideal, but Jack was physically fit and mentally clear, so he could endure stresses which bothered many of the other workers. He was also a very hard worker who'd developed highly evolved powers of concentration.

Those powers helped him succeed in the job where many others had failed. When the temperature in the main boiler room got over 130 degrees Fahrenheit, he overcame heat exhaustion by pure mind power. One day, two miners collapsed due to heat exhaustion, and he rescued them by pulling them outside and splashing cold water all over their faces. Another time, a heavy anvil fell onto an employee's leg, pinning him to the ground, and Jack was able to lift it off his leg. That anvil weighed 225 lbs!

"How the hell did you do that?" asked his boss.

"It's a secret," laughed Jack.

But his secret was simple: it was the way he'd developed mystical powers of concentration through hundreds of hours of meditation.

Unlike many of the workers, Jack spent most of his working hours in the present moment focused intently on the tasks at hand. He didn't get distracted, angry or tense, no matter how bad the working conditions got. He didn't move into the past or the future. This was one by-product of his long training as a vegetable gardener at the Monastery.

From an outside perspective, each working day in the mine might appear monotonous. But not for Jack. He'd stumbled onto a musty old book in the Stewart Public Library entitled *Contemplative Practices For The Modern World* by Padre WF Symington. The library had only four shelves of books at the back of the Post Office, but the postal clerks did loan books out to trusted readers, and Jack was one of them. This particular tome contained a whole chapter devoted to creating 'flow' in the workplace, and the formula was simple: take control of your actions and make the work more complex.

Influenced by Symington, Jack went ahead and created complex routines, even for the most mundane tasks. He timed how long it took him to clean one oil filter and strived to improve his speed on each one without sacrificing work quality. Then, he graphed the results. He experimented to see how he could get the staff room floors to actually shine and the toilets to flush more efficiently-- with a stronger draw. This required detailed drawings and making repairs. To enable him to lift heavier weights when the mechanics required it, he started lifting a twenty-pound barbell--expanding the number of lifts weekly. Each day repeated itself endlessly in exactly the same way, but Jack experienced the daily events as constantly changing and expanding. He was manifesting high levels of job satisfaction for himself by being creative and proactive.

In the morning, after his alarm went off, he showered, meditated for thirty minutes, dressed--with a new shirt every day--and walked through the kitchen on his way out. There, he'd find a special lunch made by Suzie, which he picked up after leaving an inspired love note to her, stuck to the fridge magnets.

While bumpily riding up the mountain, he closed his eyes and counted up and down to one hundred, over and over again, ignoring the chatter, the smoke and the cold. Once he started work, he used his conscious mind to create more and more complexity around his jobs.

That monk Symington was a genius, he thought. With his knowledge, I can make any job fun and stimulating.

One day, when the work was slow, and his boss was angry at him, he made Jack climb into an air receiver the size of a Volkswagen Van and chip rust off the bolt heads inside without ear plugs—it was just like he was a prisoner of war that day. He was given four hours to do the whole container. Jack ripped his handkerchief in half and stuffed each part into his ears. He worked quickly, finishing all the work in two hours. That gave him time to meditate for the final two hours and crawl out of the hole in a very calm, peaceful state.

"Did you clean every bolt, Jack?"

"Yes sir, I did—twice."

"How do you like your job?" his wife asked him when he got home.

"It's great, honey--time is passing very quickly—I can't believe it'll be Christmas in a month.

Chapter 23   The Power to Heal: November, 1991 to April, 1992

Carl Tara Sandheim was right about the mining lifestyle. There was a continual chorus of bickering amongst the employees, and their conflicts were exacerbated by their boss, Bill Dougherty. He was constantly berating the workers and belittling them publically, which added to the tension of working in a hot, noisy, and dirty environment.

Luckily, he finally stopped punishing Jack and yelling at him for three reasons. First, he admired his work ethic and detached manner. Second, Jack found Bill lying in a pool of oil outside the main building one morning and was able to sit him on a bench and assist him in getting clean before anyone else saw what had happened—a sprained ankle on slippery concrete and liquor on the breath. Finally, he caught Bill kissing another man one day in Stewart City Park and then promised him he'd never reveal the secret. And he never did.

Every Friday night, all the inside workers went drinking at the King Edward Hotel in downtown Hyder. It was part of the work culture, so Jack was forced to join them. Dougherty frequently bought him extra drinks. It was a rowdy bar frequented by hippies, miners off-duty and the occasional tourist. Jack saw the buck-shot holes in the front door and thought, *This place looks like something you'd see in a fourth-rate Western.*

There were American license plates tacked up all over the wall (some going back sixty-five years), two broken-down shuffle boards that were still in use and a chubby bartender who loved to 'hyderize' anyone that was visiting for the first time. 'Hyderizing' meant giving the customer a free drink; an ounce of Newfoundland <u>Screech</u> mixed with an ounce of beer that was lit on fire. You had to down it in one gulp as soon as the flames burnt out. This concoction inevitably made the recipient wobbly.

"Do you enjoy going to the pub on Friday nights, Jack?" asked Suzie in early December that year.

"No, I hate everything about it—especially the Saturday morning hangovers. The only part I like is having a drink with you once I get home. Getting laid is a bonus because you're an absolutely amazing lover. It's so refreshing to be with a woman who loves sex as much as I do."

"We're a couple, Jack and married people do things *together*—back each other up, right? I'm always happy to please you."

"Yes. But I also notice drinking booze ruins my meditation sessions until Tuesday mornings."

"Let's look at the positive side of things. You're turning out to be a fabulous father."

Nothing could be more accurate than that. Jack was utterly devoted to both Rodney, who was now calling him "Dad," and Lalita. He walked with his baby if she woke up during the night, changed her diaper whenever it was needed and bathed her lovingly three times a day. He took her on long walks all over town in a collapsible stroller and put her in the Jeep car-seat whenever he went out on driving trips. He worked with Rodney on his educational program for an hour every day, read great works of literature to him and taught him how to play chess and checkers. He also introduced him to the world of music by giving him guitar lessons. Most of all, he talked Darwin into taking him and his nephew out fishing in his thirty-two-foot Kris-Kraft cruiser every Saturday morning. They never came home without catching the full fishing limit of fresh salmon, which Sue often baked and soaked in fresh lemon juice the same day it was caught. Most importantly, Rodney was introduced to the game of hockey. As it turned out, Darwin had played Junior B in his youth and was a devout NHL fan. Once his grandson was registered to play, both he and Jack went to every game they could. Slowly, Rod's association with other kids who were having a bad influence on him began to disintegrate. He no longer seemed to feel the need to be accepted by hoodlums.

As time went on, Jack settled into his routines effortlessly. He worked hard for forty hours a week at the Le Duc site and made friends with several of the workers, including Dougherty, who sometimes joined the Saturday fishing expeditions. Working in the mine and lifting weights made him physically fit and strong again.

Suzie doted on him, spoiling him totally. She cooked delicious meals, cleaned their home fastidiously, constantly complimented him, laughed even at his failed jokes and made passionate love to Jack whenever he wanted sex. On Sundays, the small family went on exciting outings and adventures. But Jack became so busy with family life that he stopped writing and meditated only sporadically.

During the winter months of 1991, he rekindled his communications with Carl Tara Sandheim. At Christmas, he wrote him a poignant email which read,

Dear Master—

I've settled into hectic family living and seem to be busy with worldly affairs all day, every day. I crave rest so badly that sometimes I sleep-in and skip my morning meditations. Work on my koan has come to a standstill. I've even allowed alcohol to slip back into my life, joining fellow workers at a pub once a week. Working in the mine is a discipline that helps nurture my awareness, but the stresses of parenting, socializing and keeping a wife happy can be debilitating. I miss the immaculate order, peace and serenity of monastic living. How can I stay mindful and aware throughout all my challenges?

All the best of the Christmas Season,

Jack

Three days later, he received a reply.

Dear Jack—

*Thanks for the update on your spiritual situation. Despite what you think, progress **is** being made. You don't need to berate yourself—just allow trust to take over your inner life. The universe is unfolding as it should, so don't change anything. Just abide in awareness and notice everything that happens to you and around you. Here's another clue to help you with the koan—"Do you have any recollections of being born?" If you get back to your daily meditations, insights will* *come. And it takes time to build a mindful life; please be patient.*

Sandheim

Communicating with his Zen master cleared Jack's head and inspired him to continue on his spiritual quest. The other element of his renewal came directly from his interactions with Lalita as the months went by.

She was a precocious child, progressing rapidly in every important aspect of development. She walked without support of any kind at nine months and started to recognize pictures a few weeks later. Jack read to her every day and picked out four well-illustrated cardboard books in full color to read to her whenever she was willing to engage.

"My friends at the baby support group can't believe she sleeps nine hours every night and never cries unless she's in pain. They say that's highly unusual, Jack," said Suzie one day.

"That doesn't surprise me at all," he replied.

Jack also played the guitar for her, and she responded by clapping her hands and singing with glee in her own baby way, like a happy nightingale at dusk. All that exposure to music when she was in utero was making a difference. But the most shocking character trait Jack noticed was his daughter's ability to facilitate healing. Sometimes, he took her to the Order of St. Luke's, 'laying-on-of hands' sessions at the Anglican Church. She sat in her stroller, watching the proceeds with curiosity.

"Jack, every time Lalita comes along to these meetings, Alvin's stuttering stops for a few days," stated Mrs. Gayle Pruit, a local barmaid who was raising her son alone. And if she's not here, it gets worse. And the church's caretaker, Spike Reynolds reported that his vision cleared and his cataracts settled down when Jack's daughter showed up at the meetings.

"Our daughter has the gift of healing others, Suzie," said Jack one cool evening in early April 1992.

"How do you mean?"

"People sometimes experience miraculous recoveries when she's present at our healing services on Wednesday nights."

"That sounds too good to be true; she's not even a year old yet," responded Suzie.

"Yes, it does—but it's true," Jack answered.

He wondered what the gift of healing really was. *Can she be a healer with no training?* He pondered these events during his periods of formal contemplation.

After many hours of disciplined meditation, he finally realised that he had no recollection of ever being born. That led him to the conclusion that he wouldn't recollect dying when that happened.

If I don't experience birth or death, it must mean they don't exist, he realised. *Birth and death must only be beliefs.*

In his email communication to Sandheim that month, he mentioned this inner opening.

Sir—

After prolonged penetration of my koan, I'm coming to strange conclusions. I don't ever remember being born, and I'm confident I won't experience dying. Does this mean birth and death are nothing more than beliefs that society forces onto us?

Jack.

Sandheim's response was quick.

Jack—

Keep working on this—you're nearing a massive breakthrough. Always remember that traditional social beliefs do have some reality. They describe a world that exists—but not in the way they say it does. Reality is different, strange, mysterious and mind-blowing. But we've all been conditioned intensely since the moment of birth. This universal hypnotism is powerful but can be broken. Stay with your meditations now that your inner wall is cracked.

Sandheim

There was always one central tension in Jack's life—a conflict between his spiritual practices and realizations and life in the world. No sooner would he feel that progress was being made than a major distraction or temptation would drain and confuse him. He was most susceptible to sex, alcohol, lack of sleep and a strong desire to please others, not to make his friends and family uncomfortable. But the spiritual life was causing him to be uncomfortable with 'normal' living. *Most people are living in an insane way*, he realized. *And I'm powerless to change that.*

Chapter 24   <u>Alicia: April 1992 to June 1995</u>

For the first four years of her life, Lalita existed in an enriched environment, something that would affect her forever in a positive way. Her father overextended himself to develop her into an exceptional child prodigy. He read to her every day and taught her how to play the guitar. When she was three years old, Jack hired a Spanish nanny to babysit while he and Sue were at work. And he gave that nanny, Alicia Mendez, a direct command—*do everything you possibly can to teach our daughter Spanish.*

"Yes, I'll do that," she said, "She'll be able to speak Spanish perfectly in one year."

Jack believed Alicia because he'd already come to know something about her. She was eighteen years old, a devout Roman Catholic, a master violin player and a straight-A student at high school. Three of Suzie's friends had recommended her as a babysitter. She was motivated to earn money for college and apparently had a special caring way with children. On top of that, she was extremely beautiful; her olive-brown Latino skin was flawless, and her black eyes sparkled with light and joy like a Greek goddess of antiquity.

Her father, Feliciano, was a mining engineer who worked at the Le Duc Gold Mine and her mother was a web developer toiling from home doing most of her work in Spanish. Her name was Gabriella. Alicia had two older brothers and a sister named Cora in Grade 4. Her aunt Pera and her French husband Lee also lived with Alicia's family in their sprawling country farm along with their only daughter

Cornelia. Pera waitressed part-time at the <u>King Edward Hotel,</u> and Lee was the Head Chef there. They were a large, close-knit and extended Roman Catholic family.

I'd like her to learn French as well, Suzie," said Jack in June 1995. "Let's register her into the *French Immersion Program* at <u>Stewart Elementary School</u>. Alicia speaks French too and can help us with this."

"If that's what you want, I'll go along with it, Jack—you never know when extra languages will come in handy."

Suzie was so in love with Jack that she'd do anything for him and agree to any plan he cooked up. To her, he was the ideal man: virile and full of energy, smart yet sensitive-- someone who was both practical and intellectual. And he was devoted to the development of her children. She even tried to be open and understanding about his spiritual practices, although she herself was an outright atheist. By the time Lalita turned four, Jack and Suzie had grown very close and were both experiencing a profound love that was authentic, but rare.

Despite Sue's reservations, Jack was determined to give Lalita a religious education. He took her and Rod to church every Sunday and familiarized them with the most well-known Bible stories. On top of that, he taught Lalita how to meditate and, by her fourth birthday, had her sitting with him in silent contemplations every morning. Rod *did* go to church until he was older but didn't like it. He refused to sit in meditation. By the time Lalita entered kindergarten in 1995, Jack and his father-in-law had become very good friends. Like Jack, Darwin had a keen interest in his grandchildren and their welfare.

One Saturday afternoon, when they were having a beer at the King Eddy, he said,

"Jack, you're the son I've always wanted but never had."

After a few drinks, he tended to open up to Jack, even expressing feelings that he never shared with anyone else. He was a hard-nosed, tough criminal lawyer.

"I don't know what to do with Georgina, Jack."

"How do you mean?"

"She wants to get married."

"Well, Darwin, what's stopping you? She's an attractive woman. You've been with her a long time, so you must know what she's like."

"She's oversexed, fantastic in bed—even a bit kinky and likes it rough. She's got a bombshell body and will service me anytime in any way I want, which is fantastic. I'll never forget those terrible years living with a frigid wife. She's a good cook and keeps our home clean enough for me. But, Jack, she's not very bright. I can't talk to her about anything of consequence, and she constantly nags me about money.

"What does she want you to do with your money?"

"Spend more of it on her," he answered, frowning.

"I don't give advice, Darwin, but in this case, I'd say it'd be wise to put off marriage as long as you can."

"My feelings exactly, Jack. By the way," he continued, now slurring his words, "You're doing a wonderful job with Rod and Lalita—they're both going to grow into amazing human beings, I'm sure of it. But do you *have* to expose them to all that religious crap?"

"Consider it education, not indoctrination. I just want the kids to be aware of some of the spiritual traditions in the world, but in the end, they'll never be brainwashed. Above all, I'm teaching them to be discerning and make their own choices. Right now, I'm introducing them to the basic principles of both Christianity and Buddhism."

"Please don't turn them into religious fanatics."

"No--I promise not to."

"On another matter," Darwin continued, "I just won a major case which involved prosecuting the killer of a wealthy businessman in Terrace. His name was Fred Carpenter, and it was his partner who murdered him in cold blood with an axe. The monster was sentenced to twenty years for manslaughter. My bill was over 600k, so I'm in a position to give you the home you and Sue now inhabit, as long as you promise to stay with her and take care of her."

"You're a very generous man, Darwin, and you have my word—I'll stay with her forever and put her welfare before my own."

"Not everyone would agree that I'm generous, but thank you for your promise."

In the fall of 1995, Jack and Darwin started coaching Rodney in hockey. There was, at that time, only one Midget hockey team in Stewart and that year Darwin was named its Head Coach. Jack became his assistant. That meant he was up twice a week at 4 am for early morning practices and unavailable for anything but hockey every Sunday afternoon. Once a month, the team played in Terrace, which meant two nights in the Lakelse Lake Hotel. Rodney wasn't one of the best players on the team, but he *could* skate hard, forward and backward, and get the odd goal— not bad for a defenseman.

That same year, Jack applied for a welding apprenticeship at the mine and, largely due to his strong relationship with Bill Dougherty, got it. It was a ten-month course and would enable him to make more money, have more holidays, and experience better work conditions. He was gradually becoming integrated into the culture of hard rock mining.

Meanwhile, Lalita started kindergarten in French Immersion. She was already fluent in Spanish thanks to the work of Alicia, who had, by this time, introduced her to many members of her extended family.

"Your daughter's reading at a Grade 2 level. I've never seen that before in all my twelve years of teaching," said Ms. Emilie Chatreau at Lalita's first parent-teacher interview. "She can also print many words in two languages and paints beautiful water colors. You must have put in a great deal of time with her, Mr. Turner."

"Thank-you, yes I have. But I wonder about her social skills. Does she get along well with her peers?"

"Lalita is a definite leader, but in a very quiet, confident way. She's never loud or bossy, but others tend to mimic her and seek her approval. That's also very unusual."

"Did you know she has the gift of healing, Ms. Chatreau?"

"No, I did not. What exactly does that entail?"

"In the right setting, she can facilitate the physical healing of others. I've witnessed it on many occasions."

"Will you explain that to me," requested the teacher.

"Perhaps I could, Ms. Chatreau. Do you believe in spiritual healing?"

"I don't know what spiritual healing is, Mr. Turner."

"Let's just say when a group of like-minded people get together and enter a prolonged silence with the specific purpose of experiencing healing, many miracles can happen."

"What kind of miracles?"

Some people are cured of diseases like skin cancer or gout, others find relief from paranoia or anxiety disorders."

"Does a minister of the cloth have to be involved?" She asked.

"Not necessarily—all that's really required is a group of sincere people who are willing to enter a meditation and be open to the possibility of supernatural healing."

"And how does Lalita affect these experiences?"

"Lalita and I attend the <u>Healing Order of St. Luke</u> meetings every Wednesday evening. About thirty participants gather at the <u>Anglican Church</u> to pray and enter that transformative silence. We've noticed that Lalita's presence at those meetings tends to facilitate rapid recoveries," replied Jack. "No one knows for sure why that is, but it has been noticed over the years that some people have the gift of healing. That means they were born with it."

"Do you think my chronic hip pain could be cured in your group?"

"I'm confident attendance in our group could end your hip issues, Ms. Chatreau."

"Could I come to the next meeting then?"

"By all means," said Jack.

The following Wednesday evening, Ms. Chatreau entered St. Matthew's Anglican Church on Spring Ridge Drive and was greeted in the oak-floored lobby by both Reverend Blaine Stephens and his wife, June Red Eagle.

"Welcome to the Healing Order of St. Luke," said the minister. "My name is Blaine, and my wife's is June. I understand you have a physical problem you'd like us to pay attention to."

"Yes, Reverend, I do. My name is Patrice, and my hip has been sore and tight ever since my replacement surgery nine and a half months ago."

"Come downstairs with us into our largest meeting room and get ready to have a significant healing experience. Your part is just to believe it can happen without a medical intervention. All we ask is that everything that happens tonight is kept strictly confidential and secret. Do I have your word on that?"

"Absolutely, Reverend, I won't tell a soul what happens."

Patrice entered the classroom and was pleased to see about twenty smiling faces welcoming her. They were sitting on gray metal chairs in a circle.

"Have a seat on the chair in the middle of the group, Patrice. Close your eyes and relax. We'll now enter a five-minute silence."

Ms. Chatreau obediently sat down, closed her eyes and settled herself into a comfortable pose. After what seemed to her like hours of waiting, she heard the faint sound of guitar music accompanied by soft humming. After that, the whole congregation got up and walked silently towards her chair. Soon, she felt many hands on her arms, shoulders, legs and back. Those hands included those of Lalita and Jack.

"Do you want to be healed, Patrice?" whispered the minister.

"Yes, I do."

Suddenly, there were sounds entering her ears. It was as if everyone there were speaking in tongues because she didn't understand a word. Her body felt warm, and a powerful energy refreshed her and made her feel calm. She was floating in space—tranquil, peaceful and rested. When the process ended, Stephens said,

"You may get up and leave now, your session's over. Come back any time, and if you want to join our group, let me know. There'll be a two-week initiation for that, but then you'll be a regular member.

Patrice quietly left the meeting, floating on air. She never felt pain, soreness, tightness or discomfort in her hip again.

Chapter 25   The Dream: December 31st, 1995 to January 1st, 1996

On New Year's Eve, 1995, Jack and Suzie went to a small party at Darwin's palatial waterfront home. Alicia had informed them she'd be willing to babysit all night long if necessary.

"Just have fun and don't worry about a thing," she'd told them as they walked out their front door.

"She's a wonderful babysitter, that's for sure," noted Jack.

"Yes, she sure is," replied his wife.

Ten other couples, friends of either Suzie or her father, were in attendance at the party. After light cocktails and a lovely, catered meal of baked ham slathered in Dijon mustard, hot scalloped potatoes and steamed garden peas, the hard drinks started to flow. A large Sony tape deck had been set up to play favorite songs, and a space had been cleared in the living room for dancing. Darwin was doing everything he could to ensure everyone was getting drunk and wild. At midnight, Jack stood under a stock of mistletoe and kissed his wife passionately, then whispered into her left ear,

"Let's go home early and make out."

"I'd love to," chirped in Suzie, by now slurring her words. She smelled of gin. "You've finally caught on—I'm a confirmed sex addict! Let's get out of here."

After a three-hour session of intense love-making, which came close to breaking their bed and did include three orgasms for Sue, both Jack and his lover fell into a deep sleep, she woke up with a start at 10 am.

"I've never been happier than I am right now--*in my whole life*," she said, watching Jack beginning to stir. "These last few years have been wonderful, and I'll love you forever."

"I can honestly say the same thing, darling," added Jack, "Even though I just had another weird dream."

"Tell me, what happened in that dream?"

He then propped himself up on two elbows and answered, speaking slowly and sweating slightly,

"I visited hell in the dream. It was very hot down there— fires were burning everywhere. And there were ugly demons lurking behind each and every flame. Some had huge mouths and fat pot bellies, some had rat faces with puff cheeks and four legs, and others were just ghoulish creatures-- white, pasty and exhausted, like half-asleep hungry ghosts. It was very, very hot. When I tried to walk out of there, I bumped into a jail cell with you inside. It was blocking my way out. You were naked, flames were burning all around, and you were screaming and begging me to free you. But I couldn't get near enough to help. I felt powerless, watching a fire burn your skin away inch by inch. You were screeching at the top of your lungs,

Jack, do something! HELP ME!"

At the end of the dream, you were just a rounded pile of burnt ashes."

"Jack, that wasn't a dream. It was a nightmare—forget it."

"Yeah, but how?"

"Make love to me again—*right now.*"

Two hours later, Sue rolled over in her nakedness and muttered,

"Wow, that was amazing. I'm sure going to hate leaving you in mid-January for over a week."

"Where are you going?"

"Dad's working on a big case in Terrace, and he needs me there from January 16—25. He's paying all my expenses and giving me a *big* bonus."

"Oh no--I'll go crazy without you for that long, and the kids will be distraught."

"I'm dreading it too, but the money will help us right now. And don't worry about anything; Alicia has already agreed to move in while I'm gone and do all the cooking, cleaning and babysitting."

"Alicia's great, honey, but she'll never be able to replace you."

As it turned out, Alicia's parents were a little concerned that she wanted to move into Jack's home in the absence of his wife, but she insisted.

"I trust Mr. Turner totally, and he trusts me, Mother," she told her agitated parent. "Besides, I feel like I'm part of their family now. The kids adore me."

"You're too young to be moving away from your own family, Ali," she taunted. "And a man without his wife can be tempted to do bad things."

"Mr. Turner would never do anything inappropriate, Mother—he's a devout Buddhist—and I'm twenty-two years old now—old enough to make my own decisions. Besides, there's no way he can work, look after two kids, write a novel and run a house by himself. Have some compassion, will you?"

"We'll see how it goes, Ali—but your father and I will be watching developments closely."

Alicia didn't know that her mother had been sexually abused when she was twenty. At the time, she was staying with her uncle in Barcelona, helping him build an addition to his seaside cabin. She was a strong, buxom girl and was good with her hands. Her Uncle Carlos was teaching her some basic carpentry skills, and she was learning them quickly. Her parents had sent her to help him for the whole month of August 1948. Carlos claimed to be a religious man and had become a Lay Reader at St. Michael's Sacred Heart Church. No one ever suspected he could act in depraved ways at times because he attended morning mass every morning of the week.

At first, Alicia brushed off her uncle's inappropriate advances and ignored them, but when he climbed into her bed on the second night of her stay and raped her repeatedly. The next day, she demanded that he let her go back home. It was the first time she'd ever had sex with a man.

"You can't leave now, Gabriella. Your mother and father have struck a deal with me that you stay until the addition is finished, and if you ever tell anyone what has happened between us, I'll ruin your reputation forever," he yelled at her after slapping her across the face, leaving a bright red mark.

In her innocence and naïveté, she stayed on, living in fear and guilt and tried to do her best to help the man, her uncle. For some strange reason, she felt obligated and submissive. For the entire month, he invaded her bed every night until she was resigned to the abuse. Her uncle was rough with her and unfeeling. It was all about *his* pleasure and nothing else, so as soon as he had his release, he rolled over and fell asleep, snoring loudly. His niece hid her bruises expertly and wore sunglasses for the entire month. Somehow, her uncle made her feel guilty, made her feel that she had done something wrong and that she'd lured him into the depraved acts. That was why she had always kept the sordid debacle to herself.

When she did finally get to go back home, she was pregnant and had great difficulty finding a doctor who'd give her an illegal abortion. It was a back-alley operation done with no antiseptics or clean instruments. Luckily, she survived the ordeal and was able to keep even *that* catastrophe secret. For the rest of her life, she told no one of her suffering, pain and the tormented days with Carlos Ferrer. Even when her sister Pera, a very devout Catholic, told her she'd been assaulted by Father Agnasio, she kept quiet about her own trauma.

"Gabby, Father Agnasio asked me to come to his office after choir today and did something very inappropriate," she whispered to her sister one day.

"What did he do?"

"He complimented me on my singing and told me to sit on his lap. Then, all of a sudden he started kissing me and stuck his tongue down my throat. He said it was all right because he loved me and, according to him, love is sacred."

"Did he rape you?"

"Oh my God, I'm only eighteen years old. How could he do that?"

"Never mind, but please never spend time with him alone again."

"But he's always asking me to do chores for him in the sacristy."

"What kind of chores?"

"Polish candlesticks and fold vestments, that kind of thing."

"Make excuses. The next thing he'll try is having sex with you."

"How do you know, Gabriella?"

"Trust me, I know men." That was as close to exposing her own assault as she ever came.

But that month changed the fabric of her whole life. She never enjoyed sex again and was forever nervous around men older than herself. For the rest of her days, she had periodic nightmares and anxiety attacks. Intercourse was inevitably followed by migraine headaches that lasted for hours. But the most dramatic effect it had on her was the questioning of her faith.

How could a man as pious as Carlos do that to me? She kept thinking. Subsequently, she began to question the men of the church. They were so powerful, so influential, and so full of authority. *Why do women have such an inferior role in the church?* She wondered.

Her mother noticed Gabriella stopped going to confession and stopped attending the mid-week mass.

"You're not confessing your sins anymore, Gabriella."

"Maybe I don't have any," she replied in a cheeky, rebellious voice.

When she grew up and became a mother herself, she was always over protective with Alicia. She wouldn't let her go to school dances or date any boys. Her curfew right up to the end of high school was strict—8:30 pm. Alicia was never allowed to wear make-up and always had to dress in plain clothes—pants or skirts down to her ankles and heavy sweaters that tended to hide her potentially seductive figure.

Luckily, she married a man who was kind, understanding and compassionate. He never criticized her phobias or pushed her into unwanted activities. Alicia noticed her mother's hang-ups but didn't protest the restrictions placed upon her. However, she was very different than her mother, being a very feminine creature with an open, trusting nature. She was also strongly attracted to handsome men. Men like Jack Turner.

Chapter 26 Nanquat Bay: January 16th , 1996 to March 15th , 1996

It was raining heavily on the sixteenth of January, but Suzie was making good headway in the Jeep along the highway from Stewart to Kitwanga, en route to her legal assignment in Terrace. She drove past three magnificent glaciers, two fast-flowing rivers and a seven-mile strand of majestic Douglas Firs with her windshield wipers slapping time against the heavy weather. It was a two hundred kilometer trip, and she was driving very fast, trying to make up time, like a race car driver a lap behind.

Nine miles out of Cranberry Junction, she rounded a hairpin turn just as Dave Sullivan was barreling along in the opposite direction in his semi-trailer with a full load of fresh logs chained to its deck. Sue took the turn wide and didn't have time to swerve completely out of Dave's path. His truck hit her passenger side hard enough to send the Jeep over a steep cliff, down the mountainside and into the deepest and coldest glacier in the area. Sue's vehicle hit the water upside down with a thud and sank six hundred meters to the ocean's bottom. Unfortunately, Sue was strapped inside, and her safety belt jammed. But even if she'd made it out the window, she'd never have made it to the surface. The Jeep was never recovered.

For the rest of his life, Jack remembered exactly where he was when staff sergeant Mike Simpson called him. He was sitting at his kitchen table with Rodney, drinking black coffee. They'd both just got home from church.

"Are you Jack Turner?" The officer asked.

"Yes."

"This is Miles Simpson of the RCMP, and I'm sorry to have to bring you bad news. Your wife has been lost in the Nanquat Bay Glacial waters. Her vehicle crashed, rolled off the highway and sank over six hundred meters into the sea with her trapped inside it."

Jack fell to the floor and moved into a fetal position, covering his head with outstretched hands.

"What's the matter, Dad?" cried Rod, but Jack couldn't respond. He lay on the floor crying tears of desperation for over two hours. Finally, he roused himself, grabbed a bottle of Johnny Walker and headed to the master bedroom. After polishing off what was left, he crawled under the covers and pulled the Persian eiderdown over his head. Just before darkness swamped the room, Darwin showed up.

"Jack, get out of bed—we're going to police headquarters *right now*."

When his son-in-law didn't move, he pulled the covers down and pushed Jack to the floor. His eyes were bloodshot, and his whole upper body was puffy and red, like an infected wound.

"Get up—we're meeting the Police Chief in ten minutes."

At the station, Jack sat with Darwin, the Chief of Police and Dave Sullivan.

"I'm so, so sorry," moaned Dave. "The road was narrow, and your wife was travelling fast. My semi hit her vehicle in a hairpin turn and careened down the mountain into

Nanquat Bay—eight hundred meters below the road. There was nothing I could do to save her; the Jeep sank immediately, and that Bay is deep, very deep."

"There'll be a thorough investigation, Mr. Turner, and a comprehensive accident report will be generated," stated the Chief. "At this point, we don't have any evidence to charge Mr. Sullivan, and he has co-operated with us fully—so now he's free to go."

Jack was given a month's leave from Le Duc to handle his family's affairs, which was helpful because he'd fallen into a deep depression.

The hardest thing Jack had to do was tell Lalita about the death of her mother. He took her for a long walk along the edge of the Portland Canal, shuffling slowly over the remnants of what used to be a series of sturdy wharves servicing a mining community of over 10,000 people at the turn of the twentieth century. Now they were just creaky, old pillars and platforms full of worm holes, like an abandoned medieval ship rotting in the sand at the bottom of the sea.

"Your mother's gone to a better place," he whispered after a long silence when all that could be heard was the soft lapping of sea water against the rotting support beams.

"Where's she gone, Father?"

"Into the next life--her Jeep crashed and sank to the bottom of the ocean while she was in it."

"Did she suffer?"

"Only for a brief moment—but let's sit on this bench and meditate on death and the *impermanence of life*."

An hour later, Jack told his daughter,

"Lalita, I'll always be here for you and never abandon you. We will work through this tragedy and have a wonderful life together. That's what your mother would want."

From then on, Jack redoubled his efforts to be an exemplary father to both the children in his care, but something inside of him had shifted. The grief was too much to bear, and he started to drink again. He never got drunk in front of Lalita or Rodney and mustered every bit of discipline he had to parent them. But late at night, when no one was looking, he drank whiskey or beer. It was the only way he could get to sleep. He stopped meditating, writing and exercising.

Susan's funeral was heart-wrenchingly sad. Darwin invited most of the people of Stewart to her graveside, and over sixty people showed up, although hundreds of others sent their condolences. The rite was held on a rainy, dark Saturday afternoon. Jack read several Buddhist sutras, and Darwin gave a heavy speech.

"My heart is broken," he stated, touched by emotion, "Susan was not only a wonderful daughter and the apple of my eye--she was my best employee. Her loss will leave a black hole in me and my company, a hole that'll never be filled. Please join me in a ten-minute silent tribute to her." When that ended, he invited all present to a solemn wake at his home. Refreshments were served, and all the guests had time to mingle and tell their favorite Suzie-stories. And there were hundreds. After most of the guests had left, Darwin addressed Jack in a serious tone of voice,

"This must be very hard on you too! As long as you stay single, I'll support your life in Stewart, and your name will remain on the title deed of Suzie's home. Let's help each other get through this. We can do it if we stick together."

"Thanks, Darwin, your support makes all the difference," spluttered Jack.

Just as he went to leave, Alicia brushed up beside him. Turning to look at him, with tears in her eyes, she said.

"Mr. Turner, I just want you to know that I'm happy to stay on as your nanny until I start college next September. And my salary of one thousand dollars and full room and board are totally adequate until then."

Jack didn't notice the love and adoration in Alicia's eyes, voice and manner. He was too busy grieving and looking after his children. But inside the nanny's heart lay a powerful desire to become the woman in her new home, as well as Suzie's replacement as Jack's lover. So she began developing new habits designed to make her man happy.

Jack went to bed every night at 9 pm so he could get up early to meditate in the Zen way. Alicia started a new routine—bringing him a cup of steaming hot chocolate just as he was going to bed.

"Thank you for bringing me this delicious drink every night, Alicia; I'm finding that he helps me get to sleep."

"Yes, I know you sometimes have trouble falling asleep, so I added a five mg tablet of melatonin to the drink," she whispered back to him one night.

"That's so thoughtful of you, and I appreciate it."

But there was something else Jack subconsciously liked about this new tradition. Alicia entered his room wearing a transparent silk nightgown, which revealed all the parts of a body any heterosexual man would enjoy seeing. Her body was fully exposed to Jack when she came by with the drink—and she had a magnificent twenty-three-year-old figure.

She also started to cook Jack's favorite meals. Each one included a lean gourmet meat dish such as fresh halibut sprayed with lemons, chicken breasts with spicy batter, or turkey sausages stewed in whole tomatoes. These delicacies were always served with Thai brown rice and a full salad made with every vegetable Jack loved—tomatoes, spinach, avocados, celery, peppers and cucumbers.

"You're a wonderful cook, Alicia. We all love your meals—thank you so much. But you don't have to work so hard to please us," he told her.

"I don't mind doing it at all, sir."

After every evening meal, Alicia did all the dishes, cleaned the kitchen counters and polished the floors until they shone. On top of that, she was constantly complimenting her boss. To her, he was handsome, athletic and smart, and she continually let him know how she felt in colorful but somewhat subtle detail. And all these new habits included her help raising Lalita and Rodney and teaching them both the Spanish and French languages as well as how to play the violin. She was also willing to babysit on a moment's notice. Jack's children loved her above everyone else, including Jack. Before long, Alicia had become an integral and extremely important member of the family.

"Do you love Alicia, Daddy?" asked Lalita one day.

"Let's just say I love all the things she does, my dear," replied Jack.

"Why does she always wear strong perfume when you're around?" she continued.

"I hadn't noticed," said Jack.

"Do you miss Mommy?"

"Yes, I most certainly do. She can never be replaced and her passing has left a black hole in my life. I lie awake every night wishing she were beside me. There's a huge piece of my heart that's gone missing, actually."

Even at a young age, Lalita was very intuitive. Her father's comments about Suzie were real, she knew that. But she could also feel the heated energy being generated between her father and her nanny.

Chapter 27   May 1st to June 1st, 1996

Jack went back to work on May 1, 1996 and struggled to resume his regular life. But it was difficult. He missed his wife's company, her support, her love, her passion for life, her love of sex and her adoration of Lalita and Rodney. He stopped meditating, exercising, writing and playing the guitar. In the end, it was a Friday night dream that broke the spell that was stifling his life and choking off his spirit, like a man's body slowly ebbing away when he's hanging at the end of a rope dangling from a tree while his neck's in the noose.

He dreamt he was sitting in the company of Siddhartha Gautama, listening intently to the *Enlightened One* who spoke slowly and directly to him, dressed in an orange robe, sitting motionless—calm, tranquil and poised.

"The drama of life is a mirage," said the Buddha, "All that exists is the awareness beneath all of that drama. Death is like a river whirlpool. When the circle of spinning water dissolves, the river remains unchanged and continues to flow. Once the whirlpool is gone, the river remains untouched.

Jack woke up with a start and saw Lalita in the corner of his room. She was sitting with her eyes closed in the full lotus position.

"What are you doing in my room, Lalita?"

She then slowly opened her eyes, smiled and said,

"I'm trying to retrieve your soul, Dad."

After breakfast, Jack sat down to write his master a letter.

Sandheim—

I apologize for not writing you for six weeks, but the shock of my wife's death has knocked me off my stride and sent me into a deep depression, which blocked any spiritual progress. I haven't wanted to meditate or exercise for many weeks.

But last night, I solved the koan:

Nothing real exists independently except infinite awareness, and even it has no objective existence--it's empty but transparently alive and functions as pure knowing. Everything's a modulation of that awareness, and death is actually an illusion.

Now, the fever has broken. I can start living again after this amazing realization.

Over the last few weeks, a few things have come up that are very disturbing. One is that I'm a sex addict and crave sexual gratification constantly. Another is that I'm a dormant alcoholic. That means I'm tempted to drink whiskey when any heavy upset occurs in my life. It's like any agitation triggers a demon within me that gets activated and starts to act in habitual, uncontrolled and self-destructive ways.

But I feel the urge to communicate with you now and start meditating again.

Jack.

That very morning he did one hundred push-ups and played some folk songs for his children after serving them a nutritious breakfast of scrambled eggs laced with green onions, rye toast slathered with white creamed honey and hot chocolate with whipped cream on top.

Later that afternoon, he received his teacher's reply:

Dear Jack—

*Thank you for rekindling our communication threads. Yes, you **have** cracked the shell of the koan! But don't stop meditating because there's much more reality to discover. I'm very sorry to hear about your wife. Her loss will take time to process and fully understand.*

Just as you say, addictions are like demons alive in you, triggered into action by your weaknesses. I had many addictions before becoming a Zen adept. The demons aren't independent evil entities. They're clusters of pain-energies or traumas from your past, trapped within you, that have never been healed. The secret to transforming inner pain bodies is to stop fighting them! You must become still, enter a meditative state and study them, just like you were examining butterflies or spiders. Notice when they arise, when they start to grip you, what triggers them and when they leave. If you can notice the inclinations of your demons and stay aware of everything they do, they can actually become powerful allies."

*Just get back to your daily meditations, and much more will be revealed to you. You **are** making progress despite your recent setbacks.*

Sandheim

After reading this note, Jack thought he could restart his life and make a difference in the lives of others, and that's what he wanted to do.

As spring came to Stewart, new energy and life emerged in the Turner household. As it turned out, Alicia was a masterful surrogate mother. She was teaching Rodney and Lalita the Spanish language, as well as how to play the violin. Rod had no aptitude for music, but Lalita did and was soon playing children's songs on her teacher's fiddle. Alicia told lovely stories, made up from nothing, about giants and fairies, leprechauns and wizards. Both Jack's children loved them, so she began to write and illustrate children's books and taught Lalita how to read them.

"Will you teach me how to speak Spanish, too?" Jack asked one day.

"Why yes, of course, Mr. Turner. Why don't we start speaking Spanish *only* every morning until noon in this home?"

"Yes, let's do that," responded her boss. "By the way, I love your cooking. You seem to understand all aspects of the *Mediterranean Diet*, which is delicious and full of essential nutrients."

"Thank you, sir," Alicia replied. "My cooking has its roots in the cuisine of Spain."

You've also become a stunningly beautiful woman, he thought. *I must make sure I never allow myself to fantasize about anything erotic with her.*

Rodney completed Grade 12 at the end of June and got a summer job at the only Tim Horton's in town."

"Now I'll be able to afford gas, Dad," he said one morning in early July. "Will you teach me how to drive?"

"As long as you keep up with your job and all your household errands, I'll do it, Rod. We'll start tomorrow."

Two weeks later, on his eighteenth birthday, Rodney was given a 1978 Chevy truck by his grandfather.

"It's yours once you get your license, Rod. But if you get even one speeding ticket, I'll repossess it," said his grandfather. "Also, I don't ever want to see your girlfriend in that vehicle. Is that understood?"

"Yes, Gramps, it is."

Rod had by this time formed an intensely close relationship with Sally Carson—too close for his grandfather's taste.

"Are they sleeping together, Jack," he asked his son-in-law one afternoon over a few beers.

"I haven't seen any direct evidence, but there's no doubt in my mind they're having sex."

"The next thing you know, we will have another baby in this family," said Darwin.

"That would be a disaster for sure, Darwin."

"They're too young for this kind of seriousness, in my opinion."

"I totally agree with you," replied Jack.

Two weeks later, on a cool night in mid-May, loud groaning sounds coming from Rodney's bedroom woke Jack up. With some hesitation and strong feelings of guilt, he tiptoed half-asleep to the edge of his son's door and peeked through a crack beside the upper hinge.

Sally was buck naked, her white back shaking while she sat on Rod, gyrating her rear end up and down upon his horizontal body.

Oh my god, he thought, *I've got to put an end to this before it's too late.*

The next morning, after a light breakfast of pancakes, blackberry syrup and orange juice, he spoke up clearly to the boy:

"Rod, I need to have a serious conversation with you after work today. Meet me in the parlor as soon as we finish our supper tonight."

"Yeah, sure, Dad. I will do," Rodney curtly replied.

When they finally met, it was late, and Jack was very tired.

"Rod, I don't want to hurt your feelings or tell you who to go out with—but you're too young to be having hard sex with a girl who won't be nineteen for another ten months."

"Dad, I'm sorry about last night, but it was all her idea. She's been pushing me toward this for a month."

"Do you have any idea about the kind of problems having a baby with her right now would cause?"

"I haven't really thought about that, Jack," answered Rod.

"Is she taking birth control pills?"

"I don't know, I didn't ask her."

"Rodney, you have to stop this right now. It's time to start playing the field a bit, son, and there are lots of fish out there in the sea."

"What does 'playing the field' mean?"

"It means dating lots of different girls."

"Okay, I get it. I'll commit to stopping the sex but not to breaking up with Sally. We get along really well. She's my best friend right now."

The next Saturday, Jack met Darwin at the King Eddy for a beer, as usual.

"Did you know that Rodney's having full-on sex with his girl friend?" Jack asked him.

"That's insane. Do you know this for sure, Jack?"

"I saw it with my own eyes."

"I'm pissed off, but it doesn't surprise me knowing Sally's background. You know her mother's a hooker, don't you?"

"Surely that can't be true," replied a stunned Jack, "I thought this town was too small to have *ladies of the night.*"

"Believe me, it's true. She also sells heroin and cocaine on the side. I know that because a friend of mine defended her on trafficking charges last year. Somehow, he got her off."

"How are we going to get Rod out of this relationship, Darwin?"

"I've got an idea, but let me think my plan through before we actually do anything."

"Rod, how would you like to go shopping for fishing gear tomorrow evening at Gary McLeod's General Hardware and Sundries," pleaded Darwin on the phone to his grandson the very next day.

"I'd love to go--which day and when?" screeched Rod in an agitated voice.

"Tomorrow," said his grandfather.

Darwin's plan, which he'd carefully described in detail to Jack, was to bribe his grandson with a brand new fiber-glass fishing boat with a motor—the one currently on sale at McLeod's. In exchange for that boat, Rodney would have to break up with Sally.

Chapter 28   Energy Blocks : July to November 1996

Over the summer, Jack noticed a change in the Wednesday evening meetings of the Healing Order of St Luke at the *Anglican Church*. More and more townsfolk were attending because the word was out: spiritual healing works.

Minster Stephens was putting more energy into the sessions, making them longer and more intense. Jack had told him on more than one occasion about the miraculous healings that had taken place in the Order's events in Richmond at *Infinite Healing*. Each meeting started with the priest and Jack playing gospel music on their guitars while all the participants sang along. Then, any person who wanted to be healed stepped into the middle of the circle of the assembled people, while each member placed their hands on the afflicted person's body. After requesting a healing, the patient was ready.

Spontaneous prayers followed with a direct call to God: asking Him to expel the demons that were causing the sicknesses or injuries. Jack's understanding of the nature of those demons was different from the Christians present but it didn't matter. What mattered was the movement of healing energy from the current context into the injured parties. During prayers he generated feelings of love for any pain-body inside himself or the patient. For Jack, demons weren't external beings—they were repressed inner energy balls or pain-bodies, lying internally dormant from past traumas. Nevertheless, the healings continued to be more powerful when Lalita was present.

In mid-July, Alicia was stung by a massive Asian wasp and her wound quickly became swollen, red and infected with puss.

"Would you like to come to our healing session tonight, Alicia—to heal that wound of yours?" asked Jack.

"Will it take the swelling away, Mr. Turner?"

"Yes, it will, if you believe in the process."

"Then I *will* attend, and I *will* believe," she replied.

When Alicia sat inside the circle that night, Jack placed his hand on her right shoulder and went into a deep meditation. He could feel her pulse through a light summer smock and smell the sweet sunscreen on her bare arms. At times during his contemplation, he couldn't help opening his eyes and staring at her—she was an extremely beautiful woman in the prime of her life. Right at the crescendo of Alicia's circle time, Jack was overcome by a desire to see her naked and make love to her.

"Demon of lust, I see you, and I'm not afraid of you. You've got some wonderful qualities and can stay right where you are. I want to know you and be your friend," chanted Jack to himself. At that moment, he saw the apparition: a demon inside himself with a pointed chin, huge leg and arm muscles and a penis that was twenty inches long and swung like a pendulum between its legs. Instead of fighting the demon, he wanted to be friendly, accepting and supportive and possibly then turn the being into an ally.

He then focused his total field of awareness onto this wayward character and poured feelings of love from his heart into the lusty ghost in his head. Slowly his errant desires receded into pure love for his nanny, and then he only wanted what was best for her. The demon had disappeared.

During the entire episode, Lalita stood on a chair behind Alicia with both hands on her head. When the nanny woke up the next morning, the swelling in her arm was completely gone, and there wasn't a mark on her body.

"I can't believe the infection's gone," she said to Jack. "You've made me a believer in the power of spirit."

"Then you'll most likely want to become a regular member of the Order of St. Luke—is that right?"

"Yes, it absolutely is!"

By this time, unbeknownst to anyone other than her father, Lalita had become a secret apprentice to the minister's wife, Julie Raven-Heart.

"Your daughter has natural healing powers--which are a gift from the Creator, Mr. Turner," Julie told Jack one evening after a session of the Order. "If you let her become my student, I can expand and develop that power."

"How will you do that?" Jack asked.

"I'll do it by teaching her the secrets of a shaman's way of healing. Will you allow that?"

"Julie—isn't she too young to do this kind of thing," asked Jack.

"Not at all," replied Julie. "As long as a person has innate healing ability, I can start to train them as soon as they can talk."

"Then I *will* allow her to train with you. But--please let me know if anything starts to go sideways."

"I absolutely will. Now, bring her to my home on Sunday mornings at 4 am, starting next week, and I'll take her on as a disciple."

From then on, Lalita went with the Indigenous priestess to a secret hideaway in the forest, early every Sunday morning. Ms. Raven-Heart started the training each week by lighting a huge bonfire in a forest clearing amongst some very tall, very majestic Douglas Firs.

"Sit and stare at the fire for thirty minutes," Lalita, she'd say, "And imagine it contains many powerful beings that can become your allies in healing. Those beings are just projections of your own inner voices, and it's important never to fight with them."

Inevitably, Lalita's body became hot, inside and out, and she learned to absorb the healing powers of fire. After that, she mastered ten different esoteric chants as she and Julie danced around the fire.

"Now lie down and let the power of the earth flow into your soul. Once that happens, you'll be able to see energy blocks and instruct them to leave an infected body."

Slowly, over a period of many months, Lalita learned how to heal *the shaman's way*. Once she was empowered by fire and earth, she could clearly see energy blocks in the people around her. Julie then taught her how to use specific chants to dispel them.

"Everyone has at least one energy block, Lalita," said Julie, "And once you master your own voices, you'll be able to use the right chant to free those in others."

"Yes, that's why human beings have so much trouble staying healthy and reaching their potential—they never speak with one voice."

In September, on the first day of Grade 2, Lalita was informed that she was being skipped into a Grade 3 class. She was also placed in the school band at the age of five when, normally the minimum age was eight. But, by this time, Jack's daughter could play several pieces of classical music and many well-known folk songs. She was also fluent in Spanish. Teachers told Jack she was an exceptional student—displaying the qualities of poise, quiet leadership and extraordinary powers of concentration. Jack, Alicia and Lalita played music together every evening after supper. Rodney had recently joined them, playing the set of expensive drums his grandfather had bought him.

For Thanksgiving, Alicia cooked a twenty-five-pound turkey with all the traditional trimmings, so Jack invited his father-in-law and Georgina over to help celebrate.

After dinner, while Alicia, Georgina and the children were cleaning up, Jack and Darwin retired to the parlor for a drink of Peruvian port.

"Georgina and I are getting married on Remembrance Day, Jack, and I'd like you to be my best man."

"Congratulations! Yes, I'd be honored to serve as your best man. Will it be a large wedding?" At that moment, Jack's smile was superficial because he had feelings of dread pushing at his heart. *This union will never work out,* he thought.

"We're sending out two hundred invitations and plan to rent the entire fourth floor of the King Edward Hotel for our reception. The actual ceremony will take place at the Anglican Church."

"I'm impressed, Darwin—this will be one of the major events in Stewart in 1996."

"Do you think Alicia would be a bridesmaid?" Georgina wants someone young and beautiful to be in the wedding party, and some of the guests speak Spanish as their first language."

"You'll have to ask her, but I'm sure she'll do it, my friend. She's extremely compliant and always willing to help our family."

"Would you ask her for me, Jack?"

"Sure I will--no problem."

When Jack asked her, she agreed instantly, which made him very happy. What he hadn't yet fully realised was that Alicia had fallen in love with him. Her dream continued to become his wife.

Just before Halloween, Jack was having a nap to get ready for an evening of fireworks and trick-or-treating. All of a sudden, he woke up, rolled over and looked toward his bedroom door, responding to a light knocking sound. Standing in the doorway was Alicia, completely naked, which made Jack gasp audibly. She was a physically perfect specimen, standing six feet tall with measurements of 38-22-34, flawless white skin and a dark but large pubic triangle. After staring at her for over a minute, he rolled over to face the wall.

"I must never touch that woman in lust, and I won't," he muttered to himself.

Alicia knew it was wrong, but she couldn't help pursuing Jack as a lover. She was intensely attracted to him and was experiencing sexual urges that were beyond her control. Often she lay in bed at night, visualising him making love to her for hours on end. Her usual routine was to massage her vagina softly while she whispered sweet nothings to an imaginary Jack. This caused her to have frequent orgasms and to experience peak experiences based on the workings of her imagination. She prayed for relief, but it just never came.

On November 2nd, the day after Rodney's nineteenth birthday celebration, Jack entered his home limping badly.

"What happened to your right leg, Mr. Turner—it's been bleeding," asked Ali.

"A flying piece of metal hit my knee at the mine and knocked me down. It was bleeding profusely then. Luckily, our first aid attendant was available, and he bandaged it up so I could get back to work."

"Oh no!" She responded. "Let me massage it for you. Just take your pants off and go lie on your bed. I'll be upstairs in a minute with some healing Spanish balm."

When she got to his room, he was surprised to see her in a low-cut dress. When she bent over to apply the ointment, her breasts were almost completely exposed.

"That feels great, Ali," moaned Jack as she gently massaged his knee. As her hands travelled onto his right thigh, he felt an electric current run right up to his ears, like a string of Christmas lights when they get turned on and light up.

He knew her massage was getting slightly inappropriate but just couldn't summon up the will to make her stop. When she was finished, Alicia applied a fresh band-aid on the wound over a paste that smelled like an Australian eucalyptus tree.

"There—that'll take your pain away—just give it time, sir."

Jack did give it time, but two days later, his leg still hurt, and he continued to limp.

"Lalita, can you do something with my knee?" He asked his daughter the following weekend.

"Yes, I think I can," she replied. "Come and sit in the rocking chair by the fireplace."

Lalita rolled up his right pant leg and slowly detached the dressing. Then she closed her eyes and went into profound meditation.

"There's an ugly creature pinching your knee, Father. Let me chant a special mantra to make him relax."

That chant was silent, occurring inside Lalita's consciousness, lasting for ten minutes.

"Ah, the pressure's finally gone, Ali. I feel so much better. Thank you!"

The next morning, when Jack woke up he was shocked. The wound on his right knee had disappeared, and he was completely pain-free.

Chapter 29 <u>Georgina: November 5th to November 8th, 1996</u>

On Saturday, November 5th, 1996, snow fell in Stewart and covered the whole town in a three-foot white blanket, like a silk eider-down over a king-sized bed. It was the deepest one-day pile of snow since January 1947.

"I'm going out to shovel the walkways," said Jack after a breakfast of fresh fruit salad, brown German rye toast and black coffee.

"Can I help?" returned Alicia.

"If you want to—once the kids are dressed and set to their chores."

It took them four hours to clear a three-foot path from the main road up the front steps and all the way round the house.

"We'll stop now and have some lunch before our backs give out," said Jack.

Later that day, he noticed his nanny was bending over.

"Your back is sore from shoveling isn't it?"

"Yes, it does hurt a bit—but only when I walk," she laughed.

After the kids go to bed, go to my bedroom, and I'll give you a massage," Jack stated, matter-of-factly. "It'll be pay back for when you worked on my knee."

"Okay, I'll do that."

"Just take your shirt off and lie face down on my bed. Leave your brassiere and pants on," he whispered to her.

After a light supper of fresh garden salad and steamed, organic rice, Jack went directly to his contemplation room and sat down on his homemade meditation bench, facing the wall in Zen style, softening his gaze and noticing each incoming and outgoing breath. During his contemplation, he visualized massaging Alicia's body, like a baker kneading high quality, pure-white dough.

"I'll treat her physique like the sacred body of a saint," he thought.

Then he conjured up the image of his sleeping lust demon.

"You're beautiful, Butch, you can watch me treat Alicia--but please don't touch her. You can stay still but if you make one move I'll stop working on her."

Then he sat silently working on his koan for two hours.

At 9 pm precisely, he entered his bedroom. Alicia was laying face down, completely naked and exposed. Her derriere was raised two inches into the air and her long, flawless legs extended over the full length of the bed. Her red-painted toe nails were completely hidden from Jack's view.

He moved slowly to her side then pulled the Persian quilt up to the edge of her back and applied warm olive oil to her shoulders. He slowly caressed her back, pushing his thumbs gently into her knotted spots as she quietly moaned with pleasure. When he reached her lower back he began to press harder, but with a great deal of sensitivity.

"That feels so good, sir—my back is full of pain. It feels like nails have been driven into me."

During the whole process, Jack prayed for a healing and poured love into his patient's body all the while being aware of a lurking Butch--but keeping him at bay through an acute awareness of the space of healing created by the purity of his intent.

"I'm a virgin, Mr. Turner and I'll *never* have sex with anyone I don't love."

"That's wonderful resolution to make, my dear."

"Thank you—and I now want you to know something—*I love you*."

After ninety minutes of working on her back with compassion and altruism, Jack stopped and asked her,

"Do you feel better now?"

"All the pain has disappeared. I can't believe how good I feel."

"I'm going to leave my room now. When I'm gone, you can roll out of bed and get dressed. It's gratifying to hear you're feeling so much better."

The next morning, Jack sent a short email to his teacher.

Sandheim—

Last night I gave my nanny an upper body massage to relieve her back pain. During the whole session I was aware of Butch, my dormant lust demon. He knew beforehand that I'd

*stop if he got involved so I could treat the girl with a pure heart. As you said, I was able to do this through the power of awareness. It allowed me to watch the demon continually, rendering him powerless. Work on my koan has revealed an essential truth: human suffering is neutralized by abiding in awareness, and **I am that awareness.***

Jack.

Just before bedtime, he spotted Sandheim's response and read it.

Jack—

*The koan **is** working for you. As I predicted, more breakthroughs are happening. Just remember not to make **abiding in awareness** a discipline, or a practice. Only an ego would do that. Just relax and fall back into your own nature, the original self—it's the easiest thing in the world to do. **Awareness knows itself by being itself.***

Sandheim

Just before sleep arrived, Jack's bedside phone rang.

"Jack, we need to meet tomorrow night to discuss final plans for the wedding. Can you be at my place by 7 pm?"

"Yes, for sure, Darwin," replied Jack just before he hung up the phone and fell into a deep sleep.

When he arrived at his father-in-law's home, Darwin was drinking Crown Royal and slurring his words, like an old record skipping parts of the song.

"I've been dating this woman for many years now, and it's time to fish or cut bait. I want the biggest wedding celebration in the history of Stewart, Jack. Can you make it happen?"

"Why, of course. How many guests do you want?"

"At least one hundred twenty-five at the reception--and I want tons of delicious food, an open and free bar and lots of dancing."

"There's only one place we can hold a party like that, Darwin."

"Where's that?"

"The arena."

"Then book it and place the food order with *Foodcare Caterers*. They'll give me a 20% discount. Now have a drink."

"By the way, are you leaving town on a honeymoon?"

"Yeah, we are. I want to go to Honolulu but Georgina insists on Mexico. Anyway, we'll be gone for three weeks over the Christmas Season."

Jack was taking notes as fast as Darwin spoke. Occasionally, he glanced around the living room and was surprised to see how messy it was. Books were strewn all over the floor, a coffee table lay on its side, and two curtains were torn and looked ragged. *Perhaps there'd been a physical fight in there*, he thought.

"Georgina—get Jack a cold beer," yelled Darwin at his fiancé, who stood in the adjacent kitchen washing dishes.

Soon after, she entered the room, dressed scantily in a see-through negligee carrying a round tray with an ice-cold Lucky and two empty beer steins on it.

"Which mug do you want, Jack, the gold one or the silver one?"

"Gold, please," muttered Jack as he extended his hand to take the tray.

Once Georgina left the scene, Darwin lay back in his Lazy-Boy chair and stared at Jack for a long time.

"Is there something going on between you and that girl who looks after my grandchildren?"

"Why do you ask?"

"Because Georgina walked by your house last week and saw you holding her hand in the open garage."

"There's nothing to worry about, Darwin," said Jack as he sat down on the red sofa next to his father-in-law while sipping a cold beer.

"Alicia seems to have a love interest in me, but I've discouraged it. After all, she's only half my age. My true love was your daughter, and that's the end of it."

"Jack, just to remind you, everything changes in our relationship if you get involved with another woman. I'd be very careful. That nanny of yours is incredibly attractive, and if she wants you she'll try hard to make it happen."

"You don't have to worry about that, my friend," murmured Jack rather unconvincingly.

As he left Darwin's home, he had the unmistakable feeling that there was something strange, inauthentic, perhaps even suspicious about Georgina. Her behavior was erratic and puzzling. She put up with her fiance's insults and orders and made a fuss of him—but there was no love in it. She was obviously interested in Darwin's wealth, his possessions and his status.

She's a gold-digger for sure, but why can't Darwin see it? He thought.

The next Saturday, he started off his conversation with his father-in-law with a direct question:

"Darwin, why does your woman insist on going to Mexico when she knows you have a condo in Honolulu? She also knows you love Hawaii and hate going to Mexico."

"Mexico is where all her family lives, and she misses them terribly—I can understand that."

"But remember what happened last time you went to Mexico—those parasites you picked up bothered you for two years."

"Yeah, but this time, I'm promising myself never to drink their water--so I'll be safe."

"Darwin, can I ask you a personal question?"

"Go for it," he replied.

Why are you so smitten with Georgina?"

"It's very simple, Jack—sex. She gives it to me whenever I need servicing, and nothing is off the table. You'll never know what it's like to live with a frigid wife for thirty years, my friend. I was starved for affection for a long, long time."

"I relate to your need for lots of kinky sex, but that's not enough to hold a marriage together. I think you should postpone the wedding for awhile. Then, let's watch how she reacts. She seems to be in such a hurry to get married--it just doesn't sit right with me."

"I've held her off for four years, but it's too late to cancel now—the invitations have already been printed and sent out, Jack."

"Let me ask you another question."

"Sure, go ahead."

"Have you noticed anything strange or unusual about her lately?"

After a lengthy pause, he answered,

"I thought it was strange that she owns a Remington 516 Supreme pistol. One day, I saw it sticking out of her purse, so when she wasn't looking, I pulled it out and noticed it was fully loaded."

"Darwin, that's not normal for a woman in these parts, especially one who's sixty years old!"

Chapter 30   A Suspicious Death: December 12th to December 15th , 1996

Jack continued to think it was very strange that Darwin and Georgina went to Puerto Vallarta for their Christmas honeymoon instead of Honolulu, and it continued to bother him and interrupt his sleep. Much later, he learned that Georgina had a brother living in Bucerias—a tiny fishing village two kilometers east of Puerto Vallarta, which you could access by walking two kilometers from the big city, along a narrow pathway through a snake-infested jungle. And there were other things creating stress in his life at that time.

Two weeks after he'd driven Darwin and his wife to the *Goose's* dock on the waterfront, his control of the lust demon was put to an ultimate test.

Jack was showering late one night, just before retiring, his head and face full of shampoo, when a soft, warm hand began caressing his back and shoulders. When he sprayed the soap away and slowly turned round, he could see Alicia—stark naked--standing in front of him through a hazy mist. She then moved right up to him, placed her trembling lips on his and inserted her tongue straight into his mouth. She then pressed up against him, her large, bare breasts rubbing up against his soaking wet chest. She stopped kissing him long enough to whisper into his left ear.

"I love you, Mr. Turner. Will you take me now?"

Jack couldn't resist his nanny's request this time, but he swore to himself that any *secrets of the flesh* he taught her would be done absolutely untainted by lust.

"I love you too, Alicia," he moaned.

The next morning, after a long night of physical perfection, Alicia rolled over and spoke softly but directly into Jack's left ear,

"I'm so happy about losing my virginity to you. I never dreamed a man could make love to a woman for that long. You gave me my first six orgasms, Mr. Turner. It was definitely worth waiting all these years for that. Please let me sleep in your bed every night now."

At that precise moment—6:32 am—the bedside phone rang, it's screen indicating the call was coming from a Gonzales Hotel in Mexico.

"Jack, please help me, what should I do?" screamed Georgina into the phone. "Darwin died during the night— and he's lying beside me right now--stiff as a board."

"Phone the police, George—right now! Then, make sure he gets to the nearest hospital. This is an emergency. I'll be there as soon as I can—probably tomorrow."

Jack arrived at the Puerto Vallarta International airport at 6:37 pm the next evening. After passing through the long lines of an inefficient customs process, he found Georgina waiting in the lobby, standing beside unending rows of condo sellers in their colorful cubicles, like colorful circus barkers at a thousand different games.

"Good to see you Jack," she said, "Let's go—I'll take you straight to the *Bucerias Village Hospital.*"

Speeding down the highway toward their destination brought back many memories for Jack. The towering cacti, dry desert sand, stale hot air and rows of tourist hotels created images in his head based on several of his past Mexican adventures. It was all so familiar.

The hospital was a small, whitewashed series of huts, built on white sand—all of which badly needed painting. Each building had a sloped roof and a rusty sign hanging outside its front door. Georgina's 1967 over-sized Cadillac stopped in front of the last one--the one that had a poster that read, "El Mortuoria."

Georgina spoke Spanish to the guard at the front door and immediately gained entrance to a long hall, at the end of which was a set of steep, narrow stairs. At the bottom of these stairs, Jack and Georgina met an orderly who took them directly into the morgue. Jack could hear Georgina's metallic heels clicking as she hurriedly clipped along the polished stone floor. The morgue itself was ice cold, like the massive walk-in vegetable fridges at Costco stores.

Darwin was pulled out of the east wall on a metal stretcher. His face was white under a silk sheet, and his legs were frozen stiff, like long, narrow icebergs.

"He looks ghastly," muttered Jack under his breath. "Can I see the <u>Death Report</u>?"

Georgina took the clipboard down from *Chute 14* and began quickly glancing through it.

"It's written in Spanish but just says that Darwin died of a massive stroke in the early morning hours of December 14th, 1996, 1990.

On the way back to Jack's hotel, Georgina asked,

"I'm staying with my brother right now but I can take you back to the airport when you have to leave. When are you flying back?"

"Tomorrow afternoon," replied Jack. "My plane leaves at 4:20 pm."

"I'm available to drive you then," she said, "Here's my brother's business card with my phone number on the back."

Jack's hotel was inside the *Marriott Puerto Vallarta* complex—an all-inclusive resort that he was only able to book for three days. Once inside, he went straight to his room to get a bathing suit and then went for a swim in an adult-only pool. After that, he had supper sitting on a stool in an all-night hamburger stand out on the beach. As he slowly sipped his lemonade and ate his chips he looked out over the crashing waves into the expansive Pacific, just as the blood-red sun was setting.

"There's something very peculiar about Darwin's death," he thought.

Early the next morning, before he had time to go down for breakfast, Jack received a call from a hospital specialist.

"Mr. Turner, I hope I didn't wake you up."

"No, I've been tossing and turning for hours."

"My name is Jose Castro, and I'm an internist at the hospital. I'm in the hotel lobby right now and would like to speak with you for a moment. It's important."

"C'mon up to my room right now, then, sir," replied Jack.

Once seated on the room's soft, turquoise sofa, Dr. Castro started the conversation.

"First—you must promise not to mention my name to anyone."

"I promise," replied Jack, as he saluted the specialist.

"I saw the original *Death Report* on your father-in-law. It mentioned a yellowish-brown stain on his chin and the cause of death as heart failure caused by arsenic poisoning."

"What happened to that report?"

"Darwin's wife got it and gave it to her brother. Two hours later, the stains were gone, and the current report showed up in the morgue."

"Dr. Castro, can I ask you something?"

"Yes."

"Is Georgina's brother involved in the Mexican drug trade?"

"Mr. Turner, his name is Miguel Galle, and it's well known that he's a member of the Tijuana Cartel. I must leave now. Remember to keep this conversation secret at all costs. My advice to you is to leave Mexico as soon as possible and **do not** investigate Darwin's death in any way—now or in the future."

Having said that, the doctor walked briskly to the room's door and disappeared into the hall, like a silhouette vanishing into the night sky.

After a complimentary breakfast of fruit salad, pork sausages, toast, two helpings of scrambled eggs and a cup of black coffee, Jack decided to sit in the hot sun beside a quiet swimming pool under the shade of a majestic palm tree.

"I have to make some decisions, now," he thought.

Before long he fell asleep and dreamt that he was being chased by a rabid pit bull. In the dream, no matter how fast he ran, the frothing dog was gaining on him, its teeth gnashing and throat growling. When a waiter asked the curvaceous Mexican woman sunbathing next to him if she wanted another drink, Jack woke up with a start. He quickly noticed that she had a very skimpy bathing suit on.

"Yes, I'll have another drink, amigo," she said, "And bring one for my friend lying beside me too."

"Thanks for ordering me a drink," noted Jack, "But I'm not consuming alcohol right now."

"Ah, don't worry, Amigo - there's only one ounce of rum in it. It'll help you relax and enjoy yourself. You seem overly tense right now."

And when the liquid refreshment came, Jack *did* enjoy it.

"That margarita was good, ma'am, but it felt like a double. Was it?"

"No, Amigo, actually it was a weak drink. Are you an American?"

"No—I'm from Canada—what about you?"

"I live in Puerto Vallarta with my husband, two daughters and five dogs. Our beautiful home is right on the waterfront. You'll have to visit me sometime," she added, smiling seductively.

"What's your name?" asked Jack.

"Teresa-Marie, and you?" she inquired, sticking out her golden brown right hand.

Jack took her hand and shook it before saying,

"Just call me Jack. By the way, do you know anything about the Tijuana Cartel?"

"Mama Maria!" She blurted out. "They're terrible men. Right now, they've pretty well taken over the south end of town. This past week alone, there've been three murders in broad daylight and a kidnapping. They must be desperate for money right now."

"Why would they be desperate for money right now?"

"There's a rumor out there that they're trying to buy the *Sands Hotel and Casino* and expand their drug empire into gambling and prostitution."

"That's very scary," said Jack.

"Yes, it is Amigo. My advice to you is **get out of here as soon as possible**."

"Well, that's good to know," stated Jack, "Luckily, I'm leaving Mexico tomorrow morning."

At that point, Jack got up and went back to his room to get ready to leave. Then he phoned Georgina.

"I'll be on my way to the airport on the hotel bus in ten minutes, Georgina—so there's no need for you to drive me. I'll see you back in Stewart."

Chapter 31   Eviction: December, 1996 to January 31st, 1997

When Jack's seaplane landed in the harbor at Stewart, Alicia and Lalita were there to greet him with open, loving arms.

While away in Mexico, Jack's perspective had shifted significantly. He now entertained thoughts that Stewart was not where he wanted to live and his new relationship with the nanny, although it had been full of ecstasy, might now actually be inappropriate. She was seventeen years his junior, but, under the circumstances, it was going to very difficult for him to extricate himself from the illicit affair he was having. For one thing, Lalita absolutely adored her 'step-mother' and was learning a great deal from her. And Alicia was now living as his full-blown wife. She saw herself as the woman of the house--sleeping with her man, cooking his meals and looking after his children. Jack knew that his destiny did *not* include mining or living in a dusty, dirty hick town; a place that looked like something you might see in a B-grade Western. He needed to reconnect to his spiritual quest and get grounded again in his creative activities.

"I think Darwin was murdered in Puerto Vallarta," he said to Alicia as they drove home along the waterfront.

"What?—How could that possibly be?" replied Ali in a shocked voice.

"Georgina's brother's a member of the outlawed Tijuana drug cartel and I'm convinced she had him kill her husband.

Now that she's officially his wife, Darwin's entire estate will be hers. That's not good news for me."

Jack's premonition proved to be entirely correct. Soon after Georgina arrived back in town, he received an official letter from her law firm.

James Melville
Senior Partner
Maddux & Company, LLD
Terrace, BC

Dear Mr. Turner—

We regret to inform you that your current residence is not legally owned by you at this point. In fact, the title deed for 2185 Sundown Place contains a clause stating,

"...should Susan Fitzgerald ever leave this home and the relationship she now enjoys with Jack Turner on a permanent basis—for any reason—its ownership will effectively revert back to the estate of her father, Darwin Fitzgerald."

We now take recourse to legally evict you from this property, effective January 31st, 1997.

Please address any questions or concerns directly to our firm, by mail, before February 14th, 1997.

JR Melville
Maddux Law

"This gives us exactly six weeks to find a new home, Alicia."

"If we start preparing right away, a move should be no problem, Jack."

"I'm going to move to Richmond and get back into writing for a living, my dear. In that city, I'll be close to my spiritual mentor and many of my best friends. The welding lifestyle in a mine is not really my destiny."

"I'd love the chance to live in a big Canadian city," added Alicia.

"Will that pose problems with your extended family?"

"I can go wherever I want now because I'm an adult. I no longer need my parent's permission to marry. I no longer require their permission to do anything."

"That's good to know, but first, many things will have to be worked out if you're going to join me in Vancouver."

"Now that I'm pregnant, those things should be easy to resolve."

"You're pregnant! How can that possibly be?"

"I've missed my period twice now and got a positive reading on a pregnancy test. Dr. Simpson says our baby's due in mid-June."

"I'm shocked, but happy, Alicia. You'll be a wonderful mother."

"Darling, there's something you need to know about my family," said Ali.

"What's that, my dear?"

My mother and father are not happy with me living here now that your wife is gone. They think you're going to try to sexually assault me."

"Oh no--what have they said?" groaned Jack.

"If I don't move out of your home, they'll disown me. Even the priest at our church has spoken to me about this. If they find out I'm pregnant, I'll be cut out of my family and excommunicated from the church. But I don't care. You, Rodney and Lalita are my life now."

"Are you absolutely positive you want to marry a man almost twenty years older than you?"

"Yes, of course, I'm positive. I beg you not to abandon me. You can't dump me now—I'm carrying your baby."

"I'm not interested in abandoning you, Ali. But if you did decide to stay here, I'd pay for an abortion."

"How can you even say those words? I'd rather die than break-up with you."

"Alright then," countered Jack, "Let me try to make all the arrangements. Please be patient, though—this will take time."

Following up on a connection he had with the *Richmond Gazette*, Jack was able to secure a six-month contract with the *City of Richmond* to report on and write about all the activities of the *Municipal Council*. He also started working to complete his novel, which was about ninety percent finished.

When Rodney found out about the move, he refused to leave Stewart.

"I'm moving in with my girlfriend, Jack. Her mother and I get along really well."

"Doesn't it bother you that her mother, Dolly Pulford, is a heroin addict and a prostitute?"

"That's in her past. She's been clean now for over two months. Besides, Sally doesn't do drugs. She wants to go to college."

"Rod," interjected Jack, "You're only nineteen years old. You're too young to live with a woman."

"Well, if you won't give me your blessings, I'm sure Alicia's parents will be happy to know she's pregnant with your child."

"How did you know that young man?"

"I listen closely to your conversations with her," replied Rod in a cheeky manner.

At this point, Rodney know that Alicia's mother would do anything she could to stop her daughter marrying a man who was seventeen years her senior and a pregnancy would drive her to distraction.

But before Jack left Stewart he met with all of his daughter's teachers.

"Lalita is a very special child, Mr. Turner," said Mrs. E. Gordon, her Grade 3 teacher. "She's the youngest student in my class, a three-four split, yet she's virtually the top academic performer. And she's now almost fluent in French."

"She also speaks Spanish and plays the violin," replied her father.

"I recommend she be placed in a class for gifted students when she gets to Richmond," said the teacher.

Lalita's music instructor told him,

"Your daughter's an advanced violinist for her age—and she can sing too—with a perfect and natural pitch! You're a very lucky father."

"Thank you, Miss. Harper," he answered. "Lalita and I play music and sing together every day."

But Lalita's most accomplished talent was her ability to facilitate spiritual healing. Reverend Stephens held a full-day session of healing, in the context of an *Order of St. Luke* agenda, on Saturday, January 15th, 1997. Thirty-five people attended, two of whom were very sick.

James Lerner was a ten-year-old boy with pneumonia and Leanne Gardner was a young waitress in town who'd come down with German measles. Both patients were prayed over several times during the healing process on that Saturday and, as well, experienced the laying-on-of hands three times. When she put her hands on them, Lalita said she could see energy blocks in both cases, like big bricks damming up the flow of a stream. In her silent prayers she directed intense love and acceptance at those blocks, chanting her favorite mystical songs under her breath. It came as no surprise that both James and Leanne were completely healthy when they woke up the next day.

"I hope you'll be able to continue your healing work in Richmond, Lalita," said Reverend Stephens.

"My dad says he knows of a strong healing order in the city, so I expect so," she replied.

With only two suitcases, Jack boarded Air Canada flight 2719 from Terrace on the last day of January and the day of his eviction from Darwin Fitzgerald's home.

"As soon as I get settled in Richmond, I'll call for you, Alicia. For now, you'll have to move back in with your mom and dad. But don't worry, we'll be together again before Easter," Jack told her.

"Where will we be staying in Richmond, Dad?" asked Lalita.

"At my old haunt, the *Savoy Hotel*. I've booked us in for a month."

"Is it a nice hotel?"

"Let's just say it'll do for now. It's an establishment specializing in longer-term stays for people in transition."

"Make sure you write me every week, Rod," said Jack, just before he waved good-bye to the misguided boy. "And for God's sake—stay out of trouble."

"I will for sure," he yelled back.

Alicia stood at the airport gateway when her two favorite people in the world departed. She was crying unreservedly, a steady stream of tears running down her flushed cheeks. Before Jack took leave of her, he hugged his lover tightly and said,

"Be patient, honey; you'll be out of here in a few weeks. But please don't tell anyone in your family about the baby."

"I won't--but I'm already starting to show a bit, so I'll have to wear baggy clothing, Jack."

"Hang in there for a month and I should be able to send for you—but first, I have to get re-established in Richmond."

"How do you mean re-established, Jack?"

"I mean finding a place to live, buying a car, starting my new work and getting Lalita set up in school and the Richmond branch of the *Order of St. Luke.*"

After kissing her deeply, Jack moved away jerkily and rushed down the hallway to Gate 35-- B, holding Lalita's hand tightly all the way.

He was going to miss Alicia and all that she'd become in his life: a companion, a lover, a cook, a parent and a house-cleaner. But somehow, he had a strange premonition that he'd never see her again.

Chapter 32   The Governor's Suite: February 1st to February 7th, 1997

Some of the staff at the *Savoy* remembered Jack, and not much had changed with the hotel, inside or out.

"We've booked you into the *Governor's Suite* at a discounted rate, as per your request," stated the desk clerk when they arrived.

"Thank-you, that'll be great."

The *Governor's Suite* had two bedrooms, a small kitchenette and a view of the Fraser River out of two large double-pained windows, through a grove of massive weeping willow trees.

"You'll have your own bedroom, Lalita," said Jack, "So you *will* get some privacy after all."

"I'm certainly grateful for that," she replied."

Once settled into the hotel, Jack knew exactly who he had to contact. The first person on his list was Cara, so he lost no time phoning her.

"Hi Cara--its Jack Turner. I'm back in town for good now and really have to talk to you. Can we meet for coffee?"

"Well, hello, Jack—welcome home—we've really missed you at the *Center*. Why don't we make it a lunch date? Can you come to the Infinite Healing Juice Bar tomorrow at noon?"

"I'll see you then and there, Cara. We've got a lot of catching up to do."

Cara was waiting for him when Jack got to the busy shop. There were more tables in it than Jack had remembered, and all the walls were covered with exquisite art work, most of it of a spiritual nature. But a large print of Van Gogh's *Sunflowers* and Leonardo's *Mona Lisa* were hanging just inside the front door.

"Cara, this place looks so alive and yet sacred. It's also busier than I remember it. And you look vibrant and happy. How've you been?"

"I'm doing really well Jack and so is *Infinite Healing.* We've expanded our meditation programs and added another therapist with a new modality."

"What kind of modality?"

"Chiropractic—under the leadership of Harold Pascal who's a local expert."

How's the healing work going?" asked Jack.

"Let's just say we still miss Sarah but there *are* lots of miracles taking place. She taught me well."

"What about the *Healing Order of St. Luke*—is that Group still happening?"

"Unfortunately, the minister was posted to *Washington State,* so we had to discontinue his meetings."

"Cara, my daughter and I have been working with Reverend Stephens and his wife, Julie Raven-Feather. He's an Anglican minister, and she's an indigenous Shaman, and they're both doing amazing healing work. And you'll have to meet my girl Lalita—she's a magical healer at the tender age of six!"

"Would you two consider starting up the group again, Jack? We still have the space available."

"We absolutely would. When do you want it to get going again?"

"How about next week?"

"Consider it done, my friend."

"How's your personal life been going, Jack?"

"We've had some real challenges over the last five years. Suzie, my second wife, died in a horrific car accident, and her father was murdered in Mexico. Those events had a terrible effect on all of us. We're just coming out of the grief and turmoil now—two years later."

"Are you single now, then?" Cara asked.

"I'm not married at the moment, but my nanny has become the new *mother* in our home. She wants us to get married, but there may be problems with her parents and extended family. They still think she's still just my nanny and have absolutely no idea she's pregnant with my baby."

"Oh my God, Jack, you've been through shockingly difficult times. But congratulations on the new child."

"Yes, the times have been challenging—but what about you?"

"I married my best girlfriend two years ago and we're incredibly happy. She's not involved with any *Infinite Healing* programs, but is definitely my soul mate."

"What do you two do together?"

"We're both marathon runners and love romance novels. So we run and read together!" said Cara laughingly.

"She's also a gourmet cook and financial analyst for *Edward James*, so our finances are in tip-top shape. She keeps all the books for the *Center*. Last year our profits doubled from the previous year."

"That's very encouraging, Cara—Sarah would be delighted."

"Yes, she would. And there's something else that's really changed my life, Jack."

"What is that?"

"My father, who was 91 years old, died of lung cancer six months ago. He'd been ill for three years, so in some ways, his death was a blessing."

"I'm terribly sorry to hear that."

"Don't worry about it. He lived a very full, productive and happy life and he was suffering a great deal at the end."

"I understand," responded Jack, "The truth of the matter is—everyone's going to die, sooner or later."

"Yes, that's true. My father was a successful oil executive and ended up quite a wealthy man, and I was his only child.

I inherited his ten-acre family estate in the British Estates and a small fortune in oil stocks."

"It couldn't have happened to a better person, Cara."

"Thank you, but its only money which, as you know, does *not* affect the quality of one's life. By the way, where are you staying right now?"

"Lalita and I are at the *Savoy*, as per usual. Alicia, my nanny, will join us in a few weeks."

"Jack, my new home has lots of space on the two top floors along with two self-contained suites in the basement. One of them is empty right now and you're welcome to stay there until you get completely re-established. I won't need any rent money, so you and your family can stay there for free."

"That's incredibly generous of you. How big is the available suite?"

"It's got twelve hundred fifty square feet of space—three bedrooms, a large kitchen and a granite fireplace in the living room."

"Consider it taken, my dear. When can we move in?"

"Any time you want Jack."

After a long conversation and a lunch of shared cheeses on a silver tray along with mounds of juicy seedless Mexican green grapes and several cups of delicious hot Starbucks coffee, Jack left to go back to the *Savoy*, feeling very satisfied about his relationship with Cara. The connection between them remained strong, and he was extremely happy about being back home and getting involved with *Infinite Healing* again.

The very next day, he began searching for Jennifer. It took him six hours to track her down through a mutual friend.

It turned out she was living in a trailer park in Surrey, which was entirely surrounded by the *Willis Auto Wrecking Company*. This meant derelict automobiles and scattered car parts lay all over the properties adjacent to Jen's abode, creating a slum-like environment. He caught up to her after banging hard on the unhinged door of Trailer # 51. He could hear someone walking around inside but no one was opening the door.

"Are you in there, Jen?" asked Jack before hearing a feeble voice and some shuffling feet.

"Yeah, I'm coming, just be patient, for Christ's sake."

Jack was shocked when she slowly opened the door. Jennifer looked much older and unkempt. Her luscious black hair was full of gray streaks, and her face was puffy and red. The kimono she wore was dirty, and her slippers had holes in them. Her figure was gone, and only a baggy nightgown hid her sagging, obese body.

"Can I come in, Jen? It's me, Jack."

"Yeah, sure, but please excuse the mess," she muttered before turning around and limping over to what was once a cream-colored sofa. Have a seat, Jack," she said, lighting a cigarette.

"How have you been doing, Jen?"

"Not well, I've got COPD and have a sprained ankle. That's why I'm using this cane."

"What caused the lung problems?"

"Ten years of smoking two packs a day—but I've really reduced my intake now—had to."

"How about the ankle?"

"I turned it two weeks ago, walking down my front steps."

No doubt drunk as a skunk, thought Jack.

"Are you married, Jen?"

"I was until six months ago. My ex-husband's in the Navy. After his last deployment, he wrote me a 'Dear John' letter. Turns out he's living with another woman who's also in the Navy. They're residing in Halifax now, and she's pregnant. But the good news is he gave me this trailer. He signed it right over to me when I asked him for it, no questions asked."

"Are you working?"

"No, I'm on a disability pension and go to the *Open Door* once a week for groceries."

"Jen, Lalita and I are going to be running the *Order of St. Luke Meetings* at *Infinite Healing*, starting next week. Why don't you come along and participate in them?"

"Because I've got no way of getting to Richmond," she answered morosely.

"How about if I pick you up?"

"Then I might consider it."

Jack couldn't forget the promise he'd made to Sue about keeping an eye out for Jennifer. She'd be shocked to see her daughter's condition now. For some reason, this woman descended into dysfunctional living unless she was surrounded by caring, capable people who were willing to support her emotionally and financially. Left to her own devices, she inevitably became self-destructive. It was just a matter of time before she surrounded herself with gamblers, drug addicts, alcoholics or homeless beggars.

"It'd be really good if you'd come back to participating in the work of the Healing Center, Jen," Jack told her, "You were always healthy when you hung out there." Your current lifestyle doesn't seem to be working for you."

"I've just had a string of bad breaks since you left town, Jack. But I'll get through it—somehow," muttered Jen through a veil of tears that were sliding down her rosy, swollen cheeks.

When Jack checked back into the Savoy, he told Lita,

"I've got one more person I've got to see right away."

"Who would that be? She asked.

"Carl Tara Sandheim," replied Jack.

"Is he your Buddhist teacher, dad?"

"Yes, he is."

Chapter 33   The Priesthood: January 10th to January 17th, 1997

Once Jack was back in his master's office, he felt relaxed and centered within his own being. Sandheim had that kind of effect on all of his students.

"Thank you for responding to all my emails when I was away, sir. Your advice and counsel was always perfect for me."

"Think nothing of it, Jack. Now let's talk about your spiritual progress. What are your current observations?"

"There's such a stark contrast between life in the world and in the monastery."

"Precisely, but what do you specifically refer to?"

"There's no peace, tranquility or order at the heart of worldly living today. No--at the center of current social living lies *chaos*. Everyone seems to be so self-absorbed and self-directed that continual conflicts and accidents keep happening. Just watch the news on TV every night. It's the story of one disaster after another. I fear for the state of the world."

"Yes, I understand your insight. It's true. But don't romanticize about monastic living. We have to confront conflicts and human power struggles every day."

"But at least monks are aware of what's happening in a conscious   way   and   work   hard   to   confront   these dysfunctional human traits. And their whole life is bounded by discipline, work, contemplation and service to humanity."

"That's true, Jack. The secret to conscious living is to focus all of one's attention on the tasks at hand—those that are occurring in the present moment—and then, when not occupied with daily problems, *abide in awareness.* That's to say, when the practicalities of life are taken care of, it's time to relax and fall back into the reality of our own being. That reality is pure awareness itself—an objectless field of complete transparency. At first, doing this may feel uncomfortable due to all the stresses and traumas of daily living. But if you're patient, and don't allow yourself to get distracted, a kingdom of peace, joy and compassion will become your experience. Deep inside is where true happiness lies."

"Let me write that down so I'll never forget it," Jack stated in awe.

"You won't forget it, and remembering this is ultimately not that important. The key is to **do it**, not think about it."

"Thank you, master."

"On another topic, Jack—we're starting up a *Phase Two Program* for serious students who want to become Zen priests but are unable to live in the *Monastery* for prolonged periods. I think it would be an ideal plan of study for you. Let's not forget you've already completed *Phase One.*"

"How would it work?" asked Jack.

"You'd be required to attend a *Study and Meditation Session* one evening a week, work and meditate in the *Monastery* all day Saturday, as well as do some written exercises each and every week."

"How long does the training last?"

"Just six months, Jack."

"Sandheim, you know I want to become a Zen priest, so this idea is very attractive to me. But I'll have to meditate on it because it'll affect every member of my family."

"Take your time Jack. This is a program that has a continuous intake. You can start any month you want."

Jack knew in his heart that he wanted to enroll in *Phase 2* of the *Zen Training Program,* and he also knew it couldn't happen if he married Alicia.

Later that week, he received an email from his lover that expressed no small amount of distress.

Dearest Jack—

I miss you so much and can't stand sleeping alone. I crave the touch of your naked skin. The pregnancy is coming along nicely, and I'm feeling great. But I do have to tell you there are problems here. My mother's now aware that I'm having a baby, and she knows you're the father. She's adamant that I stay in Stewart and break up with you, and she's got my dad on her side. They say if I marry you, they'll disown me, take me out of their will and ask our priest to excommunicate me.

*They've even gone so far as to find me a boyfriend with a Spanish background. He's an apprentice heavy-duty mechanic at Le Duc and keeps asking me out. Please send me some money so I can fly to Richmond and be with you **immediately**. I'm desperate, so please do something.*

All my love,

Ali.

Jack let this note sit on his computer for two days before responding.

Dear Ali—

Thanks for your recent email. I'm glad your pregnancy is proceeding well, but the actions of your parents are very stressful for both of us. I want you with me in the worst way, but you must get everything right with your parents first.

Let's take time to think this over carefully—we don't want to make any impulsive decisions. I've decided to enroll in a part-time Zen Priesthood Training Program next month so a few weeks of celibacy will help prepare me. Don't worry--we'll still have lots of time to be together.

If you want to go out with that heavy duty mechanic, it's okay with me. There's no way he's going to change the way we feel about each other.

I've found a wonderful suite in the estate of one of my old friends. You're going to love it.

Jack

Deep down, he knew their relationship was in trouble. Lalita, on the other hand, was flourishing. She started attending Grade 4 in a French Immersion Elementary School and was moved into the 1st violin section in her new school's band after only two weeks in attendance. One of her school friends could speak Spanish so she continued to learn how to become fluent in that language by talking to her constantly and visiting her family.

As they settled into their new life, Jack and Lalita became immersed in the Infinite Healing Center and especially the Order of St. Luke. Jennifer Black was by then a regular attendee and began to experience some healing transformations. She started to take better care of herself, lost some weight, applied effective make-up and slowly began to look like an attractive woman again.

Alicia's response to Jack's latest email was immediate.

Dear Jack—

I can't believe you're encouraging me to go out with Paul, the heavy-duty mechanic. Aren't you even a bit jealous? He's young and strong and good-looking. There, how does that make you feel? He's pressuring me constantly to date him.

Signing on to be a priest doesn't sound like the life a married man would undertake. Jack, I want you to be committed to our family above all else. How's that going to work if you become a priest?

If you don't wire me money, I can't get down to see you. Please, Jack, I'm desperate. Help!

Love and kisses, Ali

Jack didn't reply for a week. During that week he was overcome with the idea that a marriage to Alicia just could not work. *She belongs with her family and her heavy-duty mechanic, and I'm much more committed to the spiritual life than I am to her. The only question remaining is--how do I tell her?*

Two days later, he phoned Cara and asked her to have coffee with him at the *Healing Center's Juice Bar.*

"I really feel the need to talk something over with you, Cara," he said, "Can we meet tomorrow at the *Juice Bar?*"

"Why, yes of course, Jack—what's on your mind?"

"It's all about Ali, my fiancé. The situation has gotten out of hand."

"Can you be there at 1 pm? She inquired.

"Yes," was Jack's immediate reply.

I can trust this woman's wisdom, thought Jack. *She's really advanced spiritually in the last two years.*

When Cara arrived and sat down at his table, Jack couldn't help but notice how beautiful she was—and it wasn't just her physical appearance. She had a clear, unblemished face with huge blue eyes that made direct contact with the pupils of anyone she was speaking to. And when she conversed with someone, she was totally present. She was the best listener he'd ever met.

"Alicia's gorgeous and serves my every need. She's also pregnant with my second child. I love being with her because she's so alive, trusting, loving and compassionate."

"What's the problem then, Jack?"

"She's almost twenty years younger than me and deserves to be with someone in her own generation and culture. When she retires at sixty-five, I'll either be dead or in a rest home. That's not fair to her. Besides, what I really want to do is become a Zen priest. The Buddhist way of life is not conducive to being married to a pregnant twenty-three-year-old."

"What do you refer to regarding her different culture?"

"She lives in a very traditional Spanish extended family. The entire clan is a group of devoted Roman Catholics. She says the church isn't important to her now—but it will be, someday--I just know it. I'm not a Christian, Cara. How's that going to affect the raising of our child and all the religious events her family will be attending?"

"Oh, I see. Yes that **is** problematic."

"Can you give me any advice?" asked Jack.

"I don't give advice, especially in critically important matters like this. But I'll answer by telling you a story. Once upon a time, there was a very handsome swan who was so lonely he started spending time with a wayward group of turkeys. One of the young turkeys—actually the most beautiful--fell in love with him and begged him to live with her group permanently. Under pressure, he bent to her desires. Two years later, he'd forgotten how to swim and fly. All he did all day was eat corn husks and waddle around in circles. By that time, the young turkey had found another lover and disappeared."

"Thanks for that story Cara. I've just made a very important and irrevocable decision: I cannot marry Alicia."

Chapter 34   Changes: Easter 1997 to Summer 1997

By the time Easter 1997 came around, many changes had happened in Jack's life. The *Order of St. Luke Group* had grown quickly and now had up to sixty participants on a busy night. Lalita was playing a leading role in the meetings by her healing presence. Her training now included *Christian* healing modalities, *First Nation's* shamanism and *Buddhist* mindfulness techniques. Her father had taught her how to do Zen meditations and engaged in this practice with her every day.

"I think you're ready for your first koan, darling" he told her one cool April morning."

"What's a koan, father?"

"It's a puzzle that can't be solved by normal thinking. You have to live in the question it poses and let that enquiry penetrate your being. Then it will begin to generate wise insights."

"What is my first *koan, then?"*

"How can I be happy all the time?"

"That's it?"

"Yes, just stay with that one question, and your life will start to become magical, as if a fairy godmother was guiding you."

"Thanks, Dad—I'll work with it and let you know what happens."

Jared Peterson was a Grade 4 student in Lalita's class at school. After attending an *Order Healing Session,* as Lita's guest, his chronic tooth ache stopped hurting.

"How did you stop the pain, Lalita? He asked her.

"When I meditated on your teeth while you were in the middle of the healing circle, I saw a mean, black goblin hiding inside your mouth. He was pinching your back right molar with a pair of rusty pliers—a look of glee on his contorted, ugly face."

"How did you get rid of that goblin?"

"That's easy. It was nothing, really, and I didn't actually need to do anything dramatic or violent. I just kept my eyes on him and stared him down. Then I poured love from my heart into his body and he began to relax and let go of your tooth. All of a sudden he morphed into a beautiful white dove and flew away. I never fight with goblins and you shouldn't either. Just relax, let them be and try to understand what they need. Then they'll become your friends and maybe even support you. This guy required a lot of love and acceptance."

"Are there really such things as goblins?"

"Of course—you'll start seeing them if you become quiet and observant."

Lalita also started using music as a healing medium. She was able to play simple melodies on her *Gudendorf* violin. Sometimes she was inspired to play improvised tunes and hum, or chant at the same time. People often found her musical interludes calming, subtly energizing and even healing. Her best friend, Cheryl Sampras, was once laid up in bed with strep throat, and it was sucking out all the psychic energy out of her. Lalita snuck into her bedroom one afternoon, when her parents were away at a PTA meeting, played original music with her for two hours and chanted several of her mystical songs. The next morning, Cheryl's throat was clear, and her energy was back at full strength.

Just before the holidays, Jack received an email from Alicia. It read:

Dear Jack—

I'm sorry to have to tell you that I had a miscarriage after having sex last week. Our son would have been a beautiful baby—I've seen many pictures of him in my womb.

I've dated Paul a few times but ended that relationship recently because he turned out to be an abuser and a sex maniac. My father has introduced me to a four-year medical student who's doing a residency in Stewart with Dad's GP. His name is Jeremy Potter, and he's asked me out a couple of times, but I keep turning him down, even though he speaks Spanish fluently.

If you're still planning to marry me, please give me a definite date and wire me some money so I can fly to Vancouver.

My love, as always,

Ali.

Jack noticed that Jen Black was slowly starting to transform her life, perhaps due to her participation in the *Order*. She'd recently signed on as a Member in Good Standing, which meant she was now committed to attending all the regular meetings. Over a two-month period, she lost twenty-two pounds, bought a whole new wardrobe and started wearing make-up again.

"I officially got a job today," she told Jack while they were having coffee at the *Juice Bar*.

"What kind of job?"

"I'm now the permanent janitor at *Champlain Heights Elementary School*, which means I'll be able to afford to put my old beater back on the road once I save some money.

"Jen, why don't you sell your trailer and buy a *new* car?"

"Because then I'd be homeless," she answered quickly.

"Well, Cara tells me her bachelor suite will be coming available next month. If you'll do some part-time work at the *Infinite Healing Juice Bar*, like the old days, she'll subsidize your rent."

"Let me think about that and fully process it—makes me a little nervous, but it might just work."

Jen moved into Cara's empty suite on July 1, 1997, after selling her trailer and buying a 1992 Toyota Corolla from *Budget Car Rentals* in downtown Vancouver. She was given $1000 in trade for her old jalopy.

Cara's estate was conducive to personal growth, relaxation and contemplation. It was situated on a ten-acre parcel of prime land—secluded from neighbors, full of towering evergreen trees, covered in many large spaces of lush green grass and replete with a swimming pool and tennis court. On Sundays in the summer, Jack, Jen, Lalita and Cara lounged by the pool sun tanning, swimming and chatting endlessly, often about nothing special, or important. Cara's wife, Gertrude, had a twelve-year-old daughter named Teresa and they were usually present by the pool on Sundays as well. Soon Lalita and Teresa had become good friends.

Over that summer, three very important turning points occurred in Jack's life. Sandheim officially accepted him into the *Zen Priest's Extension Training Program* that was starting in September and his novel, *The Lonely Stranger*, was accepted for publication by *Singular_Press* out of St. Louis. His editor, Lyle Johnson, started creating online events such as book launches all over the southern states and putting the work in best-seller space in every *Chapter's* store in America.

"We sold 1200 copies in July alone, Jack," said Louis to him on the phone.

"Wow, maybe I'll make some money on this one," he replied enthusiastically.

"You most definitely will," responded the resolute editor.

It was during this period that Cara invited Jack to buy some shares in *Infinite Healing* and work with her to expand the business.

"If you'd be willing to come on board and take on a larger role in the operation, I'd offer you a basic wage and a generous percentage of the profits," she said to Jack one day.

"What would that expanded role look like?" He asked.

"Running a meditation program and a creative writing course," she responded.

"I'd love to do those programs—my answer is an unqualified *'yes.'*"

Jack postponed replying to Alicia as long as he could. But as his priest training was drawing near, he had to let her know that the marriage was off. So, he finally sent her an email.

Dear Ali,

I'm so sorry I've delayed writing you, but it's been extremely busy down here for the last two weeks.

It's important for me to tell you that I've definitely decided to enroll in the part-time Priest's_Training Program and to become much more involved in the Infinite Healing Center.

I'm devastated by the news that you lost our baby—he'd have been a beautiful love child, that's for sure. Under current circumstances, I must tell you that our marriage is cancelled and I don't think you should come to Vancouver.

My life is heading in a different direction, and so should yours. You are young, beautiful and intelligent and deserve a man your own age in your own culture--a man like Jeremy. I hope we can stay friends and keep in touch.

Sincerely,

Jack.

Her reply came quickly.

Jack—

*I **have** started to date Jeremy and am happy to tell you that he's a far better lover than you. My parents are ecstatic that we've broken up. I wish you well in life.*

Please give my best wishes to Lalita and tell her she can visit me when she gets a little older.

Alicia Mendez

Even though he was upset at the prospect of never seeing Alicia again, he knew deep down the break-up was appropriate. As time went by, he began to forget all about the passion she generated in him because he got very busy in his healing work.

On Saturday mornings and Wednesday evenings, he and Lita ran the *Order of St. Luke* meetings. They worked on penetrating what lay at the heart of spiritual healing. Over time their results kept improving.

"Father, I can't find a technique or a formula for healing," noted Lalita one day, "All I know is that healings are impacted by the level of peace I'm experiencing."

"How do you mean, Lita?"

"If I've been meditating well and have no distractions in my life, I seem to enter a very calm, tranquil state. The quality of that state seems to affect healing--the higher the quality, the better the healing. The older I get the more I love meditating in the Zen way you taught me."

"That makes sense to me, my dear. And what I notice is that healings don't happen at all unless the injured party requests them."

In the afternoons on Saturday, Jack ran a *Zen Meditation Class*. He offered training in formal meditation, followed by lessons on the Buddhist way of life. The class manual had been written by him and illustrated by Lalita.

Every second week on Monday evening, Jack taught an eight-week creative writing course that he'd developed. As time went by, it became more and more popular. Several of his students began to get their work published.

Chapter 35   <u>Sainthood: September 5th to September 7th, 1997</u>

After the Labor Day weekend and Lalita was settled into a Grade 6 class at *Windermere Elementary School,* Jack received a strange phone call from Jen Black.

"Will you come over to my place for supper this Saturday? I've got a proposal for you."

"Why don't you just give me the proposal now?"

"It's a little complicated and I'll need more time to explain everything."

"Alright then, sure—what time?"

"After supper at about 7:30—and come alone."

When he entered her apartment, Jack was surprised to see how tidy and spotlessly clean it was. He could vividly remember how decrepit and dirty her trailer was. The furniture was sparse, simple and esthetically pleasing. He immediately noticed a bookshelf crammed full of self-help books.

"Something smells delicious, Jen—what is it?"

"Turkey sausages, green peppers stuffed with mashed potatoes, Bree cheese and sage-tinged apples along with homemade cherry pie for dessert. While you're waiting, how about having a glass of vintage Red Bordeau?"

"That'll be just fine," answered Jack.

After supper, they retired to a Danish teak sofa with pink cushions which was sitting in the corner of the living room next to a stain glass window.

"Don't worry about the dishes; I'll do them before I go to work tomorrow morning."

"That was the most delicious meal I've ever eaten, Jen. I didn't know you were a gourmet cook. But now I'm going to have to loosen my belt and rest awhile."

"Go ahead, Jack," she mused coquettishly, "My proposal's a bit strange, but please, hear me out. I've thought about this for a long time and beg you not to interrupt me until I've finished speaking. Can you agree to that?"

"Okay, shoot."

"I want to have children."

"That sounds like a noble goal and one I can fully understand and appreciate. What's holding you back?"

"I don't have a man, Jack."

"Well, I know many ways you could find a man. You've come a long way back to full health in the last few months-- and don't ever forget you're basically a very beautiful woman with an incredibly sexy body. Sorry for embarrassing you, but I'm just being honest."

"Jack, I want you to be the father."

At that point, Jack spit a full mouth of wine onto the glass coffee table in front of him, and his face turned beat red. Some of the wine hit the carpet and stained it.

"Jen, that's impossible--we've been down that road together before, and it just **did not work.**"

"I'm not looking for a relationship, Jack, and you'll have no obligations to help me in any way, assist in raising our children, or give me any money. A legal contract will be drawn up that'll fully protect you. I just need to be inseminated by a handsome man with good genes, someone smart who I know and trust. It's that simple."

"You said *children*, Jen, why?"

"I want three, and you could father all of them."

"Jennifer Black—I'm' starting a Zen Priest Training Program in seven weeks. One of the first rules is strict and absolute celibacy throughout the entire period of training."

"What the Zen people don't know won't hurt them."

All of a sudden, Jack noticed Jen's breasts jiggling slightly because she wasn't wearing a bra. Her blouse was transparent enough that he could see the color of her areolas and the tiny bumps on both of her taught nipples. Blood rushed into his loins.

"Let's start trying to get me pregnant tonight, Jack," she whispered seductively. "After I have a shower, I'll be in my bed, waiting for you," she added, heading into her compact bathroom after winking at him and touching his bare arm before she disappeared.

Jack was abruptly left sitting on the sofa, sweating.

I can't do this, he thought. *She'll bring me down again, just like last time.*

Unfortunately, he hadn't had sex, or any kind of sexual release, for over six months, and his body ached for a woman. He knew exactly how voluptuous she was, how sensual, how erotic. She was like a masterful, experienced geisha girl, fully trained. Her bed could produce the feeling of a thousand orgasms all at once, and *he knew it.*

Jack scurried out of Jen's apartment before anything physical developed, but thereafter, he was full of inner conflict. He didn't want to get intimately involved with any woman, did not want to father any children and did not want to distract himself from the intensity of Zen training. But, on the other hand, his body longed for physical contact with an attractive woman. Over the next few weeks she magnified this conflict by becoming openly flirtatious with the man she wanted to father her children.

On another front, Jack received a disturbing letter just before Halloween that year. It was from Dolly Pulford.

Dear Jack—

I hate to write with bad news but I must. Rodney is now in the provincial slammer in Prince George. He and two of his goon buddies knocked out the cashier at a Petro Canada *gas station and stole $55. (That's all there was in the till at the time.)*

I know he's only twenty years old, but they processed him through adult court and sentenced him to two years less a day. Sally's trying to save some money so she can visit him, *but so far, she only has $18, and the return bus fare is $182.50. She's getting nowhere fast.*

We've tried our best with him, but he's been out of control for a while. Sorry.

Dolly

The next day, Jack called the Prince George Regional Correctional Center and spoke to Rodney's parole officer, George Pakos.

"Can I visit Rodney Fitzgerald, George?"

"By all means, Jack, the more support he gets, the better it'll be. Just so you know--he's been here for seven weeks and hasn't had a visitor yet."

"I'll be in Prince George next week for a few days and would like to meet with you. Can we talk about getting Rod into a Trades Program?"

"I'll be happy to sit down with you to discuss Rod's situation," replied George. "As soon as he turns twenty-one, he'll qualify for one of two trade programs: cooking or bricklaying. So far, he's expressed no interest in either."

It took Jack two days to set up care for Lalita while he was gone. Cara and Jen agreed to make sure she ate her meals, got to school, practiced her violin and did her daily meditations.

"I'll be back in three days, darling," he told his daughter.

"That's great, Father," she responded, "I'll be fine. Rod's in trouble, and no one else can help him but you."

"Thank you for being so understanding. Will you pray for him while I'm gone?"

"Yes," answered Lalita with tranquility and peace in her voice.

She's on her way to becoming a saint, thought Jack.

He thought about making love to Jen constantly. Images of her naked body rose up before him throughout the days. The enforced celibacy of Zen living was creating intense pressure in his mind and body. He even started to dream about sleeping with her and had a couple of wet dreams. For her part, Jen continued to tempt him whenever she could.

"Would you like a back massage?" She asked him one evening when they were sitting alone in colorful beach chairs at the side of the pool.

"Thanks, but not tonight, Jen," he replied while noticing her bikini tops were hanging low.

Late one Friday night, she walked unannounced into his apartment holding a rolled marijuana joint, thick and pointed at both ends and asked to borrow some sugar.

"Thanks, Jack," she said after he gave her a pound of Demerara. "Did you know I'm naked underneath this kimono?"

"No, I didn't," he replied curtly while trying to look away from her bright orange nightgown.

"Will you smoke some weed with me tonight?"

Without waiting for his answer, she sat down at his kitchen table, lit up the stogie and took a long, deep puff.

"This stuff is Columbian gold, and it's very strong. You're going to love it, Jack."

She then stuck out her right hand, the one holding a joint, and without thinking, Jack took it and sucked on it until both his lungs were full of heavy, green smoke. He held his breath for ten seconds before exhaling deeply. After that, he began to relax.

"I'm in control of myself," he thought, *"And this feels good."*

Once the whole stick had been consumed, Jen started laughing at her own inane statements.

"You'd make a damn good father, Jack!"

"Then why are you laughing Jen? Are you mocking me?"

"No--I'm laughing because I'm hungry—do you have any salty potato chips?"

"No, but I'm hungry too," he mumbled, "How about some pancakes and blackberry syrup?"

"Sound fabulous," she winced.

Somehow, Jack was then able to toast a dozen Eggo waffles, slap them with Becel margarine and pour a whole bottle of Smith's Sweet Syrup over the square artificial flapjacks.

"Wow, these taste great, Jack. I didn't know you were a gourmet cook."

"I'm not, Jen—but I *am* tired and have to lie down."

As soon as he pulled his couch into a hide-a-bed, his body fell on it and passed out immediately. When he finally woke up, morning sunbeams were shining through his living room window, lighting up his entire apartment.

"Jen, wake up," he stated authoritatively, as he poked her right arm. She was sound asleep at his kitchen table.

"Where am I?" She groaned.

"You just slept all night at my place, sitting in a chair at my kitchen table.

"What happened last night, Jack?"

"Nothing—Jen--absolutely nothing."

"Do you want to drive over to McDonald's for breakfast?

"No, Jen, I've got a lot of work to do today. Good-bye."

Chapter 36   <u>Sex—September 8th to September 12th , 1997</u>

Jack continued to be astounded by his daughter's personal growth. She was most definitely mature beyond her years. By the time she was eleven years old, she could look directly into the hearts of the adults around her, see their energy blocks and the ego games they played. When she meditated, a peace beyond all human understanding descended upon her, and she came to love that peace--to dwell in it as long and as frequently as possible. She was confident yet humble; wise yet innocent; calm yet full of energy. Her father was sure that her prayers for Rodney would have an impact.

When he arrived at the prison in <u>Prince George</u>, Rod had to be summoned to meet him and George from an isolation cell.

The probation officer met Jack in his very small and cramped office, like a walk-in closet with too many clothes. It had faded mahogany paneling, one small window covered with dirty Venetian blinds and a tiny desk for George, full of papers, files and bits of stale, moldy food.

"Welcome to our *Institution*, Mr. Turner. I'm glad we finally have someone in Rodney's family to consult with," said George.

"What's the problem with him, sir?" replied Jack.

"He flaunted the rules two weeks ago, so we had to separate him from the other inmates," said George. "What we're dealing with here is someone with a personality disorder."

"How do you mean?"

"He's got two people living inside him. It's a Dr. Jekyll, Mr. Hyde situation. On the one hand, he can be polite, articulate, sensible, helpful and smart. But sometimes, a demonic personality arises in him, which he doesn't seem to be able to control. Then he becomes crude, violent, impulsive and completely self-absorbed."

"That reminds me of his father," thought Jack.

"What did he do to get put into solitary confinement?"

"He sold cigarettes to half the prison population."

"Can I have five minutes with him alone?"

"Yes, but only five," stated the officer curtly as he sauntered out of the meeting room. "I only have so much time to deal with this."

Jack was shocked by his nephew's appearance. He had tattoos all over both arms, and his face was gaunt, whiskered and full of pockmarks, along with two long, fresh scars. He'd filled out and had a small pot belly. He actually looked like a long-term convict.

"Rod, you're no longer a child, so you're going to have to face up to some of the responsibilities that come with adulthood. I can't judge or criticize you because I did some time in prison on a robbery charge once too. But trust me, we've got to get your life back on track *right away.*"

"It's Dolly's fault, Dad."

"How can that be true?"

"She told me to get her rent money any way I could one night when she was drunk—knowing perfectly well I'd have to pull off a robbery to pay her, because she always talked about taking down that gas station. She also made me smoke grass and screw her when Sally was delivering newspapers in the afternoon, and she fucked all my friends too."

"Forget about Dolly and her daughter, Rod—you're never going to see them again. Once you're out of here, you're going to live with me and your sister in Richmond until you get your feet back on the ground. She's already started praying for you. In the meantime, you have a choice to make, and I want you to make it **now**: do you want to become a cook or a bricklayer?"

"A cook," he blurted out quickly. "By the way," he continued, "Two days ago, I dreamt about Lalita. In the dream, she was massaging my chest, and my heart kept getting bigger and bigger as a result. When I woke up, I was full of peace and had a calm energy inside me that lasted for two hours."

"That's great, Rod. Now I want you to start an exercise program. Make it simple—do some push-ups before breakfast and at bedtime, and keep increasing the number you do each week until you feel confident in your body again. By doing so, you'll lose that belly fat in a few weeks."

"Okay, I'll do it!"

"Rod, I have to go back to Vancouver tomorrow morning, but I want to be in communication with you. Can you access a computer here to write emails?"

"Yeah—there's email access in the library. I'll write you as soon as I'm back in general circulation."

"Good—I want a one-page report on your progress—every week! I'll respond to everything you write."

Jennifer and Lalita were waiting for Jack at the airport, and both hugged him tightly as soon as he cleared the baggage exchange.

"I missed you, Dad, and I'm sure glad you're home."

"I missed you *too*, dear, and I want to talk to you about Rod," replied Jack.

"How is he?" she asked.

"In bad shape, but I think we made some progress in two short days. I'd like you to start praying for him on a regular basis. Will you do that for me?"

"Yes, of course."

"I'm really benefitting from the *Order* meetings, Jack," blurted out Jen as they sped along the Fraser Highway and over the *First Narrows Bridge*. Lita's presence there is very helpful—she's an authentic healer--no doubt about it."

Later that night, after Lalita was asleep and Cara's estate became quiet as the sun went down, Jack got a phone call from Jen.

"Can you drop over for a minute, Jack? My toilet's plugged?" Do you happen to have a plunger?"

"Yes, I do. I'll be over in a few minutes."

When he got there, he found excessive amounts of fresh, clean paper stuffed down her only toilet. After removing most of the obstructive material, Jack was able to get the water flowing again by using his plunger.

"Will you have a glass of wine with me? I'm very lonely tonight, Jack."

When he glanced over at her, his eyes flipped open very wide. She was wearing bikini briefs and an utterly transparent blouse. He immediately saw both her oversized breasts swinging under her clothes. Nothing was left to his imagination.

"Just a very quick sip of English port, Jen--then I must go."

After placing a small, one-ounce tumbler in his hand, Jen started rubbing his bare neck and moved her breasts two inches away from his face.

"You're staring at my boobs, Jack. Would you like to kiss them?"

Without waiting for a reply, she unbuttoned her shirt and pushed her right nipple into his mouth. While he was sucking it, she started massaging his penis, which had by this time grown to its full length and thick width.

"I've always admired your size, Jack. Now be a man and show me what you can do with it."

By this time, Jack's body had completely overruled his mind, so he pulled his jeans off and let Jen have her way with his manhood. She wasted no time placing it deeply into her mouth—an aperture that quickly began sliding up and down along its long, wet length.

He was so sex-deprived that he managed to satisfy Jen through an intense session of intercourse that lasted for a full forty-five minutes. During that time, she experienced three significant and very intense orgasms.

"Wow, that was amazing," she squealed when Jack rolled off her sweat-covered body. "I've never had sex so long and so hard, Jack. You were rough with me, and I really liked it."

"I guess I got carried away, Jen. I haven't had sex for a very long time."

"I went off the pill last week, Jack and I desperately hope you just impregnated me with your seed. Now, that would give this little episode a very happy ending, wouldn't it?"

"I can't do this again, Jen—it just isn't right for me."

"Did you enjoy it?"

"Not really."

"Then why did you have such a big climax and fill me with a liter of hot, sticky sperm?"

"It *was* nice on a physical level."

"Well, let's do it again as soon as possible—just to make sure I do get my baby. Why don't you sleep in my bed until you start your Zen program?"

"My preparation for spiritual living is supposed to be ongoing, Jen. Let's call this a once-in-a-blue-moon experience."

After he got home, Jack sat down on his Lazy-boy chair and closed his eyes.

He was depressed and racked with guilt.

Having sex with Jen feels more like an addiction than a love-fest, he thought. He'd craved her body and satisfied himself totally on a physical level. But now he felt as though all his psychic energy had been drained away like someone cleaning out his entire savings account to gamble it all away.

"I did experience a flash of egolessness at the top of my climax," he remembered, "But there was no love in it."

Then he drifted into a reverie, remembering the sex acts he'd had with Sarah and Suzie. With them, there was no pressure to perform. He wasn't controlled by his body because he loved them and only wanted their pleasure and satisfaction. The sex itself was simply an expression of his love for them. That's why it always proceeded slowly, mindfully and tenderly. Sarah loved to be massaged, so Jack would give her long Shiatsu Treatments before proceeding into love-making. He appreciated the softness of her skin, her beautiful legs, her long blonde hair and how she whispered loving words at him while looking directly into his eyes. Suzie liked her feet treated, so he'd give her an acupressure session before he even kissed her. Her scent was always powerful, heavenly, even, yet subtle. When it was all over, he felt energized, whole and grounded in love.

With these women, it was like a spiritual experience. The sex uplifted him.

As he prepared mentally for more formal Zen training, he remembered the instructions of his teacher—*celibacy will enhance your meditations and increase your insights; alcohol and sexual release will pull you right off course, so avoid both at all costs when training.*

Chapter 37 <u>Preparations: October 1st to November 15th, 1997</u>

In early October, Jack got two very interesting emails in his computer's inbox. The first was from his nephew. It read:

Dear Dad—

I finally got out of solitary and joined the general population again. Thanks so much for visiting me—you've given me hope that my life can really change.

I started Cook's Training this week, and it's going to be fun. I've been posted to kitchen duty in the mornings. My job is mostly to clean up and wash dishes but yesterday, they did teach me how to make porridge for two hundred people.

Like you suggested, I've started doing sixty push-ups daily— thirty before breakfast and thirty at bedtime. They make me sweat a lot! Everyone's treating me better now. I wrote Sally and broke up with her—good riddance.

Rod

The second was from June Eagle-Feather.

Dear Jack—

I'm coming to Vancouver to do a Shamanic Retreat over the Christmas holidays and would like to request that your daughter assist me for the full week. It'll involve spending six days in a sweat lodge fasting and doing sacred purification exercises to encourage the sweating out of toxins and negative energies which create disorder and imbalance in a person's life. The sweat lodge experience cleanses the body, mind and soul. Intense heat is generated inside the lodge by steam created from pouring water on heated rocks. The fee is either a gift of sacred clothing or one of the special kinds of tobacco that I sell--but if Lalita will help me, she won't need to make any contributions. The purpose of a sweat lodge is not to make money but to heal and cleanse the participants. She's already a natural-born healer, and this Retreat will take her deeper into a transformed life.

Love and peace,

June

Then he responded immediately to Rod's letter by writing:

Dear Rod—

Thanks for your first weekly report. It sounds like you're turning things around now. Consider yourself an apprentice cook, and be patient. It takes time to learn a trade, but you'll get there!

Your push-up regime is a good one, so keep it up. I'm glad you ended your relationship with Sally. She was no good for you. Keep your nose down, work hard, and you'll be free in no time at all.

Jack

In answering June's note, he wrote:

Dear June—

I like the idea of Lalita doing your Retreat and assisting you. This work will surely deepen her metaphysical healing abilities—adding a whole new dimension to them—and she'll have time for this at the Christmas break. I'll speak to her about it and get back to you shortly.

Jack

He approached his daughter the next day after their evening meal.

"I've received word from June Eagle-Feather that she'll be doing a Sweat Lodge Retreat later this year in Vancouver. She'd like you to participate and assist her. Would you be interested in doing that?

"Yes, I would, Father," she replied without hesitation. "But what exactly would be involved?"

"Sweat Lodge Retreats are sacred purification events. The steam from pouring hot water on granite stones will penetrate an enclosed space. After the participants have fasted, she'll lead them in healing changes, visualization exercises and esoteric movements. As a result, negative energies are expelled, and the attendees are released from any psychic blockages and dark thoughts they've accumulated. The ultimate purpose of a sweat is to purify the spirit and body to facilitate communication with the Great Spirit. If done properly, this gives the participant true power."

"Do you think I should do this, father?"

"Yes, I absolutely do. I trust the leader, and this will add a whole new dimension to your healing abilities."

A few days later, Jack was able to tell June that his daughter would be able to participate in the Retreat activities. Her main role as an assistant would be to help the Shaman set up all the exercises and support her in individual counseling sessions.

As he prepared for his next phase of Zen Training, Jack was mentally tormented by Jennifer Black's behavior. She continually flirted with him and constantly invited him over to her place to "talk."

"You can make love to me however and whenever you want, Jack," she whispered to him as he sat in a lounge chair at Cara's pool one day in early August.

The next day, he sent his mentor an email which read:

Dear Master—

I'm now preparing for the Priest Training Program and would like to meet with you to discuss my final thoughts on what will happen in the program and to ask you a few questions. Is there any way we can meet next week?

Jack

When he did meet with Sandheim in his office, his teacher had, as usual, set up a sacred tea ceremony. The stillness pervading that office created tranquility in Jack's mind and body, like the smooth glass-like surface of a duck pond in August. As the monk slowly sipped his cinnamon tea, he asked Jack.

"What are the questions you want to ask me before starting *Phase Two* of the *Priest Training?*"

"The first one is: How strict are the rules for celibacy during the Training?"

"Absolute abstinence from any sexual activity is one of the most important vows you'll be required to make. Why do you ask?"

"An old flame of mine wants me to father her child, and I'm tempted to get physical with her."

"Jack, it's way beyond the purview of Zen to make judgments on anyone's sexual conduct or family plans. However, when you're training for the priesthood, it's critically important to avoid leakages from your seven chakra centers. The two worst possible energy drains are caused by releasing sperm or drinking alcoholic beverages. This is not a moral issue but a spiritual one."

The meeting lasted another hour, but Jack had received the information he needed to make some decisions. He knew that tension and inner conflict were going to follow, but he also knew what he had to do.

In the middle of November, June Eagle-Feather arrived in Vancouver in her motor home to set up her *Retreat*, make all the final arrangements and meet with Jack and Lalita.

After a few hours of warm greetings and drinks of iced tea and lemonade by the pool, Lita asked the Shaman exactly how the *Sweat Lodge* would be run.

"I have access to a wonderful forest on Wiersmaq Band property three miles north of the University of BC, Lita. On a clearing in the woods, we'll dig a pit in the earth, about a foot deep and two and a half feet wide. Then, willow branches will be cut and bent over the hole to form a wide dome, many feet across. A large piece of canvas will then be stretched across the structure, and a fire will be built outside the lodge. In that fire will go the rocks that will eventually heat the interior. At all times, we'll treat the lodge as a sacred dwelling--after all, building it is one way to honor the Creator."

"Why do you need a fire, June?" asked Lalita.

"The fire will heat five rocks, which will be taken into the completed lodge. These particular rocks represent the four essential directions: east, south, west and north. In the middle will be placed the biggest stone—the one that signifies God's creation."

"Once the event starts, how do you heal the participants?"

"I don't heal anyone," June replied. "All I do is present a mirror so people can see themselves *as they truly are.* I tell them they're like icebergs floating on the sea of life. If they look down deep inside themselves, they'll notice they're made of water just like the ocean—except they're frozen."

"How do you mean frozen?" asked Lita.

"I mean, they're frozen in their approach to life. But if they have the courage, they can look at themselves *as they are* and see where the precious life force is leaking out. Their addictions to money, sex, food, alcohol, TV and ambition drain them of natural energy or heat—so they become cold. When those leaks are closed, they'll hold that energy and heat up. When that happens, the iceberg that they were melts into the aliveness of the sea of life. Do you understand what I'm saying?"

"I think so," said Lita.

"Well, you'll know for sure when the event is over," stated June out of a narrow smile on her round face. "The most important thing to know is that our job is to make every participant feel unconditionally accepted as they are."

"Thank you—that I can understand," replied Lita.

"Would you like to join us for supper tonight, June?" asked Jack. "We'll start eating at 7 pm."

"Yes, I'd love to join you, Jack. Thank you."

Later that day, the shaman showed up for a dinner of Idaho baked potatoes, tomatoes stuffed with Mexican green peppers, Greek salad and steaming hot Japanese herbal green tea.

"June, I'd like you to meet Cara Shrum," said Jack just before she sat down at the long pine dining table. "She's the owner-operator of *Infinite Healing*."

The meal was served to Lalita, Cara and June before Jack sat down to join a discussion that had ensued.

"What kind of healing work do you do, Cara?" asked June.

"Well, I'm a massage therapist by trade so I work to physically manipulate injured muscles and bones. But I also work on a spiritual level by pouring my own awareness and love into all my clients. That's why I have to be totally present when working on people."

"That sounds divine," replied June. "I use Christian prayers and chants to create a sacred space in my retreats. But the fundamental healing practice is based on First Nations' traditions, which include fasting and strategically using heat from hot stones to purify all my participants."

Jack then interjected by saying.

"Lita and I work with Cara at *Infinite Healing* along with Father Jerome Santoro and specialize in the laying on of hands. I also conduct Zen Buddhist classes, which focus on long periods of formal meditation connecting aspirants to themselves, which is ultimately to their own field of awareness. In our *Order of St. Luke* meetings, we notice that a group of devoted Christians can produce powerful healing results when they fervently believe in the healing power of Jesus and all lay their hands on a sick person at the same time."

"I'm impressed with all these modalities," offered June. "The only point I'll add to this discussion is some people are natural-born healers. No one knows why this is so, but there's a person sitting at this table right now who is proof of this."

"Who is that?" asked Cara.

"Lalita," answered June. "And we're hoping our upcoming *Retreat* will add more strength to her already powerful abilities."

After the nutritious meal, which everyone found to be delicious, they all retired to Jack's deck to watch the sun go down over snow-clad mountains in the distance. Soon, they all became silent, falling naturally into a meditation on the beauty of nature. The red-orange-black sunset had a powerful impact on everyone present.

Chapter 38   A Beautiful Woman: May to September 2007

Lalita Fitzgerald grew up to be a remarkable woman. She was exquisitely beautiful with deep blue eyes, long jet-black hair, a classic nose and slender but well-proportioned legs. She stood six feet two inches tall and towered above most other women. By the time she was twenty, she'd become fluent in three languages—French, Spanish and English. She handled the violin with full mastery and could play classical, jazz, country or folk. Most significantly, she'd become a powerful, intuitive, mystical healer.

In the summer of 2007, she was living in Pine Grove, a town of 25,000 inhabitants in the northern interior of British Columbia. She worked as a waitress at the White Spot restaurant there. On weekends, she often busked just outside the City Park under a stand of majestic pine trees. Strangely, she liked to play her own music, music that flowed harmoniously forth from the depths of her heart, music that never repeated its patterns. On Sunday afternoons, she might attract up to sixty onlookers who generously filled her wooden wine keg with significant amounts of loving donations. Many spectators broke into spontaneous dance. Lita gave all of the monies she collected to the Dandelion Food Bank.

Since the first Sweat Lodge she assisted at with June Eagle-Feather, she'd participated in ten other week-long Lodges over the years. When she was eighteen, her mentor became an assistant and allowed her to lead the event. After that, she was officially initiated into the Quimsuten Society as a fully-fledged Shaman. She chose the lavender plant as her link to open the healer's heart so that her ego could be

309

transcended during the event. That consistently put her in touch with the miracle-producing power inherent in the universe. Utilizing the time-tested processes of fasting, repeated heavy drumming and exposing herself to excessive heat, Lita could enter an altered state of consciousness and take a journey into the hidden dimensions of existence—a non-dual reality. On such journeys, Lalita received aid from spirit guides. She was then able to bring back knowledge for the benefit of healing others. Each Lodge was different, but the essential principles were always the same:

All beliefs have to be dropped. When the heat gets intense, a special rattle made of compressed buffalo hide is used repeatedly until all cultural values and ideas are expelled. During this process, the stomach must be completely empty.

Each participant has to be naked and then painted with horizontal red lines up and down their entire body.

A potent pipe full of special tobacco is smoked, and the smoke is rubbed all over the body.

The lodge must be kept in total darkness, representing the darkness of the soul—an ignorance from which purification must take place so that light permeates one's entire being.

A rope of hemp must be wrapped around the body and tightened until pain is experienced throughout the entire body.

The pain must not be avoided but absorbed and welcomed until a final breakthrough occurs.

The result always leads to power. This power bestows many special gifts, including the ability to heal.

Her training as a Shaman was complimented by years of Zen practices that her father taught her. She'd been a devoted student of meditation for over fifteen years and felt most at home in the contemplative state. At the tender age of fifteen, she'd cracked the koan, How Can You Stay Permanently Happy? After meditating for forty-eight hours straight, she told her father,

"Happiness has nothing to do with anything going on in the outside world. It happens as soon as you discover that it's the very nature of consciousness. Abiding in awareness is permanent happiness."

Her daily routines continued to include meditating in the Zen way for three hours—from 3 am until 6. Those times were the highlight of her day.

Her various spiritual modalities included extensive work in the Christian healing Order of St. Luke, which proclaimed healing powers through the laying on of hands and speaking in tongues.

But the main reason she moved to Pine Grove was to be near her most important teacher—Chief Gray-Cloud. He was a Grand Wizard and had taught June Eagle-Feather all the secrets of Shamanism. June had only ever referred two apprentices to Gray-Cloud, and Lita was one of them.

"This man will teach you how to do miracles, Lita," June had told her. "He can heal anyone of any disease. He can also do a rain dance and make the showers come when times are dry. But I must warn you—his training sessions are intense, and you must be very strong to endure them. Are you willing to submit yourself to this kind of training?"

"Yes, I am," said Lalita without hesitating.

This master lived in a villa embedded in the caves of Mount Pringle. She first met him in the summer of 2005.

"You've been recommended by my best pupil, June Eagle-Feather," he told her. "She says you've got exceptional healing powers given you by the Creator. Do you want to develop those powers and use them to help others?"

Lalita looked directly at him before answering. He was sitting on a hand-carved, massive wooden chair, like the throne of a medieval king, and he was wearing a long red-felt robe, hand-stitched with hundreds of animals in black knitted patterns all over its surface.

"Yes," she said fearlessly.

"Your training will begin next Sunday," he responded in a deep, baritone voice. "Please fast from now until then and come prepared for many grueling exercises. Arrive at 4 am precisely."

On her first formal Lodge with Gray-Cloud, she showed up at the agreed-upon time. A massive fire was burning outside a large enclosure made from bent pine tree branches and tar paper. The four essential directional stones were already in place inside the Lodge. It was extremely hot in there.

"Have you fasted for these past four days, Lalita?"

"Yes," she replied.

"Good—go inside now, remove all your clothes and sit in the middle of the four rocks. Paint your body in straight horizontal lines with the red ochre I gave you. Close your eyes and wait for my next instructions. Do you understand me?"

"Yes," she said.

At that point, she pushed aside the buffalo hides hanging in the entrance, stripped naked and sat down in the middle of the stones. Then she painted her body.

My God, it's hot in here, she thought.

Six hours later, Gray-Cloud entered the Lodge and sat on a pine stump in the south-west corner.

"Are you awake, Lita?"

"Yes," she mumbled faintly.

"All your beliefs and cultural training must be dropped. I will chant many Cree songs and shake my buffalo rattle until you are completely empty inside. Now, wrap yourself in the magic rope beside your feet and pass me the loose end."

When she'd fully complied with his commands, he began to pull the rope tighter and tighter. Soon, her body was turning red and chaffing.

"Do you feel the pain?"

"Yes," she cried out.

"Do you want to become a master medicine healer?"

"Yes," she mumbled.

All of a sudden, a thunderbolt of excruciating pain went up and down her spine, and she lit up like a Christmas tree. She shook violently all over for ten minutes, then flopped onto the sand floor.

"Don't move, and don't avoid the pain. Go right into it," said Gray-Cloud.

For forty minutes, Lalita withstood the torture until, at last, the pain subsided. She felt an incredible peace descend upon her, and a sense of calmness enveloped her entire body. She could clearly see three spirit guides sitting beside her inside the circle of sacred stones. The one to her immediate left—a fairy-like woman dressed in a pure white silk robe started speaking to her in a soft, melodic voice.

"We'll be here to guide and help you when you need us. But first, remember our seven absolute rules which must never be broken"--

Drop all your ambitions and never do anything that'll benefit you or bring you profit or advantage.

Never engage in any form or kind of sexual activity.

Never drink alcoholic beverages.

Never eat meat.

Spend three hours every day in silence.

Keep your healing powers secret.

Speak from your heart when communicating.

"Do you promise to obey these commandments?"

Lalita paused for a long time before responding. And then, looking Gray-Cloud directly in the eyes, she stated emphatically,

"Yes, I will obey them—always and forever."

The second guide, who was a saint-like looking man dressed in a long purple gown, then spoke,

"If you're ever in trouble, or in a crisis, or need help healing anyone, call us from your deepest silent prayer, and we'll be there for you."

Finally, the third spirit spoke. She was the tallest of the three and the most beautiful.

"If someone asks for healing, you can cure them by calling on us. But don't do anything other than be present. We'll do all the work."

From that day forward, Lalita was a transformed person. She walked slower and more deliberately than she used to and spoke less. For some reason, the clothes she wore, although plain, were always impeccably clean, and her apartment was washed down and scrubbed bare every day. She got rid of most of her furniture except for a bed and a kitchen table with one chair. But the biggest change was how she affected other people.

When Lita was at work, her boss, Rick Jones, noticed it was always quieter than at other times, and no arguments or complaints ever occurred. His restaurant became busier, and sometimes customers had to wait in line to get served. The food tasted better when she served it, and no one could explain why.

"Men are always asking you out and fawning over you," her friend and fellow waitress, Ruby Macmillan, said one day. "You're so incredibly beautiful—why don't you ever date or go to dances, Lita?"

"I'm too busy doing other things," she'd invariably say.

Sometimes, for no particular reason, strangers would ask her to pray for them. When that happened, she'd always agree, and those prayers were always answered.

"I'd like you to become the manager of our coffee shop, Lita," said Mr. Jones in September 2007. "Cheryl's leaving us, and we need to replace her. You'll be getting a set salary, and the income will be thirty percent greater than what you're making now."

"I love my job, Rick," she replied, "And have no desire to be promoted."

A little while later, one of the cooks came down with double pneumonia and was off work for two weeks. She told her husband to ask Lalita to visit her.

"I'm terribly ill, Lita, and not getting better. Can you help me?"

At that point, Lalita just smiled and sat down on a chair in the corner of the room. She then just closed her eyes. Ten minutes later, she walked back to Sally's bed and said,

"You've just got a minor cold. It'll be gone tomorrow."

Two days later, Sally was happy, healthy and back at work.

Chapter 39   Chaos: December 15th to December 27th, 2007

In the spring of 2005, Cara Shrum sold off Infinite Healing and paid out all of her shareholders. From that sale, Jack Turner received forty-four thousand dollars. She also sold her estate and donated over half a million dollars to various charities of her choice. Even though she was still a wealthy woman, she'd decided to become a medical doctor and had been accepted into UBC's Medical School for the term starting in September of that year. Two years later, she was leading her class and loved every minute of her intense training programs. Her new home was a luxury two-bedroom condo on the edge of the UBC Campus. She and her wife Gert broke up in 2004 because the latter became a Roman Catholic nun and went to Africa as a missionary.

On December 15th, Cara phoned Lalita with some rather urgent news.

"Lalita it's Cara. How are you?"

"Just fine, Cara, and you?"

"Well, I'm rather concerned about your father. Jennifer Black kicked him out of his townhouse and is threatening to charge him with wife-beating and sexual assault. Their kids—Ricky and Randy, are staying with Jen's aunt in some kind of trailer court. Social workers from Burnaby Social Services have visited the boys and may take them into care as wards of the province. I think you need to come to Vancouver this Christmas to help sort out this mess. You're welcome to stay with me."

"Where's my Dad living now?"

"He's living with me for the time being."

"Cara, I've got a week off at Christmas and was planning to attend a Sweat Lodge with Gray-Cloud. But now I must cancel those plans. I'll be in Vancouver early next week."

"That's great news, my dear. Just let me know your flight times, and I'll pick you up at the airport."

As promised, Cara was there right on time to meet Lalita on the 18th of December.

"Wow, you're even more beautiful now than the last time I saw you," said Cara.

"Thank you! How's my Dad doing?"

"Not particularly well, my dear. He's into the sauce pretty heavy right now."

"What happened to his marriage?"

"After he came home early one day and found Jen in bed with one of the neighbors, things started going downhill fast. He started drinking heavily and fighting with his wife. The twins went out of control, and both got suspended from school until the New Year."

"How are you doing?"

"Breaking up with Gert and selling Infinite Healing were very hard to deal with, at first. But I've become so immersed in Medical School that my former life feels like a dream now."

When they arrived at Cara's home, Lita found her father sitting on the living room's thick, soft, plush carpet, leaning against a shiny black leather sofa. He was sound asleep and had an empty bottle of Johnny Walker in his right hand.

"Dad, wake up," Lita stated firmly.

Jack slowly opened his puffy, bloodshot eyes and exclaimed,

"Lita, my God, you look radiant—it's so damn good to see you. How are you?"

"I'm fine—but what about you? What's going on?"

"I never wanted to marry Jennifer, and you know that. I did it because she was pregnant with my identical twin boys," he moaned as tears watered his face, "It was a bloody mistake from the beginning. I wanted to become a Zen priest, not a welder."

"Yes, I get it," said Lita.

"Anyway, one night, she swung a heavy corn broom at me in the garage and just missed my head. I pushed her away to protect myself, and she fell down and scraped her knee on the concrete floor. After that, she charged me with sexual assault and battery. It's insane. Ricky and Randy are staying with her alcoholic aunt."

"Dad, you're shaking. Calm down; it's going to be alright. Let's go into your bedroom and meditate," responded Lita.

The following day was a Saturday. Cara made them all a nourishing breakfast of local fruit, homemade sourdough crusty rolls and hot orange herbal tea.

"You seem much calmer today, Jack," noted Cara.

"Yes, I'm feeling much better, thanks."

"What's happening with Rodney, Dad?"

"He's working as a cook at some diner in East Vancouver and living in a flophouse."

"I'm so glad he's working in his trade—he worked hard to get his journeyman's papers," responded Lita.

"Me too—but don't ever forget he's a heroin addict and can't keep any girlfriend for more than a month."

"I want to visit him—can you set that up?"

"Yes, okay, I'll call him."

Rodney was living in a basement suite on Pandora Street. It was situated under a broken-down house that had definitely seen better days. The windows were filthy, all covered in black smoke like a Halloween decoration. The main door rattled and shook when Rodney opened it.

"Lita, you're gorgeous—thanks for coming by. You look so alive!" Rodney yelped.

"So good to see you again, brother," responded Lalita calmly. "Can we come in?"

"Ah, well, I guess so—sure."

His apartment was in a mess. Empty Lucky bottles were strewn all over the floor, and ashtrays full of stinking butts littered the living room.

"It's wonderful that you're working in your trade Rod. Being a cook is one way to help others—by ensuring the food they eat is nutritious and of a high quality."

"Yeah, true," drawled Rodney, "But most of my customers order greasy fries and cheeseburgers."

"Rod—how about introducing us to your friend," said Jack as he looked straight at the slovenly woman smoking weed on the filthy couch adjacent to Lita.

"Sure—I'd like you both to meet my girlfriend, Sammy. We met during a Thanksgiving community supper at the downtown Salvation Army."

At that point, Sammy smiled a drowsy smile and then promptly fell asleep, snoring loudly. As Jack and Rodney continued talking, Lita excused herself and quietly disappeared into the bathroom. Standing next to the shower, she closed her eyes and entered a profound contemplative state for over fifteen minutes.

"Lita, Rod has to go to work now, and he's running late—we've got to go," Jack shouted through the bathroom door.

"I'll be right out," his daughter replied.

On the drive back to Cara's, Jack's voice was sad.

"He just can't seem to break out of a very depressive lifestyle, Lita. I think those years in prison really hardened and corrupted him."

There are lots of positives with Rod, Dad—I think he's going to be alright in the fullness of time."

"I sure hope so," Jack answered.

The next day, when Jack and Lalita arrived at the Springfield RV Park in North Surrey, they were both struck by how downtrodden the place looked. Garbage was strewn all over the property and several of the office windows had plywood in them, rather than glass, making it look like a company gone bankrupt.

Stopping at #51, Jack banged hard on the trailer's door. Soon, a morbidly obese woman dressed in a raggedy housecoat and smoking a cigarillo opened the door.

"You're not welcome here, Turner. You're a bastard—now get lost!" she screamed, slamming the door quickly in his face.

"Well, I guess you're not going to see your nephews today, Lita," moaned Jack.

"Let's just sit here on that bench for a while–maybe she'll let them come out and visit us."

Lita sat perfectly still for twenty minutes with her eyes closed. She could feel the cold breeze on her cheeks and smell the pine needles in the breeze.

Presently, the trailer door to #51 opened a crack. Randy and Ricky then pushed their way onto a porch and looked around for their visitors.

"You boys look exactly like your father," Lita said, smiling at them. "Come over here, sit down and talk to me."

The twins were alive, bug-eyed, full of displaced energy and clearly agitated. Beneath the rags they were wearing, Lita could feel and see their charisma and beauty. Both boys had identical red, curly hair and big, bright blue eyes.

"What are those welts on your arms," she inquired.

"Auntie's cats scratch us all the time, Aunt Lita," blurted out Ricky.

"I heard a rumor that you boys do well in most of your school subjects."

"Dad helps us a lot," said Randy.

"When can we come home, Dad?" the boys echoed. "We hate it here."

"We'll have the situation under control in no time, boys. Just be patient."

"Thank God," cried Ricky, as he leaned over and started hugging his brother.

Later that evening, while Cara, Lita and Jack were eating a delicious meal of homemade vegetarian pizza, Caesar salad and fresh tomato juice, the phone rang.

"It's for you, Lita," said Cara, "And you better take it now— sounds important."

On that call, Lita learned that her master, Gray-Cloud, was near death with terminal colon cancer.

"I have to fly back to Pine Grove tomorrow, folks—Gray-Cloud is dying, and he's calling for me."

At the airport, Jack hugged his daughter tightly just before she boarded Flight 17021—PGP. While in that hug, Lita couldn't see her father's tears, but she could feel the trembling in his heart.

"I'm so glad you came to see us, darling," he whispered into her right ear. "Everything feels so much better now, but I don't know exactly why. At last, I feel there's some hope."

"I'll be back at Easter, Dad--to see how everything's progressing. In the meantime, let's stay in very close touch."

"I'll email or phone you every couple of days. Now, can I ask you a big favor?"

"Yes, of course."

"Will you pray for us?"

"Yes," stated Lalita most emphatically.

Chapter 40   Miracles: December 29, 2007to April 7, 2008

When Lita reached Gray-Cloud's villa, a somber, sad mood enveloped the entire community. His people were moving about slowly, heads bent so as not to make eye contact. Several black-dyed buffalo blankets were strung around his home on a long wire frame.

Two female indigenous nurses were present as she entered his bedroom, catering to their master's every need. He was hooked up to an IV solution, attached by a needle penetrating deep into his left arm.

"Lalita--thank you for coming to see me so quickly," he whispered—talking slowly, hesitatingly. "It's important I speak with you at this time--but first, let's smoke my Peace Pipes. Nurse Ms. Silver-Joe Carver then handed Gray-Cloud a large, long, colorful pipe with attached eagle feathers and various hand-carved animal etchings along its side. Its pit was full of fresh, green and very poignant tobacco. Then he gave Lita a similar but smaller pipe, all ready for smoking. After several draws on the robust tobacco, Gray-Cloud and Lita fell into a deep silence. Both of them closed their eyes as they held hands. The smoke was pungent as it wafted up to the pine rafters and settled along the entire ceiling.

Presently, the Teacher opened his eyes and, looking at his pupil lovingly, said,

"The spirits have spoken to me. You're the apprentice with the strongest power to heal. Therefore, I give you permission to hold Sweat Lodges in my name whenever you want and to have access to all my connections. Will you work with anyone I send you?"

"Yes, teacher, I most certainly will," whispered back Lalita.

"Thank you, my dear. I bless you for all time."

At that point, Lita's master stopped breathing, and a pure white light descended onto his face. Lita felt a powerful transmission of inner power move into and permeate her entire body.

When she got home, there was only one thing to do: fast for five days to integrate all aspects of her being. This was difficult to do working all day in a busy restaurant that served delicious foods—but she persevered until Friday night after her shift had ended. The following day, she stripped naked and sat before her electric fireplace turned to its highest level until Sunday. As darkness fell, she turned off the fireplace, showered and immediately went to bed.

The next morning, she woke up in a state of ecstatic presence. The entire universe appeared perfect in every way to her.

"Heaven is right here, right now," she thought, "If only people could see it."

"I must now be in communication with my family," she muttered to herself.

What follows are the email communications between Jack and Lalita Turner from January—April, 2008.

January 17th

Dear Lita—

I'm so glad you came to visit us at Christmas. You seem to have brought us a spate of good luck.

Cara and I are getting along really well. I've been able to help her with some of her medical school papers. Believe it or not, we're both attending the Zen Buddhist Monastery in Richmond for the Sunday Meditation Service, and we now both get up at 6 am daily to meditate for one hour before breakfast.

She says I can stay with her until all my marital issues are settled.

Dad

January 24th

Dad—

I'm ecstatic that you and Cara are getting along so well— and it doesn't surprise me. She's a very conscious person with strong spiritual gifts—and so are you! Spending time meditating together will build a strong bond of trust between you.

How are Randy and Ricky?

Love,

Lita

February 1st

Lita—

Somehow, Cara got Jennifer's permission to send the twins to boarding school at St. Michaels' Academy in Victoria for both the winter and spring semesters. Their marks were high enough to gain entry into that prestigious institution, and they got to come home on long weekends and all the traditional holidays.

Cara's paying for their entire tuition and says if they do well, she'll keep them there until the end of Grade 12.

She's also paid for Jen to move into a supervised transition home for three months. After that, she'll go into her own apartment with support from two psychiatric nurses. I'm a little embarrassed that Cara's footing all these bills—but she just keeps on insisting—you know how she is.

Jen even told Cara she was willing to meet with me when she gets out of transitional housing to discuss an amicable divorce. After that, I plan to sell my townhouse and give half the proceeds to Jennifer so she can start a new life and maybe even buy her own condo. That's only fair.

Dad

February 10th

Dad—

As I predicted, some of the chaos I witnessed at Christmas is evaporating, and the universe is now definitely unfolding as it should.

But I'm very curious about Rodney. Is he still living with Sam?

Love,

Lita

February 21st

Lita—

As strange as it may seem, Cara's in the process of buying a vegetarian restaurant on Nelson Street in downtown Vancouver. Rodney will become the manager, get a substantial salary and profit bonuses and will have full authority to run the place his way. She's been meeting with your brother constantly for over a month now, and they're on very much the same page. Rod's is currently drawing up plans for a new menu, a change in decor, and the hiring of several new staff.

Sammy's moved into the YMCA on Burrard Street, and Rodney says he wants to stay single at least until the café's fully up and running. He has, however, hired Sammy to be a part-time janitor at the restaurant, which will be called <u>Veggies For All</u>. That act made it a little easier for Sam to handle the break-up with Rod.

Cara works very hard at school during the day and gets assigned tons of homework. But we still have time to go for lovely walks after supper and sit by her fireplace, talking energetically before bed.

Dad

March 5th

Dad—

I've become very busy all of a sudden because many of Gray-Cloud's disciples keep booking appointments to see me, and I try my best to accommodate them.

I'm also creating two CDs of some of my best violin songs. Several members of Gray-Cloud's community tell me my spontaneous violin sessions have a healing effect on them. One of the most important indigenous musicians in Pine Grove has connections and is going to market my CDs internationally, but more on that later.

Here's hoping you and Cara continue to experience each other as kindred spirits.

Love,

Lita

March 25th

Lita—

Cara and I are truly kindred spirits! We love to talk when we're alone about so many subjects that we have in common and share an interest in. She likes to discuss spiritual healing, mindfulness meditation, modern Buddhism and Christianity and all the esoteric arts.

But I must now confess something to you—a romantic element has entered our relationship for the first time. She's always considered herself to be gay, but all that is changing. For the first time in her life, she's become attracted to a man in a physical way. And that man is me!

We now seem to be living as man and wife, and Cara doesn't want me to move out any time soon. I don't know where all this will end up, but I'm certainly enjoying the present situation.

In fact, I'm enjoying it so much I've started writing a new novel, which is turning out to be a sequel to my first one. There's already an interest from my publishing company to write and market it.

Dad

March 27th

Dad—

I'm overjoyed that you and Cara are now a family unit. All that suffering you've endured over the past few years is behind us. Now, we can all move on to exciting new adventures.

Unfortunately, I won't be able to visit again at Easter because I have to organize a massive Sweat Lodge at Gray-Cloud's community for sixty people.

However, my prayers will be with you all. In my place, I'm going to mail you two of my violin CDs. Try playing this music in the silence of the morning—before your day starts getting busy.

Love Lita

April 7th

Lita—

I'm disappointed you won't be coming down for Easter, but we did receive your wonderful CDs, and everything you said about them was true. The music is heavenly, healing, enchanting and mystical. Listening to it for thirty minutes each day definitely improves the quality of our lives.

Cara and I did a two-day retreat last weekend at the Monastery, and it was very enlightening. It involved lots of Zen meditation and five lectures from Karl Sandheim, who's now ninety years old. His experience in the spiritual life and his esoteric wisdom are incredible. After all that mediation, we walked for hours in the forest grove adjacent to Buddha Hall.   The sun was shining as we moved amongst the towering pine, fir and maple trees, holding hands. We stopped to rest on a bench beside Kaliper Creek and stared at the flow of the water together. Then I started to speak to her, and I'd like to share some of that conversation with you.

"I feel totally happy at all levels of my life, Cara," I told her.

"This is the best relationship I've ever been in," she replied.

"Cara, I'd like us to get married."

"Are you proposing?" she asked.

"Yes—will you marry me?"

"My answer is an unqualified yes," she countered.

So that, Lita, is how it happened. We're getting married at the Monastery on July 8th this year—with Sandheim officiating. It's very important to both of us that you attend, be Cara's bridesmaid and bless the whole event.

In the meantime, I'm sending you a gift. It's a simple question that's actually a koan that's generated a lifetime of valuable spiritual insights for me, and I'm hoping it'll do the same for you.

What is the sound of one hand clapping?

Dad.

Lalita smiled broadly when she read that last statement. She was utterly content. All the sacrifices and spiritual training she'd undertaken had powerful effects on the world. *One thing I now know for sure*, she thought.

Mystical healing works.

About the Author

RP Mickelson is a natural-born storyteller whose tales take many forms: short stories, novels, children's books, and lively oral encounters. His first novel, *Stone House*, was published in 2021, and his collection, *Inspirational Short Stories,* was published in early 2023. This work is the first book in The Mystical Healing Trilogy series.

He lives with his wife in Victoria, BC and has three adult children and seven grandchildren.

While his current athletic passion is the game of table tennis, he loves all racquet sports.

www.ingramcontent.com/pod-product-compliance
Lightning Source LLC
Chambersburg PA
CBHW071203020726

47502CB00002B/524

9 781927 848913